FEAR
OF
FALLING

CATH STAINCLIFFE

CONSTABLE

CONSTABLE

First published in Great Britain in 2018 by Constable

This paperback edition published in Great Britain in 2019 by Constable

Copyright © Cath Staincliffe, 2018

1 3 5 7 9 10 8 6 4 2

The moral right of the author has been asserted.

A CIP catalogue record for this book is available from the British Library.

ISBN: 978-1-47212-543-9

Typeset in Times New Roman by Initial Typesetting Services, Edinburgh
Printed and bound in Great Britain by Clays Ltd, Elcograf S.p.A.

Papers used by Constable are from well-managed forests and
other responsible sources.

Constable
An imprint of
Little, Brown Book Group
Carmelite House
50 Victoria Embankment
London EC4Y 0DZ

An Hachette UK Company
www.hachette.co.uk

www.littlebrown.co.uk

In loving memory of my mothers: Evelyn Cullen, 1935–2017, and Margaret Staincliffe, 1931–2017

Part One

1985–2004

Chapter One

The first time I saw Bel she was doing the moonwalk. On ice, in the park, New Year's Eve 1985. The lake was frozen over and a gaggle of us teenagers were there, like animals come to drink at a waterhole. Except we were swapping cider and vodka and the gathering was a way-station, a warm-up (in spite of the chill) for the real destination. A party. A house party, since most of us didn't have the cash for clubs in town and taxis home, even if we had got fake IDs with doctored dates of birth. It was just a matter of finding out who was having a get-together.

Bel glided in and out of the pools of light cast from the fancy lamp-posts that ringed the perimeter. She was all angles, sharp and sculpted. Her height was emphasised by the long dark coat that eddied about her ankles and swung out as she turned, revealing biker boots, a black-and-white checked skirt shorter than mine, a shiny black top. Her hair was cut short on one side and fell in a smooth inky wave on the other. There was something androgynous about her, even with the skirt and the slash of blood-red lipstick.

The ice squeaked and groaned and people called out, teasing her, warning her.

She spun round and bowed, self-mockery in her eyes. One arm bent across her waist, the other extended, hand cocked, fingers clutching a long, tapered joint.

Whoops and whistles from the crowd.

She straightened, sucked hard on the joint and held the smoke in her lungs before passing it to one of the others watching from the lakeside.

I wondered who she was. I didn't know everyone there but no one else was so unfamiliar, so particular. She must be new. Or visiting.

I wondered if the joint would eventually reach me, if it would do the rounds or circulate only among the inner circle of her friends.

Bel stepped up from the ice onto the pathway and I turned away, remaining next to her gang but not wanting to seem needy, greedy.

Shouts and singing heralded the approach of more people, and as they drew closer, I made out friends from school and felt relief. They were late but at least they'd come. I could lose myself among them, no longer on my own, sticking out like a charity case, someone to be pitied or despised.

Before they reached us, Bel tapped my shoulder, holding the joint in thin fingers, the roach pointed my way. Her dark blue eyes glittered. She smiled, large straight teeth, pointed canines.

That night I thought it was the drugs that made her eyes like that, almost feverish with a brilliant, burning intensity.

'Thanks.' Lowering my gaze.

She watched me, I could tell, as I took a drag and felt heat climb into my face. The joint was stained with her lipstick. The taste of it, powdery and sweet, mixed with the pepper of the nicotine, the pungent rubber of the cannabis.

Around us ran murmurs, rumours and speculation, names and addresses, potential sites for the celebration. Kids shivering, feet tapping on the ground to keep the circulation going. Someone's teeth chattering. A scream of outrage cut off. Bursts of laughter. Fooling around.

Three tokes, and the effects of the smoke rippled through me, over my skull and down my spine, as if I was a cat being stroked.

Grinning, I handed it back to Bel.

She peeled away and my friends were there, pulling out bottles and cigarettes. Someone shouted the name of a street, people cheered, and the mass of us moved off.

The thrill of possibility, the joy of being here and free and young and stoned and part of it all, rose, like bubbles, in my blood.

The party was in an old villa, a student house, the music audible from the end of the street. Rectangles of light spilled from the open front door and the large windows.

In the front garden figures stood around a brazier, faces bright.

No one seemed to be monitoring arrivals. The first of our group walked in. I could see the hallway was crammed. The thud of the bass travelled through me, gave me butterflies.

A shriek to my side, and a Catherine wheel began to spin, pinned to the wooden gate that must have led to the back. Someone too impatient to wait for midnight.

I hung on outside, savouring the whirl of colour, the spokes of stars streaming into the dark.

As it finished, I made my way to the house. The door had shut. I knocked hard and it was flung open, a man there, frowning. 'Who invited you?' he demanded.

He was drunk, his eyes bleary, words thick. The sting of humiliation burned the back of my neck.

'She's with me.' It was Bel, further down the hallway, a bottle in her hand already. She beckoned to me. 'Come on. He won't bite. Not if you're quick.' Laughter from the others there greeted the remark.

The man edged aside.

Pushing through the scrum I went in search of the kitchen where I found people I knew. There was a large enamel bucket full of mulled wine, a ladle hooked over the side, a few slices of lemon floating in it and a cigarette end. All the other bottles I picked up were empty; crushed beer cans littered the surfaces. I scooped out the fag end with a bottle top, then filled a plastic cup with wine. Took a long swig. It was tepid, sour. I took another drink and refilled the cup.

Later, I was on the stairs, when the music cut out. A relay of calls, 'Five minutes, five minutes', rang through the house. People moved to the living room, some standing on the sunken sofas, others shoulder to shoulder in any available space. A few had bottles of champagne or fizzy wine, well hidden until then, and were loosening the silver wires in readiness. The air was filled with smoke and perfume and a musty, fungal smell that I guessed came from the house itself.

The countdown began and I closed my eyes, as though something might change before I opened them again, as though there was some magic coming at midnight.

A roar went up: 'Happy New Year!' Corks popped, ricocheted off the ceiling. A girl started singing 'Auld Lang Syne' – they always sang that at the New Year dos my parents dragged me to – but she was drowned out by shouts of 'Happy New Year!' and people began to kiss each other. I saw the point quickly enough, to get round as many people as possible. Like spin-the-bottle without any boring pre-amble. Most of the kisses were pecks on the cheek and swift hugs with strangers. The man who'd tried to stop me coming in grabbed me and mashed his wet lips on mine, crushing them against my teeth. I tasted blood. I pulled away, swiped the back of my hand over my mouth.

Then Bel was there. Eyes glimmering. She kissed me full on the lips. No tongues but her mouth moving, smooth and gentle, on mine and I felt an answering shiver deep in my belly.

Was she a lesbian?

Was I?

Who cared?

She stepped back, eyes dancing, the curtain of hair swinging away from her cheek, revealing a row of rings, glinting silver, in her ear. Over the shoulder of the boy I was kissing, I could see she barely touched the next girl.

Had I been singled out?

Everybody moved outside for the fireworks, the ground rutted hard with frost, creaking underfoot. The garden wasn't really big enough: we were too close and people yelped as sparks caught their hair or clothes. I couldn't see Bel anywhere. The gunpowder made me cough.

My friend Katy found me. We had to be home by one o'clock. It was time to start walking.

I could stay, I thought. I might never see her again. It's New Year's. Why shouldn't I stay longer, stay out all night if I felt like it, sixteen after all? So what if I was grounded as a result, if they stopped my pocket money? I was old enough to leave home, anyway.

Films in my head, Bel cheering me on, admiration in her expression. Defending me. We could find a place to live together. I'd wear a coat like hers, cut my hair.

6

'Lydia!' Katy complained, pulling her hat on.

Should I find her, at least, say . . . What? Goodbye? Thank you? And risk looking like an idiot?

'Coming,' I said, and followed Katy through the house and out into the street.

'That was a dead loss,' she complained. 'Not one fit bloke in the whole lot.'

Katy was hunting for a boyfriend – we all were. It was our permanent state of affairs, barring short stretches when we were actually seeing someone.

'Apart from Mark Foster,' she said, 'who's a total prat.'

'Fit prat, though.'

'You didn't find anyone?' she asked.

Those spiked teeth, the taste of her lipstick.

'Nah.'

We walked back, talking too loudly, breaking into song every so often. Our breath puffs of mist. The cold pinching my feet, my wrists, the top of my back. A light, sick feeling inside me. Unease or excitement.

What if I never saw her again?

And what if I'd never set eyes on her in the first place? Would Fate have been any less brutal?

Chapter Two

School resumed, and my social life shrank again to Saturday nights, and then only if Katy and I weren't babysitting for my little brother or her cousins. I had a Saturday job at the vet's. At that stage I wanted to become a vet myself and my dad, who did the accounts for the practice, had put in a word with Mr Egerton.

Stifled by the routine of school and study, family meals and long evenings poring over my biology and chemistry textbooks, I kept reminding myself that I'd be leaving in a year and a half, off to uni (hopefully), independence and making my own rules. It felt like for ever.

I had the attic bedroom. An old Formica table served as my desk, and by standing on the chair, I could stick my face out of the dormer window while I smoked. The room was only marginally colder with the window open. The frame stuck sometimes, swollen and spongy with damp, mottled with mould. The central-heating radiator didn't work. There was a two-bar electric fire that I was allowed to use on the most wintry days. It sizzled and whined and gave off a smell of burning metal. The heat scorched my legs. And I'd drape a blanket over my shoulders.

Some nights I rewarded myself with an hour of television at nine o'clock depending on (a) what my parents were watching, and (b) if I could bear to watch with them. Anything with sex in it was a no-no. Unless it was animal sex, some nature documentary, and even that came pretty close to making me shrivel with embarrassment at times.

I wanted to ask my friends about Bel, to see if they knew who she was, but couldn't work out how to frame the question without sounding weird.

One Saturday in May we all went out for the evening. There was a strange atmosphere, everyone stunned by the fire that had ripped through the football stand at Bradford City's stadium on Valley Parade that afternoon. We heard about it at the vet's, and when I got home they were showing it on the news. Cameras had been there to film the match and captured the inferno. People had been trapped, the turnstiles locked. Dozens were feared dead.

I walked into the bar ahead of Katy and the others, my eyes stinging with the fug of smoke. Blinking, I looked for seats and there she was, Bel, in the far corner, arm draped over some boy's shoulders, her head tilted, touching his.

I wanted to run away. I felt exposed, caught somewhere I shouldn't have been. A trespasser.

Katy nudged me and pointed to a table where a group were gathering up their coats and bags. I nodded. She gestured to the bar and raised her eyebrows. The jukebox was loud, Frankie Goes to Hollywood singing 'The Power of Love'.

'Special Brew,' I mouthed. I wanted to get drunk as fast as possible.

She probably doesn't even remember me, I thought, as we claimed the table, shed our layers, moved the empties to the centre. I was determined not to look her way again, busied myself with a cigarette and arranging the beer mats in readiness.

It was taking an age for Katy to get served and Sue went to wait with her. Alison had split up with her boyfriend (after all of two months) and was in tears, confiding in Pam.

Lonely. I was lonely. Even there in the company of friends, with the evening stretching out ahead. Lonely and fed up. My trousers were too tight – my latest diet had defeated me. Why should she remember me? Fat, spotty, with stupid frizzy hair. And how could I be so shallow when all over the city there were people who had actually lost someone, or were terribly burned in hospital? I was a horrible person.

Once the drinks had come and I'd had half of mine and listened to the latest gossip about Mark Foster, whose mother had apparently caught him shagging his brother's girlfriend, I began to relax.

Only then did I let my eyes return to her corner. Bel was talking, hands flung wide, gesticulating. The boy was listening, and smiling, a small, thin smile. Then she laughed, throwing back her head, turned and noticed me.

She gave a nod, a clear nod in greeting, and I waved. Immediately I wished I hadn't: a nod in return would have been way cooler.

She beckoned and I went, like a puppy.

They squashed up on their banquette and I sat next to her.

'Colin.' She made introductions. 'Bel.' A finger pressed to her own breastbone. She wore a dark shiny top, a different one, a V-neck with a zip up the front. 'Lydia.' She pointed to me.

She knew my name.

'You're from here?' she said.

'I am,' I said. 'Sad but true.'

Her eyes danced. 'Colin says we can get into the disco at the university, don't even need an NUS card.'

'True,' I said. Not that I'd been. 'Just proof of age.'

'Wicked! We'll go before last orders. Beat the rush. You coming?'

'OK,' I said. *OK?* I sounded so lame. 'So where are you from?' I swigged my drink hoping that I wasn't being too nosy, or too boring. It was the sort of question my parents might ask.

'France,' she said. I must have looked surprised because she chuckled and said, 'Not French. My dad worked there, then London, now he has to work here.'

'Bummer,' I said.

'Oh, I don't know.' She gave a little shrug, still smiling. Was she teasing me? 'Least if I bomb my exams, I can blame it on the move.'

Colin said nothing. He seemed content to watch her, his eyes glittering. I guessed he was smashed. He was slightly built and had dark blond hair, a long, sharp nose and a pointed chin. His teeth were crooked like mine.

'A levels?' I said.

'Yes. Yawn,' she said. 'The English isn't so bad. You still at school?'

'Lower sixth. Bradford Girls' Grammar,' I said.

'Ah, a Proddie.' She formed her fingers into a cross. 'I'm at St Joe's. For my sins. Hah!' The energy came off her, like heat. She offered me a cigarette, then handed one to Colin. Stood up with her own unlit. 'Skin up for later.' She winked.

I stood too, sucking in my stomach, feeling hot, my pulse too quick. 'When d'you want to go?' I asked her.

'Twenty past. Tell your mates,' she said.

'Yeah.'

None of my crowd wanted to come. That meant spending money on a taxi home if I missed the midnight bus. And the risk of playing gooseberry.

But there really wasn't any question.

She knew my name.

Soon we were spending most Saturday evenings together. Katy complained when I wriggled out of babysitting. 'At least you'll get to keep all the money,' I said lamely.

I felt mean, but there was no way I was going to sacrifice the thrill of time with Bel in return for a tedious evening eating cheese and crackers and chocolate éclairs, and watching B movies or chat shows on TV.

Things were awkward between Katy and me on the walk to and from school. Silent, save for the occasional exchange about homework or scandals involving other pupils or staff.

Alison and Sue confronted me about it. Ambushed me in the sixth-form common room during a free period. 'Katy's fed up,' Alison said. 'It's like you can't be bothered being friends any more.'

'She was in tears yesterday,' Sue added.

'We're still friends,' I protested. I could feel my face was bright red. 'I just don't want to babysit any more.'

What did they expect would happen? That I'd feel so guilty I'd end my new friendship and everything would go back to how it was before?

'We're still friends,' I said again, picking up my books and shoving them into my bag.

'We're thinking about skating, for Katy's birthday, a week on Saturday. Get a curry first.'

Bel, gliding, on the frozen lake.

It was a test. I felt a sullen resentment, like a lump, behind my breastbone. My jaw tightened. 'Sounds good,' I said.

'We haven't told her yet,' Alison said. 'We wanted to make sure you'd come.'

Dutifully I went and joined in the chatter, laughed at our pratfalls and even enjoyed the sensation of speed when I completed a circuit, the music deafening, the flashing, swooping lights almost blinding.

I played the part. It was a survival strategy, belonging to a clique. Those who didn't were pitied. And disliked. Lesser beings. Freaks. Idiots.

Katy maybe expected me to resume the babysitting with her but I never did. Then she started going out with Richard and I was off the hook.

Bel lived at the other side of town, across the valley. Two bus rides from me. Their detached house was much bigger than our semi. The garage had an automatic door, like something from a film. They had a cleaner. But we never spent much time there, even though her parents were out a lot, working or socialising. It was a long walk from the bus and not close to any pubs.

'It's a mausoleum,' Bel said one time, when I suggested we rent a video and watch it at hers. (We hadn't got a video player yet, despite me nagging my dad.) 'It's better at yours. And we can go to the Swan or the Queens. See who's around.'

* * *

12

One evening at the university disco, as they put on the last record, Alison Moyet singing 'That Ole Devil Called Love', Bel asked me if she could stay at my house. We were both giddy on drink.

'What about Colin?' I said. He'd gone to the Gents. Bel and Colin were affectionate with each other, tactile, but I wasn't sure whether they were definitely going out together. I was too self-conscious to ask her straight out. She'd talked about people being hung up on rigid relationships and not being free, and I didn't want her to lump me in with them.

'I can't go to his house,' she said. 'Bunk beds and a kid brother.' Then she swiped at her hair, pushing it out of her eyes. 'We're just friends. Like you and me.' So we were just friends. I was absorbing that when she said, 'You know he's gay?'

A frisson of surprise made me dizzy. 'Colin is?' Colin was an observer, watchful, rarely taking centre stage. He never said very much, but when he did he was witty, incisive. He was also unfailingly kind.

She nodded. 'He keeps quiet about it.'

'Right. I won't say anything.' I rushed on, 'You'd have to share my bed, though.'

'Lydia,' she arched her hip, planted a hand on it, angled her arm, 'I would love to share your bed.'

We reached home at the same time as my parents, who'd been at a dinner dance and were decidedly tipsy themselves.

'Nightcap?' my dad offered. And we accepted with alacrity.

Bel charmed my parents with anecdotes of French life, and one Drambuie turned into three before my mum called time.

Upstairs any awkwardness I might have felt vanished when I fell over with one foot tangled in my jeans and we both became hysterical with laughter.

In bed I turned off the lamp and the dark rushed in. Bel shifted as she pulled the eiderdown up. She was lying on her back.

I was aware of the space between us, only a couple of inches – the bed was a small double. What if I touched her by accident? Or farted? *Oh, God.*

13

'You'd better not snore,' she said, making us laugh again. Then, when we'd quietened, 'Hold hands.' And she patted the bed until she found mine and wrapped her fingers round it. 'Sweet dreams,' she said.

I was happy. So happy. I wanted to stay awake all night, feeling her hand in mine.

I was asleep in minutes.

Chapter Three

Bel called me when I was working at the vet's. 'There's a rave tonight,' she said, 'up on Baildon Moor.'

'How will we get back?' I said. 'The last bus is—'

'We won't need to. It's an all-nighter, doesn't start till after the pubs. Tell your parents you'll stay at mine. I'll do the same.'

My stomach clenched at the thought of being found out. 'What if they check?' I tried to keep my voice low – everyone in the waiting room could hear me.

She gave an impatient sigh. 'Well, I'm going. It'll be amazing. I'm getting the ten to eleven bus. Bring something to drink.'

'I'll see.'

My parents barely registered my announcement. My brother Steven's school report had arrived and it was a big disappointment so he was getting their undivided attention.

I bought two large bottles of cider from the off-licence near the bus stop.

When the bus arrived I had a moment's panic. Where was Bel? Then I saw her at the very back with a group I didn't know.

The pubs in the village were closing when we got there. It was a still night as we walked towards the moor, leaving the streetlights behind. The stars grew brighter, frosted across an inky sky.

One of the people had a torch and they led the way, the rest of us stumbling and giggling behind them.

Bel and I were sharing a quarter bottle of rum. We heard the music first. Then, when we crested the ridge, we saw a huge bonfire and an illuminated stage with DJs at the decks. I felt the rush in my veins and had an urge to run down there but I'd have broken my neck if I'd tried.

We joined in the dancing and soon it was warm enough to shed our coats.

Bel shook my shoulder and opened her hand. Two pills. Ecstasy. I hesitated only for a moment.

Time stretched and warped as the drug took hold. The music was in my bones, the beat driving my heart, filling my skull. The stars all seemed to be shining for me, for us all. The smell of grass and earth was dizzying. Now and then smoke billowed over from the massive bonfire, making me cough, making my eyes water. I loved the whole world. I loved Bel. I hugged her, then the others around us. I loved them all. My skin was tingling, like I was truly alive for the first time ever.

I pulled Bel towards me. Kissed her on the mouth. She smiled and danced away, arms held high.

I don't know how much later it was that the music cut out and we heard engines and sirens and dogs barking.

For a moment I thought it was part of the event, a light show or an alternative circus or something, but then Bel grabbed my arm. 'Run. Police.'

We scooped up our coats and ran further onto the moor, into the darkness, holding hands. When Bel tripped over, I went too, hitting my temple on a rock sending an explosion of white-hot pain through my head.

The land led down into a valley and I could just make out some trees ahead. Once we reached them we huddled down, hoping to be safe from the police. A wash of nausea made me swing away from Bel to vomit violently. Had anyone heard? We waited, but although we could hear calls and shouts at some distance, nothing came any closer.

'Move away from the sick,' I said.

Further into the wood we settled again. There was no wind but I could hear rustling in the undergrowth. A mouse, perhaps, or a shrew. My throat was sore, my face throbbing. 'Now what?' I said.

16

'Wait for daylight,' Bel said.

We were way too hyper for sleep and spent the next hours talking. It all felt incredibly deep and meaningful, but by the time the sun rose, washing the sky a peachy pink and lighting the mist that hovered just above the ground, I'd forgotten all of it.

'Shit. Your face.' Bel had a mirror in her bag, she passed it to me.

'What am I going to say?'

'Tell them you fell on our stairs. That my mum tried to take you to hospital but you didn't want to go,' she said.

It was six in the morning. We walked into the village. A milk-float, tinking as it went, the only sign of life. The first bus wasn't until seven so we began walking back to Bradford.

I felt tired out, flat; all the magic from dancing under the stars, from being in love with the world and everyone in it, had soured and drained away. I could smell sick on my clothes and my head ached. I just wanted to go home and sleep. I barely cared any more if my parents found out I'd been out all night. What could they do?

My dad was washing our car on the drive when I walked up the street, a blister on my little toe making me limp.

'What happened to you?' he said, staring at my face, more suspicious than alarmed.

I trotted out the lie, trying to make it sound amusing.

'Had you been drinking?'

'A bit.'

'Maybe that'll teach you,' he said drily.

I managed to avoid my mum, whom I could hear in the kitchen. She'd have been more observant and probably smelt the sick, then started grilling me. I went straight up to shower.

Most of the day I dozed. My parents were out for the afternoon playing golf. The headache still clung to me when I got up for tea. And a shivery feeling. What if the police had caught us? Would we have been arrested? Charged?

My mum was irritable over the meal: there'd been some falling out among people on the committee at the golf club and someone had been elected that she thought shouldn't have been. After hearing how I'd fallen she said, 'You're so clumsy, Lydia. You need to be more careful. You could have lost an eye.'

Steven pulled a face at me and I wanted to stab them all with my fork.

I rang Bel that evening. 'My face is still killing me,' I said.

'But wasn't it awesome?' she said. 'All of it?'

I tried to echo the tone in her voice, rise above the leaden feeling that had dogged me all day. 'Amazing,' I said. 'Really amazing.'

Chapter Four

Bel flunked her A levels and was told she had to re-sit in November.

For a month in the summer her family went to France and I was marooned at home. My family and I were due to have our annual holiday as usual in the last two weeks of August, caravanning in Scarborough on the east coast. As July ticked by I was irritated by everything from Steven's inane jokes to my mum's insistence that I make myself useful and 'cut the grass' or 'hoover the carpets'.

The days dragged on, deadly dull. I lay on the floor in my room listening to the radio and wanting to scream. To distract myself I took up projects: making a leather purse, decorating plant pots with stencils. The results were workaday, practically competent but not particularly imaginative.

Bel sent me a postcard. The Eiffel Tower. She'd drawn a stick figure falling through the sky from the top. And scrawled, *Wish I was there!* on the back. Had she been up to the top? I'd hate it. I'd a fear of heights, more particularly of falling or jumping from a great one.

A few days before we would leave for Scarborough, I was helping to make tea, mashing potatoes while my mum poured onion gravy into a gravy boat to go with the sausages. I asked her if I could stay at home instead: Bel would be back tomorrow and she could stay with me when they left. We could look after Harvey, our cat. Save bothering the Marsdens next door. The idea had come to me that morning and I'd been rehearsing how to broach it all day.

She frowned, mouth pinched. 'You don't want to come with us?' She was hurt.

'Please, Mum? I'm seventeen.'

'But you've been so bored,' she said.

19

'On my own, yes. It'd be different with a friend.'

'I'll have to talk to your father about it.' Coldly.

I'd disappointed her and I felt a pang of sadness mixed with a flare of frustration. She'd tell him it was a bad idea. They'd make me go. Forced marches to the beach. Wasps and a chilly wind off the sea, sand in everything, and doing the washing-up in the stupid sink with its little spigot and a foot pump for the water.

I was so sick of them all, sick of being me, stuck there. Sick of the rules and routines. They'd drag me to Scarborough and I'd show them. I'd wait for a moonlit night, run away and throw myself off the cliffs. Like Bel's drawing. They'd be so sorry. It'd be a tragedy. They'd weep at my funeral. So young. Such promise. A broken dream.

My mum must have spoken to my dad straight after tea, because when I brought the coffee in, she said, 'You'd have to look after the place.'

My heart bumped. 'I would, honestly.'

'No parties. No bad behaviour.'

'No, I promise.'

It would be awesome.

Bel's parents said no. She told me over the phone. I stood in our hall, wrapping the curls of the telephone cord round and round my fingers till they throbbed.

'They say I've got to revise,' she said. 'Like there's any point. I hate them.'

How could they be so cruel? 'You can revise with me,' I said, fretful. 'I can test you.'

'Different subjects.'

'So?' I said. 'They don't know that.' Half bold, half desperate. 'Besides, I did English at O level. Tell them.'

'They won't listen.'

'I could talk to them.' Could I? Was I brave enough?

'It's hopeless,' she said.

Why wouldn't she try? She was just giving in. A horrible thought formed in my mind: she didn't want to come. It was my plan not hers.

She was making excuses because she didn't like me and didn't want to spend a fortnight with me. I said something quickly, tears in my voice, and hung up.

It was my mum made it happen, once she saw how sad I was. I never shared my deeper fear, just told her about the revision. She rang their house and spoke to Bel's mother while I sat on the landing and eavesdropped. Mum explained how they'd hoped I'd look after the house and the cat but they couldn't leave me on my own. Boasting about my academic achievements, she said it would be a perfect way for us both to revise, that I was very ambitious and they trusted me to act responsibly while they were gone. I was level-headed and had never let them down. She even invited them over in case they wanted to see the house. As if they might be harbouring unfavourable images of where or how we lived.

I wondered whether perhaps there'd been some sort of who's-the-most-liberal competition going on. Anyway, if there was, it worked in our favour.

I was almost exploding with impatience on the day my parents set off. My mum snapped at me when I tried to hurry things along and put the box of groceries into the caravan before the kitchen utensils. Hanging offence.

Then there was the palaver of getting the caravan hooked up to the tow-bar on the car and checking the electrics. More fussing about with a flask for the journey and Steven sent to the corner shop for milk and a sliced loaf.

As soon as the caravan disappeared at the end of the road, I ran into the house. In my parents' bedroom I cleared the bedside tables, putting the books and Rennies, hair grips and alarm clock into the cupboards beneath.

I sniffed the pillows – they were OK. I shoved their slippers under the bed. The rest would do. We could sleep there, it was a bigger bed, and if we wanted to smoke in the house we'd go to my bedroom or the lounge.

* * *

21

Bel hugged me tight, made promises to her father, who was dropping her off, and groaned as she lifted her suitcase over the threshold.

'You've got a tan,' I said. She was the colour of toffee, like a Caramac.

'It was blazing, even hotter than this.' She wore a flimsy black scarf around her neck and pulled it off.

'Wow!' A huge love bite, a violet blotch pricked with red, marked the side of her neck.

'I've been sweltering, hiding it from them.'

'Who gave it to you?'

'Armand. Bit of a dope but gorgeous-looking. Sort of young Al Pacino type.'

While I'd been pining for her, she'd been with some boy. And the postcard? Had she actually meant that?

'Is there anything to eat?' she said. 'Shall I dump this?' She kicked the case.

'Did you sleep with him?' I said.

A moment's surprise flashed through her face, then amusement brightened her eyes. 'It passed the time.'

'Will you see him again?'

Did she hear the antagonism in my voice? Sense that I was upset? I think she did. Bel could read people well, even if she refused to take into account their feelings.

It had been seven months since that kiss. We'd shared a bed several times but Bel had never made an approach. Sometimes I dreamed about us, having sex together, but whenever I masturbated my fantasies were of men. Was I still hoping we'd be more than just friends?

'How about a drink?' she said. 'I've a bottle of Pernod in here. And I'll tell you all about it. Every gory detail. Have you got ice?'

She made him sound totally unimportant, this Armand, but when she launched into the mechanics of who had done what, I had to get up and start rummaging in the fridge for food so she wouldn't see how uncomfortable I was.

'He was the best so far, anyway,' she said.

So he wasn't the first. 'Out of how many?'

'Five.'

Five! I tried not to betray any shock. 'I'm still a virgin,' I blurted out.

'Yeah,' she said. 'But they say it's best to wait until you're sure. Pick the right person.'

As if they were lining up to woo me.

'I did miss you,' she said. Then, 'Two whole weeks!' And she raised her drink. 'To us!'

Her smile warmed me through. It was impossible to resent her. I reached over and clinked my glass on hers. 'To us.'

Beneath the residual sting of disappointment I think I was relieved. We would be friends, not lovers. I wouldn't be just a number in a string of conquests. They'd come and go but I'd be a constant. We would never break up.

We fell into a lazy routine, sleeping till midday and staying up till two or three every morning. The weather was relentlessly hot and sunny. We got stoned and sunbathed topless. Bel said all the women did it in France. The garden was overlooked but the Marsdens were out at work during the week. I couldn't help but compare her breasts to mine. While hers were small, neat, with dark brown aureoles and large dusky rose nipples, mine were three times the size, pillowy and freckled, my nipples small and pink.

In the sun I went a reddish brown, and burned my nose.

We ate from tins and packets. Finished the Pernod, drank cider. Bought chips and followed them with cubes of jelly and ice cream when we got the munchies.

I made sure we did some revision as promised. She knew the themes for her English lit already, likely question topics, but hadn't learned many quotes to illustrate anything she wrote. We picked out a batch, learned them by rote and I tested her at random. When we were lying in the garden, or walking to the shops, or eating a meal, I'd give her a theme – the power of reputation in *Othello*, free will and Fate in *The Mayor of Casterbridge*, imagery in Plath's *Ariel*.

I couldn't help much with the French. 'How could you fail French?' I asked her.

23

'Now you sound like my mum!' she grumbled. 'The language is fine but the rest, it's more of the same. Tomes of it. Bloody *Père Goriot* and Voltaire. On and on. *Très ennuyeux.*'

In bed she always held my hand.

One afternoon Bel and I were in my room; she was doing my hair, backcombing it into a helmet and trying to get some bits to dangle down. It was airless, the heat stifling. The window was jammed half open, and when I tried to open it wider, it wouldn't budge.

'Here, let me.' Bel banged it with the heel of her hand. There was a tearing sound, then the whole frame fell away, crashing onto the roof slates below.

Shit! I scrambled onto the chair. Bel was hooting with laughter. I peered down, ignoring the sick, dizzy feeling it conjured, but I couldn't see anything.

'What am I going to say?' I was supposed to look after the place.

'It's an accident.' She waved a hand, brushing away any concern. 'Shit happens.'

We planned a day trip. Made a picnic of hard-boiled eggs and ham sandwiches, Babybel cheeses and Marathon bars. Got the bus to town and another up to Haworth. Home to the Brontë sisters.

The Parsonage where they had lived was charging for admission, more than we could afford, but we wandered around the graveyard there, then walked over the moors to Top Withens, the tumbledown house that had inspired *Wuthering Heights*.

The moorland was open, the sky a high blue. Butterflies were flitting in the heather and grasshoppers bounced away from us. Bel had brought a ready-rolled joint along and, after checking that no one was around, she fired it up and we shared it. She began singing a wavering rendition of the Kate Bush song. Then we were running, arms wide open, racing towards and then past each other, twirling. Tripping sometimes, the ground springy underfoot, with tussocks of grass, heather and bilberry. Breathless, we stopped, lay on our backs on the ground.

'"Oh lift me from the grass!"' I quoted Shelley. '"I die! I faint! I fail!"'

'Can I have your picnic, then?' Bel said.

'Philistine.'

I wanted the day never to end.

Chapter Five

Bel had scraped through her re-sits but, to her parents' dismay, refused to apply for a course at a poly. She was living in Leeds and working in a restaurant there. In the spring she got together with Craig, a student at Bradford Uni.

I was revising hard. I'd had an offer from the new school of biological sciences at Manchester University and was determined to get my grades. I wasn't going out much but when I did it was usually with Bel and Colin.

Bel and I went to see *Witness* at the cinema. We were in the toilets afterwards, Bel flicking at her hair in the mirror, when she said, 'I'm pregnant.'

I felt dizzy. 'What are you going to do?'

'Get rid,' she said.

'Is it Craig's?'

'Yes.'

'Does he know?'

'No. Look, I need you to cover for me.' She leaned forwards, licked a finger and smoothed her eyebrows. 'I can get an appointment at the Brook Street clinic but if my parents start nosing around just say I'm with you that day.'

'Aren't you going to tell them?'

She looked away from her reflection to me. 'Are you mad? It's a mortal sin. The nuns trot out the slide show every few months, babies in shreds. At least your lot get spared that. They'd crucify me. Like literally. Force me to have the thing.' She glared. 'So?'

'OK.' I nodded. 'Do you want . . . Will you go on your own?'

'I'll be fine,' she said. 'You could meet me after, if you can bunk off. Just in case.'

I had images of her collapsing at my feet, a pool of blood on the pavement. Going into shock and dying in my arms.

'Are you sure?' I said.

'Can you imagine me with a kid? I don't ever want children. I mean, hey, what sort of world is it? We're all about to be blown sky high if we're not poisoned by Chernobyl first. Why would anyone want to bring kids into all that?'

Seeing her go through it and imagining myself faced with the same situation made me determined never to take a risk. I'd be extra careful about contraception when I had sex.

The summer before I left home I got a Dutch cap from the family-planning clinic and practised using it. I had my eye on Craig's friend, Bill. Bill was a Geordie with gangly arms and legs and a lopsided smile. Most of the students went home for the holidays but he stayed in Bradford, working at Grattan's, the mail-order catalogue warehouse.

We met up one night, Bel and Colin, Bill and I. After drinks we moved on to a club where they played lovers rock, and soul classics. Lots of slow dancing. The perfect place to pick people up. Bill danced with me for almost every number, and when I got ready to leave he invited me to his room. I had to refuse. I was expected home. A one o'clock curfew. I couldn't wait for the autumn when I'd be able to stay out all night whenever I felt like it. Answer to no one.

'Come round tomorrow,' he said, kissing me.

I knew what he wanted. I wanted it too. And when it happened, on a mattress on the floor, with the Smiths playing and the sun streaming round the edges of the curtains, I was lost in the experience. Hungry for the sensations of his hands on me, his lips too, ready when he entered me. Expecting it to hurt more than it did. I was breathless, brimming with excitement as he came. He rolled off me and we laughed at the sucking sound that made. Then, without a word, he stroked me to climax.

From conversations with Bel, from magazines I'd read, I appreciated that this attention to my needs was a rare thing in a man. I'd struck lucky. If Bill had been willing I'd have settled into a relationship with him. For a while I thought I loved him. I loved the sex and he was easy company, kind of goofy. But he didn't want strings. He didn't want a steady girlfriend. He had no interest in commitment.

A bit like Bel.

Before I left for Manchester I decided not to see Bill any more, not in that way: I was getting miserable, jealous. Bel listened to me cry about it, and fed me drinks and smokes and teased me. 'Once you get to uni, you'll have the pick of the crop. All those brainy boys and their Bunsen burners.'

Manchester was all I'd hoped for. Living in a shared house meant there was always someone I could talk to, watch telly or go to the pub with. The coursework was demanding but I loved it, I did well, one of a handful of women in my year. I didn't see Bel for weeks but I wrote and she replied with short notes and cartoons in answer to my longer letters.

The end of my first term, I was home for Christmas. Bel was back at her parents' for a while – she'd left her job. When I rang she said she had flu, she didn't want to talk, and when I tried again a couple of days later her mother answered, and said Bel was still recovering from the accident. *Accident?* Why had Bel lied to me?

The next morning I got the bus over to her house, feeling slightly foolish. What if she didn't want to see me?

There was no answer when I knocked. Then I thought I heard movement inside. I called through the letterbox, 'Bel, it's me, Lydia.'

She opened the door and I gasped in horror. Her face was terribly bruised, one eye like a purple egg with a slit across, her cheek swollen. A cut on her nostril.

'Jesus, Bel, what happened?'

She didn't reply, just turned back into the house, and I followed her through to the lounge where she'd obviously been holed up. It was littered with mugs, tissues, magazines, a blanket on the couch.

She sat down slowly, like an old woman.

'You want a cuppa? Anything?' I tried to fill the silence.

'You mustn't say anything,' she said. 'They think it was an accident, that a motorbike knocked me over.'

I waited, a chill across my shoulders.

She cleared her throat. 'It was Craig.'

'What?'

'Someone else caught my eye.' She barked a short laugh, wincing as she did. 'So he caught mine. And then some.'

'He hit you?' It was hard to believe. I'd never seen Craig angry or brooding. He seemed so normal. 'Why couldn't you tell me?'

It was hard to read the expression beneath the damage but in the slump of her shoulders I read shame or defeat. Something alien to the Bel I loved. 'You should report it. That's assault,' I said.

'No,' she said. 'It's over. I don't want to ever think about the creepy bastard again.'

'How could he do this?' I said. 'You loved him.'

'He loved me too,' she said. Then, 'The best sex I ever had was with Craig. After he'd hit me. Make-up sex. It was amazing.'

I must have gawped or gasped. She said, 'I must be tapped, right? Love hurts.' She groaned. 'I sound like a fucking greetings card. Talk about something else.'

I spent the rest of the day there and agreed to keep her secret.

Chapter Six

When I graduated, I started working as a trainee biomedical scientist in the haematology department at Leeds General Hospital, running blood counts, preparing slides when something needed further analysis. I loved it, doing something useful, learning about the different areas of lab work, earning a wage too. I had a room in a house in Kirkstall, in Leeds, which was handy for the hospital.

Unemployment was sky high but Bel always fell on her feet, changing jobs every few months. She could turn a hand to most things. 'I've a low boredom threshold,' she said one time, 'but I don't think I can put that on my application.'

She'd rented a flat in a villa near Lister Park in Bradford, all old cornices and big sash windows. Freezing in winter, baking in summer.

For her twenty-fourth Bel decided to use her birthday money to get a tattoo at a place in Leeds. I'd agreed to string along, do some shopping in town while she was having it done, then go for a curry with her and Colin back in Bradford, followed by a party at her flat in Manningham.

I thought she was mad. Bikers and sailors had tattoos, and people in prison did their own. She already had a swallow on one ankle. Now she wanted a rose, a briar rose with a bracelet of thorns, on her upper arm. What if she got sick of them?

At the tattoo parlour, designs, images and lettering covered every inch of wall space and there was a curtained-off area behind the counter. I assumed that was where the inking took place.

The guy who ran it was Irish. He had sleeves of ink up and down both arms, Celtic knots and patterns and stylised animals in the design. I'd never seen anything like it. He caught me staring. 'And yourself, are you not having one?' he said.

'Never,' I said clearly.

He smiled.

When I called back for Bel, her arm was covered with cling film, the edges held in place with adhesive strips. Pinpricks of blood smeared the plastic wrap. 'Does it hurt?' I said.

'Like buggery. See you later,' she told the tattooist.

'You've invited him?' I said.

'He more or less invited himself. Gift of the gab. He asked if you were seeing anyone,' she said.

I stopped walking. 'What?'

'You heard. I said you were unattached.'

'So you're setting me up with some sleazy, smooth-talking Irish tattooist?'

'Sleazy?'

I couldn't explain. Tattoos turned me off – the idea of doing that for a living, the needles puncturing the skin, the beads of blood. Daft, really, given what I was up to every day, handling bags full of blood or plasma, peering at samples and conducting tests.

'You'll be fine. He's not a dog,' Bel said. 'If you're not interested just tell him. He'll get the message.'

He confounded me, that evening at Bel's party. Disarmed me, not just with his easy manner, his charm, but because he listened, really listened, when I talked to him.

Usually, explaining my work in the lab to potential suitors led to them making weak jokes about vampires or AIDS and giving off a faint sense of distaste (I must be a brainbox, a nerd, a swot, and probably frigid to boot, to be working in science), followed by a change of subject. Conversation petered out and died unless it could be hauled onto safer ground, music or sport, anything the other party, the man, could prattle about easily, with me interjecting responses at strategic intervals.

Not Mac. He listened and considered what I was saying, asked me to clarify points, asked more questions. Not just about the job day-to-day, the world of the haematology lab, of counts and coagulation, cross-matching and transfusions, tests and analyses, but about the science in general.

He nodded, grinning. 'That's grand,' he said now and again, each new fact something that fascinated him, gave him pleasure.

'I'm on blood counts at the moment, pretty routine, feeding the machine.'

He laughed.

'But transfusion, the blood bank, that gets busy with emergencies. Things are needed quickly. Everything we have comes from the Blood Transfusion Service. Some blood groups are rarer – that's where the shortages are,' I said. 'And even among the main ABO group we always need B negative and the ABs.'

'What are you?' Mac said.

'O negative. I'm the universal donor – anyone can use mine, more or less. You?'

'No idea. But I'd not be welcome, would I?' He nodded at his forearms. 'This AIDS business, that'll affect the amount of donations you get?'

'Yes. Gay men are banned.' Freddie Mercury, one of my musical heroes, had died of the disease the year before. I thought of Colin, how scared he must be with it all. He was working as a teacher, and the government had brought in Clause 28, prohibiting the promotion of homosexuality. Bel called it a witch-hunt.

'And anyone who's used a needle,' I went on. 'Some people are worried they might get infected just giving blood.'

'Or shaking hands,' he said. 'I'm a republican myself, but Lady Di going round doing that, you got to give her credit.'

Mac was tall and broad, like a farmer or a blacksmith. As I thought that, I imagined him stripped off. Lost my concentration. Batted the image away.

He noticed. 'You OK?'

'Fine. Just use the loo.' I wove through the crowd, thinking, He's nice. God, he's really nice. And fit. I knew nothing about him, apart from his line of work. Had he really asked Bel if I was single, or was she being kind?

When I got back to the room, he'd gone. My stomach dropped. So he didn't actually fancy me. Just a good actor. He'd escaped as soon as he could. I felt clumsy, suddenly too big for the space. Alice in Wonderland.

Bel, who was between lovers, was holding court in one corner. A gale of laughter surged above the music.

I wanted to leave, go home, crawl into bed and cry, but I was sleeping at her place and it would be hours before the revelries stopped.

'Lost our spot.' A voice in my ear.

I whirled round. Mac was holding up two glasses. 'Bloody Mary,' he said, handing me one. 'Seemed fitting. Except it's orange juice, no tomato.'

'That would be a Screwdriver,' I said.

There was a pause. Hysteria rose in my chest, and I saw him suck in his cheeks to stop himself laughing.

I broke first. 'Seems fitting.' I giggled, trying not to spill any of my drink.

We sat up talking till four thirty when the last guests stumbled off. About all sorts. From our childhoods – he had grown up on a farm so no wonder he was brawny – to the abuse he sometimes got when people heard his accent and decided to blame him for the bombing campaign that the Provisional IRA were engaged in.

We kissed too. A lot. But went no further.

Bel and a bloke I didn't know disappeared into her bedroom, and I fetched my sleeping bag and rucksack from the cupboard in the hall.

'You can sleep here, if you like,' I said.

'No. I'd best get back. I'll ring you?'

'Yes. I'm on days at the moment. Usually home by half six.' I gave him my work number too.

'Do they allow personal calls?'

'If they're short.'

He nodded. We kissed again.

33

And again on the doorstep.

The sky was just getting light; everything smelt fresh and cool.

Once he'd gone I brushed my teeth and got myself a glass of water, hoping it might help with the hangover to come. I was retrieving a cushion from behind the sofa to use as a pillow when there was a knock at the front door.

'Hey?' He had his head cocked to one side, studying me. 'Would you say that sleeping bag will do for the two of us, now?'

Chapter Seven

After months of sharing our time between his place and mine, Mac and I rented a ground-floor flat together in a large terraced house in Woodhouse, not far north of Leeds city centre where we both worked.

While I was settling down, enjoying the warmth of a full-time relationship, hopelessly in love with Mac, Bel got itchy feet and went travelling. She'd be gone for months at a time until she ran out of money, then would come home for just long enough to save up for another trip.

Occasional postcards came from India, Afghanistan or Tibet. She never said much, a line or two about her adventures. I'd pin each one to the noticeboard until the next arrived and kept them in a shoebox along with the Eiffel Tower card and tickets from the concerts I'd been to, like Culture Club and Adam and the Ants.

One day I found myself asking Mac whether we could afford a washing-machine. 'Am I turning into a Stepford wife?' I said. The most mundane activities, repainting our rooms, buying a decent set of pans, sharing a roast-chicken dinner, made me happy.

'Is that a marriage proposal?' he said.

'No.'

'You're turning me down?' He faked being hurt, his dark eyes wide.

'We don't need all that,' I said.

'What?'

'Stuff, vows, bridesmaids.'

'We could cut straight to the honeymoon now,' he said. 'C'mere.' He kissed me. Then again. Raised a hand to touch one of my nipples. 'What about eating a bit later today?'

'Maybe. What about the washing-machine? There are places that do reconditioned ones.'

'God, woman, you're so sexy when you talk kitchen appliances. Drives me wild.' He bit my neck and we continued the fun in the bedroom.

Mac had not told his family we were cohabiting: he said they'd 'have conniptions', especially his mother, if it was to be known that not only was he living in sin but with an unbeliever to boot.

He was the seventh child and the baby of the family.

'It's 1992,' I had said.

'Not in Ireland. There's a hole in the space-time continuum. Covers the whole place, so it does. Keeps us permanently in 1955. Before Elvis.'

We were caught out the following autumn when his father and one of his brothers made a surprise visit on their way from the ferry up to Whitby where they were working on a building project.

Mac had a late appointment at the shop and I'd got in from work ahead of him. I was up a stepladder in the lounge, hanging new curtains I'd made, when there was knocking at the door.

The family resemblance was striking. Like looking at two variations on Mac, the same tangled black hair, the same deep blue eyes, small differences in the shape of the chin or nose but no more than that. I was fascinated. Steven and I aren't alike at all.

'Mac's at work,' I explained, furious that my face was aflame. 'He won't be much longer. Please come in and have a cup of tea.'

'You're Lydia?' the brother, Niall, said.

'That's right.' I couldn't think of any story to account for my presence and they only had to glance round the place, or visit the bathroom, to see I was resident.

To seal the deal Mac came in, half an hour later, calling out, 'Honey, I'm home.'

There was a lot of backslapping, laughter and joking between the three of them. Mac went for fish and chips – the pie I was cooking wouldn't stretch to four – and I thought it all seemed amiable

36

enough, but once they'd driven off, Mac closed the door, leaned back against it and said, 'I am so fucked.'

'What can she do?' I said. I remembered Bel, *They'll crucify me. Like literally*.

'Guilt trip me for the rest of eternity,' Mac said.

'Doesn't that only work if you let it?'

'Conditioned response,' he said. 'Pavlov's dogs. Hard to shake. Ah, sod them. Let's eat.'

'After all those chips?'

'That was just to put me on till later.' Another thing we shared, large appetites and a love of food.

Over the next couple of years Mac bore the censure of his mother and the extended family. There'd be periodic phone calls when he'd be grilled by one aunt or another about why he was choosing to disgrace the family and why he couldn't just do the right thing. If he respected me, surely he'd want to marry me.

When he did go home to visit, he went on his own. 'It's just easier,' he said.

'If we have kids,' I said to him, one balmy night on holiday in Lisbon, after we'd polished off a delicious seafood platter and a large carafe of dry white wine, 'do you think your mother would come round? If she was going to be a grandma?'

'Out of wedlock?' he gasped. 'I have no idea. And she already has seven grandchildren. Hey – are you trying to tell me something? Because bringing my mother into it sort of kills the romance, you know.'

'I don't want kids just yet but I am thinking about it more. I want to have a baby eventually.'

'Me too,' he said. 'Dozens.'

'One or two would be plenty,' I said.

We thought it would be so easy.

Chapter Eight

By 1995 Bel was working in Berlin. She'd met a German bloke in Tibet and gone back there with him, got a bar job.

When I went over to visit she'd split up with the traveller, moved into a squat in a warehouse where a lot of artists and musicians lived, and found work in a nightclub, one that showcased new bands, mainly electro and techno stuff.

I was so looking forward to time together, eager to catch up with her news, and to share what was happening to me and Mac – that we were hoping to buy a house together, were talking about starting a family. With my training at work complete and exams done in the different competencies, I'd been promoted to biomedical scientist, which meant a higher pay grade. Also I'd be able to take six months maternity leave.

But Bel and I were never alone. She let me have her room – she was sleeping on the floor above with an artist called Bruno, who was doing huge screen-prints: blocks of colour with photocopied news headlines stuck over them. She took me to see bands, to walk along the Berlin Wall, to Bierkellers, but we were always in a group. Wasn't she interested in me any more?

She was thinner, edgy. People were taking a lot of cocaine. It wasn't something I was into. Her friends were welcoming, chatting to me about the UK, asking about the nightlife and the music scene. When they heard I'd studied in Manchester they wanted to know all about the Hacienda. I'd only been twice so couldn't really say much. Most of them were fluent in English while I couldn't speak any German. It struck me there was optimism among them. I guessed it came from the unification of the country a few years before, from the sense of new freedoms and liberation that tearing down the Wall had brought.

On my last night, Bel and I were going out to buy cigarettes and beer before eating at the house. She was working later. I was feeling fed up, in two minds whether to tag along to the club or stay in and get a decent sleep before my coach home the next morning.

Halfway to the shop she suddenly grabbed my arm and swung me round. 'This way.'

'What?' Why were we retracing our steps?

Then she pulled me into a small alleyway. 'Wait.'

'What is it? What's the matter?'

'Martin.'

'Who?'

'The guy I met in Tibet.'

'So?'

She had her hands stuffed into the back pockets of her jeans, her leather jacket open, the zips glinting in the streetlight.

'He thinks I owe him some money.'

'Do you?'

She rolled her eyes, looked off to the side. 'He paid my fare back. Covered the bills.'

'That was months ago. Is it a lot?'

'About eight hundred sterling,' she said.

'Blimey. Can't you pay him a bit at a time?'

She glanced at me. 'He can afford it,' she said eventually.

'Bel—'

'Oh, don't act all holy,' she snapped. 'He'll give up eventually.'

I felt sick.

'I had to pay for an abortion,' she said. 'That set me back.'

'Oh.' Reactions, questions stumbling through my head. 'Maybe if you explained—'

'No way,' she said. 'He'll have gone now. Let's go.'

My irritation bloomed, prickly as a rash. 'Why did you even invite me?' I said.

'Lydia—'

39

'You've just ignored me, like . . .' How to explain? 'I thought we'd . . .'

She exhaled, scuffed her foot on the ground, swinging it to and fro, like a child being reprimanded. 'I'm working,' she said. 'I can't drop everything. You knew that.'

'I'm not going out tonight,' I said.

'Don't sulk, for fuck's sake.'

I walked away, trying not to cry, headed straight back to the house. I couldn't face the others so I went up to Bel's room and packed my bag.

Why were we even friends any more? She didn't care about me. She used people, I thought. A feeling of disloyalty made me squirm. Like Martin – she'd used him for his money. And she didn't look after herself. The abortion – hadn't she bothered with protection?

She woke me in the night, climbing into bed beside me. 'I'm sorry,' she said. 'Don't go tomorrow, stay another day. We'll go to the Botanical Gardens. Or the Tiergarten. Just the two of us.'

'I can't. I've got to get back for work.' And I was homesick, for Mac and my own space. I wanted to be back in control of things again.

There was a pause. I waited for one of her comments, *pull a sickie* or *it's only a job*, but she was quiet. 'I'm a stupid cow,' she said. 'It's pretty crazy over here.'

But she liked crazy, I realised. That was the difference between us. The risks, the recklessness that had been exhilarating when I was sixteen no longer appealed now I was twenty-five.

I felt the brush of her fingers against mine but I turned over onto my side.

When my travel alarm clock rang she was gone.

Mac got an edited version of my trip: Bel had been busy, a bit wild; I'd not enjoyed it much, though Berlin was amazing. I didn't go into detail about the tension in our relationship – it felt too personal. Even though it seemed to be at an end and there was little prospect she'd keep in touch, I didn't want to lay it out so baldly. Somehow what Bel and I shared, the friendship, our history, the way she captivated me, was private. Even from the man I wanted to spend my life with.

A couple of weeks later she turned up out of the blue, a rucksack on her back, a bottle of schnapps in a cardboard tube in one hand.

'I come in peace,' she announced, waggling the bottle. 'You got somewhere I can kip for a bit?'

Chapter Nine

I couldn't resist her. A lifting of my heart, a rush of warmth before I remembered how she had hurt me and felt the burn of resentment.

I let her in.

And she was on her best behaviour, funny, entertaining, excited for Mac and me.

She apologised to me for the Berlin business that evening when Mac left us in the living room with the last of the schnapps. We were playing mix tapes that Colin had made.

Bel was on the floor, leaning back against an armchair. 'I never meant to muck you about, you know. It was all a bit crazy. But you coming – and then going like that – made me realise . . .' Then she grew quiet. She drummed her palm against her knee. 'He died – Bruno.'

The artist. 'No! What happened?'

'Heart attack. He was doing a lot of speed, working all-nighters in his studio.'

'And they think that caused it?' I said.

'Yeah. I came in from work and he was just lying there.' She shook her head hard, as if to dislodge the memory. Then she reached to refill our drinks. 'To Bruno,' she said, chinking her glass on mine. Tears stood in her eyes. I'd never seen Bel cry and she didn't then. She blinked them away and talked about how surreal it had been, having to call an ambulance from the phone box outside and waking everyone in the squat, warning them to hide their drugs in case the police came too.

'Did you love him?' I asked her.

She looked at me for a long moment. 'He was a nice guy,' she said, 'but I don't know how long we'd have lasted.'

* * *

She stayed for a month, quickly picking up old friendships, making new ones and getting a job front-of-house at the West Yorkshire Playhouse. She found a room to rent in a house in Hyde Park about a twenty-minute walk from us. We hired a van and helped move her stuff from storage at her parents' house to the new place. The other tenants were post-grad students at the university. A Ghanaian, two Indian women and a Spanish bloke.

Our house-hunting led Mac and me to a two-bed-and-boxroom terrace in need of major refurbishment on the edge of Headingley. It had no central heating or double glazing, and the wallpaper dated back fifty years. Large maple leaves busy on a deep red background, then bouquets of roses and swags of ribbons set against lemon stripes, faded, apart from squares here and there where pictures or mirrors had hung.

When we got back from viewing it, in June 1996, I was full of excitement, imagining all we could do with it, hoping we'd be able to get a mortgage. I began to mix pastry to make a chicken and leek pie. Was Mac as keen on the house as I was? Did he need any persuading? My hands still covered with rags of dough, I sought him out. He was in the living room, standing in front of the television.

'You do really like it, don't you? Mac – what is it?'

'Manchester.' He stepped to one side and I saw pictures of the city centre, a pall of smoke. 'There's been a bomb in the Arndale Centre.'

'Oh, Jesus. IRA?'

'Yep. They're saying no one's died. Lots of people injured. Town was busy,' Mac said. 'The Russia–Germany match is on there tomorrow.'

'And it's Father's Day then too.' I'd posted my dad's card on the Friday. I watched the images, the crowds on screen evacuated from the area. All the lives that must have been changed for ever.

Everything else, the sunshine, the new house, the pie seemed suddenly both trivial and really precious. 'You never know, do you?' I said to Mac. 'You never know what's round the corner.'

* * *

43

We moved in the autumn and lived in a building site for eight months. With a few hundred pounds saved on top of our deposit we hired professionals to do the skilled renovations and dealt with everything else ourselves.

Mac taught me how to sand a floor and strip wallpaper, repair plaster and burn the paint off skirting boards. How to install a work surface and lay tiles.

My evenings and weekends were swallowed up with it all. Mac had to open the shop on Saturdays, it was his busiest day, so he left me to it then. I'd put my music on loud or listen to the radio and get stuck in. My hands became chapped red and rough from the work, and it was physically exhausting, but I loved the sense of achievement in the transformation of each room.

Bel despaired of us. DIY was definitely not her thing. She was happy enough choosing colour schemes or fabrics, looking in catalogues at bedsteads or lighting, but the actual graft she thought was beyond tedious. She managed to drag us out every so often, insisting we needed to 'get a life'.

Colin had moved into her house and the two of them went clubbing to Speed Queen or the Warehouse every week.

One night they called round to eat with us before we all went to see Blur in concert.

'I've come out to my folks,' Colin announced. 'I was terrified, expecting to be banished. I told my mum first. Said, "There's something you need to know. I'm gay." Honestly, Lydia, I nearly threw up just saying it. And she goes, "Oh, is that all? I thought you were ill or something." Then she says, "You are being careful?" And I just wanted to die. "Of course," I said. And she said, "Do you want me to tell your dad?" So she did and he was OK with it. Well, sort of. "I spoke to your mum." That's what he said. And he gave me this nod and that was it. I can't ever imagine taking anyone to meet them.'

'Is there anyone?' I said.

Colin beamed at me, his crooked smile. 'There is, as it happens.'

'Our Spanish PhD guy, Javier,' Bel shouted through from the

44

kitchen – she was fetching more beer. 'They can't keep their hands off each other. No one's getting any sleep.'

Colin flushed and laughed.

Bel was dating one of the actors in the visiting production of *Don Juan*. She had decided that show business was perfect for her love life. 'Lots of gorgeous blokes and they have to move on when the run finishes so it never gets stale.'

'She's a stage groupie,' Colin said.

'A luvvie lover,' Mac chipped in.

'We can't all be like you two,' Bel countered. 'Soulmates.'

I smiled at Mac.

'And some of us wouldn't want to be,' she said. 'Not in a million years. Yawn.'

'Come on,' I said, 'don't you want something more serious, eventually? Something that lasts.'

'No,' she said. I wasn't sure if she was being honest or just taking a position. Didn't she get tired of the whole dating game? Was sex no-strings really all she needed?

Chapter Ten

Mac and I agreed to start trying for a baby. I was thrilled. But as the months went by without any success I grew frustrated, anxious. Each time my period came, I felt an aching sadness and an increasing feeling of hopelessness.

After a year, as the new millennium began, I went to see a doctor at the family planning clinic, who suggested I monitor my cycle. A rise in temperature indicated when ovulation was about to occur, and an increase in vaginal mucus would show when I was most likely to conceive. She also said lying prone for half an hour after intercourse, knees raised, was known to be beneficial. But I'd already been doing that.

The only person who knew we were trying was Bel. And Bel didn't do advice so I was spared all the 'Better luck next time' or 'Maybe you need to relax about it' or 'Perhaps it's not meant to be' platitudes that came with the territory.

Things felt unsettled at work as well. The campaign for compensation by haemophiliacs who had contracted hepatitis C as a result of being given a tainted clotting agent had been rejected by the government, who had previously compensated those infected with HIV. It seemed monstrously unfair to me. The clotting agent, Factor 8, had been bought cheaply from the USA in the 1970s and 1980s; the blood donors had been people who desperately needed the money on offer and had no other way of getting it. Addicts, prostitutes, drug-users. The blood wasn't screened, just mixed together, the plasma extracted and sold to all comers. An entire batch could be contaminated by just one infected donor.

Documents relating to the scandal had been destroyed. It was a cover-up. It predated my time in the department, but some of my colleagues had been supplying people with Factor 8 containing those viruses. The only time I'd tried to ask my boss about it he'd said it was 'a bloody disaster'. He clearly hadn't wanted to discuss it.

I found myself obsessing about it, a distraction from my own problems. Could something similar happen again? Were the safeguards strong enough?

Eight months passed with no pregnancy. I went back to the clinic and was referred to a gynaecologist. Using ultrasound, he diagnosed polycystic ovary syndrome. I wasn't ovulating properly; there weren't healthy eggs available for the sperm to fertilise. The periods I had were false.

I was shocked, upset. I felt as if my body had betrayed me.

'We'll be OK,' Mac said. He hugged me close, then turned me to face him. He wiped my tears away with his fingers. He lowered his head and met my eyes. 'Whatever happens we'll be OK, you and me.'

I wasn't sure I shared that belief. A future without a child felt bleak, empty and pointless. I wanted to feel a baby growing inside me, to have my body change and adapt, to give birth. To nurse my baby. To delight in a new being, a magical blend of Mac and me, to watch them grow and develop, see their personality emerge. To recognise something of myself in them. Revel in the family traits, in the things we shared as well as in the aspects that made them unique. I wanted to rock my child asleep. To play and explore. I couldn't think of a more beautiful adventure.

The strength of my desire to be a parent was a hunger. I don't understand where it came from but nothing I did, nothing I read or heard or tried to tell myself, diminished its power.

In February 2001 we attended the assisted-conception unit at my hospital to find out what initial tests revealed about our suitability for IVF. There was a fierce easterly wind bringing sleet with it that day, and the maintenance crew were scattering rock salt over the hospital paths as we walked through the grounds.

The waiting room was stifling, even when I'd shed my outdoor clothes.

I flicked through the pamphlets on the table, charts and diagrams showing rates of success and contributing factors. One in three couples would end up with a baby. Which meant two thirds of us would be unlucky. The fact I was thirty-two and overweight would reduce our odds. And there was an increased chance of miscarriage for women with PCOS.

I didn't want to think about that.

'Mrs Kelly?'

My head swam a little as we went into the consulting room.

The consultant, Mrs Simpson, greeted us with a quick smile, and once we were seated, she said, 'Do you prefer Mrs Kelly or . . . ?'

'Lydia,' I said.

'And Mac,' Mac said.

'Thanks,' she said. 'It's always good to check.' She wore bright red lipstick and there was a streak on one of her front teeth that distracted me.

'We've had all the results through and for you, Mac, your sperm count and motility are comfortably within normal range.'

'OK,' Mac said.

'Lydia, we know you have PCOS and that impedes fertilisation but, looking at the results of the blood tests and the scan we did, there's no reason why you can't go ahead with IVF.'

'Great,' I said, with a rush of relief.

'The process is challenging, physically and emotionally. It doesn't work for everyone. We do know that your best chance is if you go for the full three rounds, but some people find that after one cycle or two it's not something they want to put themselves through again. It can be very tough. It's fair to say it takes over your life and if the procedure is unsuccessful it can be devastating. It's important you are both certain that this is the treatment you want.'

'We are,' I said. 'We do.'

48

'Yes,' Mac said. 'No question.'

We were given a timetable for the treatment and a bag full of ampoules and syringes, blister packs, bottles of tablets and pessaries. The nurse taught us both how to administer injections.

I told my parents we were having IVF, and Bel, Colin and Javier knew, but I didn't share it at work. I couldn't face people asking me how it was going.

Mac's family had no idea but we agreed that if I got pregnant we would tell them after the first trimester.

'And wait for the sky to fall,' Mac muttered.

Throughout March I took a contraceptive pill to suspend my cycle. Then began the injections, a cocktail of hormones that would stimulate my ovaries to produce many more eggs than normal. Alongside those I took vitamins and folic-acid tablets. The injections hurt, my bum became bruised, sometimes I bled. One day I simply couldn't face it, I felt so fragile. I asked Mac to help.

'Sure,' he said. 'Ready?'

I sucked in a breath, closed my eyes and gritted my teeth.

When the pain subsided, I said, 'You're not bad at that. No messing.'

'Well,' he said, 'we'd to inject the cattle sometimes at home. Sure, you didn't want to go flapping around and putting the fear in them. I soon got used to it.'

'You did not just say that.' I glared at him. 'Cattle?'

'I'll make some tea,' he said, choking a laugh.

One week into the stimulation treatment I had an ultrasound scan. My follicles, which would produce the eggs, were growing in response to the treatment. It was working. I was to carry on.

I lived in hope. This might bring us a baby. My mindset was determinedly optimistic. If I didn't bring positivity to the situation I might undermine the possibility of success. Any hint of anxiety or doubt I squashed straight away.

On a bright April day, with daffodils in bloom and catkins dancing on the willows, I went in to have my eggs collected. While I was under general anaesthetic, Mac was providing fresh sperm.

The first sensation coming round after theatre was a raging pain in my throat, as though I'd swallowed glass, a result of the anaesthetic. Then there was a dragging sensation in my abdomen, like heavy cramps.

'How many?' I asked the nurse, my voice husky.

'Five.'

A lurch of disappointment. Five was lower than we'd hoped. It was a numbers game, all of it, number of follicles, number of eggs, number of sperm, number of embryos. Statistics and percentages. A familiar language to me. All those exam questions I'd answered, of probability, of means and averages. The calculations I'd performed during my studies.

'Five.' The first word I said when Mac found me in the recovery area.

'We only need one,' he said. 'One good one.'

I nodded, suddenly weepy, but struggled to summon my faith in our chances. I had to believe this would work.

The clinic injected the sperm that same afternoon.

I couldn't wait for them to call so rang during my lunch hour the following day, my heart in my throat while they checked the results. Two fertilised eggs. Three had failed. Implantation in two days' time. It was up to Mac and me to decide whether to implant one or both of the embryos.

My decision was immediate – both. It might mean we'd have twins, and I knew there were increased risks with multiple pregnancies, but the whole venture was fraught with risk. And opportunity. Twins. Two babies. If we had twins it'd be like a complete family in one go. Excitement bubbled inside me. Twins. We could have twins.

Chapter Eleven

The transfer took fifteen minutes, no need for anaesthetic. It was surreal. I'd walked into the clinic with an empty womb and I left carrying two embryos.

The coming days were critical. I had to take progesterone pessaries as well as the vitamins and folic acid. In two weeks' time I'd have a pregnancy test. No heavy physical activity, no jumping or sports. And I was to minimise stress. How exactly?

Daydreams filled my head – of twins in a double pushchair, of bunk beds, of choosing names. I pictured Mac and myself each holding a baby, or grasping a toddler by the hand. Would we get two boys or two girls or one of each? Rosa – Rosa was nice. Rosa and Lance.

The wait was excruciating. We went to visit my parents and had dinner with them and Steven. He'd got an engineering job in Hong Kong and was leaving soon. He'd had a few relationships but was currently unattached. He seemed happy enough. My mum made me promise to let her know as soon as we had any news.

The day before the test, I grew increasingly anxious and rang Bel late at night when I should have been sleeping. I wasn't sure she'd be home: she often went out drinking after the evening's performance.

'What if it's negative?' I said.

'Have you felt any different? Sore tits, sickness?'

'Bel, I've so many side effects from the drugs I can't tell what's normal any more.'

'You'll have another chance, though,' she said. 'You told me it could take several goes. Fingers crossed and legs open, eh?'

'Bel!' She had no filter. But she made me laugh.

I gave the blood sample at the beginning of the day and they rang me at home a few hours later. I'd taken a day's leave, wanting to hear the results in private.

It was positive. I was pregnant! My heart flew. I burst into tears, blubbing, 'Thank you, thank you so much.'

They scheduled a scan for two weeks after that and told me to keep using the pessaries.

Mac came bounding in the door after work and spent the evening grinning like a loon.

I'm pregnant. The words chimed in my head over and over. *I'm pregnant. Pregnant.* Then, *I'm having a baby. I'm having twins.* It was hard not to announce it to the world. My mind kept racing ahead. Twins were often born early, or induced ahead of time, so it would probably be December when they arrived.

Counting down to the scan, Mac, as impatient as I was, decided we needed a distraction. Planning a holiday. We hadn't had a proper break since we'd moved into the house. He brought home brochures for beach holidays in the Mediterranean. It'd be better to travel earlier in the pregnancy. *The pregnancy!* We agreed on Italy, the Liguria region, for two weeks in early July before prices rose for the school holidays. One day we'll have to stick to school holidays, I thought, with a thrill of anticipation.

When we arrived for the scan, appointments were running late. I'd taken a book to read but couldn't concentrate. Mac had an Italian phrasebook and was trying to learn some basic phrases. '*Molto bene*,' he whispered to me, as we waited. '*Ti amo. Io vivo in Leeds. Dove si trova l'autobus?*'

'What?'

'Where's the bus?'

People's eyes flicked to his tattoos and away, just like mine had done when we first met. It altered how he was perceived: someone inked like that must be a hard man of dubious character. His Irish accent didn't help, not when there was still such prejudice and suspicion because of the IRA bombing campaign.

Finally it was our turn. I felt acid reflux as I lay back, and hoped

I wouldn't burp. The gel was cold on my belly. The sonographer slid the probe over my abdomen, pressing down towards my pubic arch, swooping back, then down again. The pressure made me want to pee, my bladder full to bursting as instructed.

It was the silence. The silence that alerted me. The lengthening silence as she repeated the movements. I heard her swallow, heard Mac breathing from his chair nearby, some hissing and a gurgle from my stomach. And silence.

She cleared her throat. Stopped moving the instrument.

'It's not worked, has it?' I said.

'I'm sorry,' she said. 'There's nothing there. They've not developed.'

'Oh, God.'

'Ah, Lydia,' Mac said.

I sat up, too quickly, went dizzy. The back of my head was burning; gooseflesh chilled my arms.

We were asked to sit in the waiting room until the doctor could speak to us. Another forty minutes. I was dry-eyed, stunned. No babies. No twins. No pregnancy.

Mrs Simpson was very kind, which I found harder because it made me want to cry. She talked about taking time to recover and how often it's impossible to know why some embryos fail. She advised having a D and C the next day to remove any debris from the womb. Though if I preferred I could wait to miscarry naturally. It would be just like a period. And then they would check whether everything had been expelled before we went any further.

My mum rang, wanting to know how I was. 'Oh, Lydia, love, I'm so sorry,' she said, when I told her. 'Is there anything I can do? I am so sorry. Will you be able to try again?'

'Yes,' I said, without hesitation. There was never any question that we would try again.

Mac and I grieved together entwined around each other on the sofa sharing a bottle of wine.

'If we hadn't used both embryos,' I said, 'we could have frozen one and tried again.'

'Who knows?' he said.

'I was greedy. I didn't think it through carefully enough.'

'Hey, we agreed. And loads of people opt for multiple transfers. They hope one will work.'

But we'd lost them both. Lost everything. I wanted them back. Our twins. I cried some more, then blew my nose.

'We'll still go to Italy,' he said. 'We'll have a break. Start again in the summer? Yes?'

'Yes.'

'You are amazing,' he said.

'Me?' Who couldn't ovulate properly, couldn't keep an embryo alive, who took selfish risks.

'You are.' He kissed my hair and hugged me tighter.

I drank too much that night, feeling mutinous and so very sad. The next morning, as soon as I woke, I had to rush to the bathroom where I was violently sick. It should have been morning sickness. That was all I could think of.

The phone interrupted breakfast. Mac answered. 'Ah, no,' he said. Something odd in his voice. 'When?' he said. Then, 'I'll be there.'

He turned, his face suddenly haggard.

'Mac?'

'My mam. Brain haemorrhage. The funeral's tomorrow.'

'Oh, God.' I went to hold him.

'Jaysus,' he breathed.

'I can come, if you want, rearrange the D and C.'

'I'll be OK. It doesn't make sense, your first visit being a funeral,' he said. 'And after what's happened . . . But I might tell the rest of them what's going on.'

'Yes, that's fine.'

When he returned, he said something had shifted in their family dynamic with his mother's death. A drawing together. His siblings wanted to get to know me. Mac wanted that too.

* * *

54

I wish I'd met her, known her, whatever differences we might have had. It's a part of his life that I never had the chance to share. And with five children safely grown, perhaps she might have taught me something. Helped us later when things grew so very difficult.

Chapter Twelve

We began our second round of IVF in August. Before starting we spent a week away – not a hotel in Italy but a static caravan on a site near Whitby in North Yorkshire. Mac's brother, Niall, the same one who had visited us, had bought it as an investment and was renting it out.

I was reluctant to go at first, remembering all those weeks in Scarborough with my parents and Steven. The squabbles and dodgy weather, the sense of being cooped up, the condensation that made all the soft furnishings damp to the touch.

But Mac challenged me: 'It can't have been all bad. Or were you a particularly nihilistic child? What about the beach? Everyone likes the beach.'

'Windbreaks and wasps,' I said. But then I admitted that rock pooling was OK. 'And collecting driftwood. Looking for fossils.'

'We always built a fire,' he said. 'Cooked sausages and potatoes.' His family would holiday on the coast in County Waterford where his mother's side were from. 'I'd hate to say no. Niall really wants us to have it. Hey, we can visit Dracula's castle.' He bared his teeth at me. The ruin of Whitby Abbey was the inspiration for Bram Stoker's novel.

It was raining on the long drive, the landscape blurred through the windscreen.

'Flamingo Land?' Mac asked, spotting a sign.

'Never been. A theme park, I think. Or a zoo?'

The weather worsened as we reached North Yorkshire, the sweeping moorland, with its covering of dark purple heather, looking desolate and unwelcoming. We passed the enormous pyramid at RAF Fylingdales, a nuclear-missile early-warning station.

'There used to be three giant golf balls there. We came here for days out when we were on holiday in Scarborough sometimes,' I said.

'To the air base?'

'No, idiot, to the moors.'

A pub serving food sat at the junction a quarter of a mile from the caravan site, and we stopped there for pie and mash.

The caravan was three times the size of my parents' tourer. The bedroom was separate from the living area and kitchen so we didn't have to assemble a bed each night by moving the table and fitting together the couch cushions, as I'd been used to. From our pitch we could see over the grassy clifftop to the sea, slate grey under the sullen sky.

As we were going to sleep, I said to Mac, 'We don't have to stay if it rains all week, do we?'

'It'll be fine,' he said. 'You'll see.'

I woke to the smell of frying bacon and when I pulled back the curtains the sun poured in. I felt a kick of excitement, a lightness I hadn't felt since the pregnancy test.

We went into town, making for the main beach on the west of the harbour. Whitby is divided by the River Esk, and houses climb either side of the steep valley, all red pantiled roofs and white walls peppered with small windows. Two piers embrace the harbour, like pincers, each with a lighthouse at the end. There were warning signs along the pier walls about the dangers of the water in rough weather. Extensions had been built to the piers to add further protection for the port.

On the cliffs above the west beach stands a statue of Captain Cook, who left Whitby to travel to Australia and New Zealand, and close by, a whalebone arch, testament to the town's importance as a major whaling port.

From the sands we could see the towering ruin of Whitby Abbey on the opposite headland.

The water off the east coast is frigid, even on a summer's day. It's the North Sea – apparently the coldest in the world – and I can testify to that: I screamed as the waves hit my back, and soon my fingertips were numb and white.

The next day we walked to see the Mallyan Spout, the waterfall in Goathland village, and back. We bought postcards and wrote them in a pub where we had crab sandwiches for lunch. I sent Bel one of the abbey: *We have sunshine, sea, chips. Good to get away.*

But there were babies everywhere, babies, children, men pushing prams, pregnant women. It was impossible to avoid them, thronging the narrow winding streets that led down to the harbour, filling the cafés, the penny-arcades and shops, clustered on the sands.

I tried to relax about it, allowed myself to watch two sisters sketch pictures in the sand with the canes of their fishing nets and to follow the progress of a baby, who kept crawling towards the shoreline. His father would scoop him up when he got close and take him back up the beach, tossing him into the air and catching him, the child shrieking with delight.

My composure broke when we walked back up the hill on the third day and met a family coming down. The parents carried folding chairs and a cool box. Older children had bags and towels. All of a sudden the mother flung down her chair and shouted, 'Stop your bloody whining.' She yanked a toddler out from the group and slapped his legs. 'Shut it,' she said. *Slap.* 'I'm not telling you again.' *Slap.*

The boy's face worked hard as he fought to stop crying. The woman picked up her things and they all carried on. The child was still weeping, but silently, snot all over his face, lip quivering, dragging his big plastic spade along the ground.

I stopped. Tears blurring my vision.

'Lydia?'

'I'm all right,' I said. But I wasn't. Mac helped me back to the car where I sat and howled. Afterwards, I was drained and sad. But it helped to cry. A valve for the pressure.

Mac dropped me at the caravan and went off to fetch fish and chips.

Niall had created a small garden with a picnic table and a white picket fence at the back of the caravan. We sat out there to eat and watch the darkness fall.

We talked about Mac's family, his mother, about his growing up on the farm. His nephews and nieces.

We made love that night. The bed squeaked but the caravan was stable enough not to rock, as far as I could tell. Afterwards, even though I knew it was in all likelihood futile, I lay on my back with my knees bent to maximise the chance of conceiving.

'We can walk from here to the abbey,' Mac said, the next morning. 'The Cleveland Way goes along the cliffs.'

I hesitated at the idea. The cliffs were high and crumbling, the land being eaten away by the sea. Whole cottages had fallen in along the coast. But there'd be some fencing – and if Mac walked on the outside I needn't look down, so I went along with it.

The path crossed from our caravan site through rough meadow. Bees and flies were busy among the wildflowers, buttercups and clover, vetch and blue gentian.

The path drew closer to the edge of the land. There were signs on the fencing: *Keep Out – Dangerous Cliffs*. My pulse speeded up and a humming noise filled the back of my skull.

It's fine. You're fine.

I tried to concentrate on the ground at my feet, the trodden earth of the path, the tough grass that could withstand the salt air.

But then the path narrowed. We had to walk single file. I let Mac go ahead and tried to follow. Sweat licked behind my knees, across my neck and my back. I could hear the crash and roar of the sea below to my right. There were just a few feet between the footpath and where the land fell away.

It was hard to get any air. My heart was pounding, like the waves smashing against the rock face.

The humming grew more intense. I felt a sizzling up the back of my neck and over my scalp. I thought I'd faint. Everything was loud and bright and warped.

59

I froze, bent over. 'Mac. I can't.'

He turned back. 'What? Lydia?'

My hands were shaking. Dread crawled through me. I was too close. It was too high. 'I can't.'

'OK. OK.'

He guided me back. I let him lead me, my hands around his waist.

As we walked further from the cliff edge my senses settled, my pulse slowed, the fear subsided.

'I thought it was just high buildings,' Mac said, when we were safely back at the caravan.

'Anywhere high, really.'

'You think you'll fall?'

'Or jump.' I laughed. It sounded stupid. 'Just lose control and throw myself off. I'm sorry.'

'Don't be soft,' he said. 'So – I'll cancel the hang-gliding session, shall I?'

'Shut up.'

On our last afternoon we browsed the antiques shops and the jewellers where they sold Whitby jet – made from fossilised monkey-puzzle trees, I told Mac, a fact I'd remembered from geography.

I bought a pair of drop earrings for Bel's birthday present and a pendant for myself, an unusual design, a single stone carved like a bunch of grapes on a silver chain. Grapes are a symbol of fertility. Did I buy it as an amulet? Hoping it would confer some sort of magic? Bring us the baby we so wanted?

They retrieved eight eggs in the second round. *Eight!* Any restraint I'd been exercising, trying not to get too involved, too obsessed, evaporated. Surely with eight we could create one healthy embryo.

Sleep that night was impossible. I lay next to Mac, my eyes closed, and tried to quiet my mind, suppress my fears, systematically relaxing my muscles, but nothing helped. Lurking deep inside me was a bleak, bitter pessimism that had grown over the months of failure. In the end I let my terrors come. Set out my stall as if I was running an experiment, listing hypothetical outcomes. All the worsts that could happen.

(a) No fertilisation.
(b) No fertilisation and the revelation that my eggs would never be fit for purpose.
(c) A deterioration in Mac's sperm quality; he was now infertile.
(d) The detection of uterine cancer requiring immediate hysterectomy.

I wove darker and darker scenarios until the alarm went off and I got up and took my medication.

The call came at eleven thirty. I was at work.

There was only one fertilised egg.

I rang Mac at the shop. 'OK,' he said, the disappointment clear in his voice. 'At least we have one. Are you OK?'

'Stupid question,' I said.

'Do you want to go home? I'll come back soon as I can.'

'No, I'll stay. I'm on call tonight.'

I functioned like a robot, fetching platelets from the incubator, bags of blood cells from fridges, plasma from the freezer.

I didn't feel hungry but I forced myself to eat a little.

I thought about that one tiny embryo, six cells becoming eight, carrying our genes.

After lunch that day there was a sudden flurry of activity in the lab, people gathering round the TV in the staff lounge. What was all the fuss? I watched planes ploughing into skyscrapers, the shaky footage of crowds fleeing, of screaming and sirens, heard the talk of co-ordinated attacks. I watched it feeling almost numb. Then I began to shake.

That night, sleeping at the hospital, I was bleeped twice: a stabbing victim first, then, just as I got back into bed, I was called again. Two men had been injured when a wall had collapsed on a construction site. With serious internal injuries they needed a lot of O neg running down to surgery until I could cross-match and work out their blood types.

While I worked I was haunted by the images of those planes, imagined how the hospitals there would be frenetic dealing with the casualties. The wholesale slaughter. And I also thought of the speck of life in the lab, dividing and growing, the promise of a baby.

The clinic called me again the following morning.

'I'm so sorry, the embryo has stopped developing. It's not viable.'

My stomach fell. I sat heavily. Ice in my veins. 'Why?'

'It may be there was some genetic abnormality. It's not uncommon. We'll arrange for you to see the consultant. Discuss it with her. I'm sorry.'

Nothing. We had nothing.

Mrs Simpson advised that if we went for another round, and fertilisation was successful, they would like to delay transfer until day five, giving the embryos more time to mature, to reach the blastocyst stage when cells start developing to form both the embryo and the placenta. It was likely that some embryos would fail between day two and day five but we would then be proceeding with the strongest ones. She told us there was no pressure to go ahead, to take a break if we wished.

'We could wait till the spring,' Mac said, as we drove home. 'You could have a rest from it all. The injections, the stress.'

'I'm not waiting a minute longer than I have to.' I raised my voice.

Mac looked startled.

'I want to do it as soon as we can, just get on with it.' I was angry, heat under my skin, my heart racing. Angry that we'd failed. Angry with my body, with the science that had let us down. An irrational, fervent anger.

'And if next time doesn't work? Do we stop?' Mac said.

I shook my head. I didn't know. After that we'd have to pay for treatment, whether it was more IVF or using donor eggs. Would we become those people who sacrifice everything for just one more chance? Who sell their houses and take out loans, borrow from family and friends, travel abroad in search of the next groundbreaking treatment?

'We've never talked about adoption,' Mac said.

'I can't, not now.' It won't be ours, I thought. Not truly, not really. It won't have our genes.

My masochistic imagination had continued to dwell on the twins, to fashion those first two embryos into children. Rosa and Lance. They had Mac's dark hair and my face. The boy was creative, artistic, like his father, the girl fascinated by how the world works. I never shared those fantasies with Mac. I was ashamed to think that way, fooling myself with sentiment, when in reality neither of them had ever amounted to more than a cluster of cells that survived less than seventy-two hours in a laboratory.

Chapter Thirteen

Bel was very bound up in a new relationship with a guest director. It had lasted beyond his stint in Yorkshire and she spent whatever time she could with him in London, where he was working in television. I assumed that was why I'd heard so little from her over the summer.

When I rang to tell her our bad news, Colin answered. She was away for a few days in Amsterdam with Philip.

'OK,' I said. 'It didn't work, Colin. Will you tell her?'

'Oh, no. Lydia, I am sorry.'

'I know.' We were all sorry. The whole world was sorry. What else could people say?

'She'll be back tomorrow,' he said. 'She'll give you a call.'

But she didn't. Perhaps she didn't know how to respond or maybe the whole thing bored her. As someone who didn't want children herself, my craving, the agonies I was going through, my obsession and neediness, must have been hard to empathise with. But she was one person I really wanted to share it with. I missed her so much.

Two months later, we met by accident. Bel was on her way to work and I'd gone into town to get a new watch battery fitted and buy a bra.

I saw her ahead of me on the Headrow. I recognised her gait, the shock of black and crimson hair, the leather jacket she wore. Calling, I hurried to catch up. She turned and saw me, and this look crossed her face. Dislike or disquiet? Only a flash before she smiled but my old insecurities were rekindled. Those feelings and memories of rejection, thinking she didn't want to come and stay with me in the summer holidays, and the time in Berlin.

'Hey,' she said. 'Been a while.'

'Yes.'

'I was sorry to hear about . . . . you know.' She kept looking over my shoulder, not at me.

'Right. You in a rush?' I was thrown by the strained atmosphere.

'Sort of. I'll give you a ring?'

She turned to go but I saw her eyes fall to her stomach, her arm curving protectively across it, and I glimpsed the swelling there. Bel who had always had a flat belly, the envy of the rest of us. Bel with her recklessness, her casual encounters, her abortions.

I clutched her upper arm and she swung back to face me. 'You're pregnant,' I said.

She opened her mouth to deny it, then tossed her head, the rings in her ear glinting in the light, and glanced away from me. Her lips tightening, she said, 'Yeah.'

I couldn't speak. There was a clamour of noise in my mind, an impulse to shout at her, to grab her and shake her. In that moment I hated her. Trembling, I stepped back and moved away, my errands forgotten, my heart thundering in my chest and an awful aching in my throat.

The one thing I wanted more than anything else in the world and she had stolen it from me.

Mac groaned in dismay when I told him. 'Lousy timing,' he said.

'I can't see her,' I said. 'I can't. Not when—' I couldn't go on. My eyes burned and there was a lump like a hot coal behind my breastbone. *She's done it on purpose.* It was a childish thought but I couldn't be rational. I'd lost all sense of proportion and perspective. Jealousy surged through me like a fever when I thought about Bel having a baby, of her and her man playing happy families.

'Ah, darlin', you do what's best for you,' Mac said.

Bel didn't make any attempt to get in touch with me and I put my energy into focusing on the IVF.

At my request, we didn't tell our families we were starting the final round. I hadn't the emotional energy to deal with anyone else.

65

I wanted to keep it private, secret. My world was narrowing. I was withdrawing. It was the only way I could cope.

It was hard at work where one colleague was coming back from maternity leave and another's wife had just found out she was expecting. Sometimes, as the talk of sleepless nights, feeding problems and childminders ebbed and flowed, and I prayed for them to shut up, I wondered if it would be easier if I just announced my situation.

The weather was atrocious the week they retrieved my eggs. A rainstorm swept across the city coming off the Pennines, bringing floods. We got soaked walking from the car to the building, the rain drumming down and rivulets of water underfoot, swirling with the first leaves of autumn.

Mac kissed me goodbye and I was wheeled into pre-op. My hands and feet were cold, the cellular blanket and hospital gown inadequately warm. I felt sick, and hungry from fasting since the night before.

Most of all I was scared. How would I cope if we failed? How could I bear it?

Then they came with the sedative and the mask and I began the countdown.

Waking, my head hurt, a pain vice-like around my temples and in my jaw. Along with the familiar raw throat from the anaesthetic.

I didn't ask immediately. I wanted to imagine great news, a high number of eggs, all fat and ripe, mature enough to permit fertilisation.

I shifted on the trolley. The nurse came over.

'How many?' I said.

'Nine.'

'Nine!' Nine was good. Nine was better than ever. Tears pressed behind my eyes. 'Thank you.'

'How are you feeling?'

'Groggy, headache, but OK.' None of that mattered. It would be all right. I'd have my baby.

That evening Mac and I were giddy with tension. He made a pan of chilli con carne and we watched *Dalziel and Pascoe* on TV.

All the next day as I went about my work I checked the clock. Nine eggs. Nine was great. Even if only half made it.

They rang at three in the afternoon. 'We have one fertilised egg.'

'One.' A slap in the face.

'It's looking healthy and dividing as we would hope. We would like to transfer on Tuesday, all being well.'

'Yes, thank you.'

'If you can come in for eleven?'

'Yes. Yes, I will.'

I put the phone down feeling numb. One embryo. Everything resting on a single try. What chance was there?

Then the counter-arguments began in my head. We had a viable embryo. It was behaving as it should. We were giving it extra time to grow stronger. It might happen this time. This was good.

Hope bubbled through me. Hope and longing. Please, please, let this be it.

The phone rang again, just before the end of my shift. I didn't answer it. One of my colleagues looked over but I ignored her and gathered my things to leave ten minutes earlier than I should have. For the intervening days every time a call came I feared the worst.

The implantation went smoothly, and over the next two weeks, as we waited for the pregnancy test, I felt like I was acting a part, pretending everything was normal: dealing with my job and trying out new recipes at home, going to the cinema with Mac on a Sunday, planning to make a raised flowerbed along one wall of our garden. Walking together through Roundhay Park.

On the allotted day I went for my blood pregnancy test. I watched the nurse draw the sample, label the vial and envelope: 2.5 mls of fluid that held the answer.

At home, while I waited to hear, I rearranged the kitchen cupboards, throwing away out-of-date cartons and packets. I had an urge to bake but I was still struggling with my weight.

When the phone chimed, my pulse spiked and my mouth went dry. My voice was unsteady as I answered the call.

Positive. I was pregnant! My hCG clearly elevated. 'Ultrasound in four weeks. Congratulations.'

During those long days, my mind danced around the possibilities, a blank screen at the scan, or a full-term pregnancy. My mood would lurch from a sort of frantic hope to a savage despair in the course of an hour. At nights, hands on my belly, I willed the embryo to grow and thrive.

There was no delay this time when we arrived for the scan. Walking into the ultrasound room I was filled with dread. A blind panic that made me almost catatonic so I couldn't reply at first to the routine questions the sonographer was obliged to ask. The stress was all-consuming as my clothes were adjusted, paper sheets tucked into the top of my knickers and the gel spread on my belly.

Mac moved his chair so he could hold my hand.

The sonographer swept the probe slowly over my stomach, rocked it in one position, then another. 'There we are,' she said.

She turned the monitor so we could see. 'The flickering there, that's the heartbeat.'

Mac let out a gasp, and squeezed my hand so tightly that it hurt.

I couldn't speak. Tears sprang from my eyes, leaking down into my ears. I drank in the grainy image, a snowstorm with a dark shape holding a tiny flame. I wept and wept. The relief, the sheer relief, like someone had lifted great stones from my back.

I knew all the caveats: it was early days, such a long way to go, anything could happen, but we *had* an embryo, we *had* a beating heart. A potential son or daughter.

'We should go and celebrate,' Mac said, when I'd calmed down and we'd picked up all the information about our next steps.

'Yes, let's. The new Italian if we can get a table.'

We ate glossy green olives and garlic bread. I had a four seasons pizza and Mac a steak. I was elated, almost manic, talking nineteen to the dozen.

'We'll have to get to Liguria sometime before . . .' I couldn't say the words and tempt Fate so just raised my hand and laughed, and he did too.

'Deal.'

'You'll have to dig out your phrasebook.'

'Sì, amore mio.'

The baby would be due in August so it would be the middle of February before the end of the first trimester. Could I wait that long before telling anyone? Say nothing over Christmas and New Year? Maybe I'd tell my mum once a couple of months had passed.

On 6 January, the Epiphany, seven weeks after the transfer of the embryo, I went to the toilet when I got home from work. Blood in my knickers. A dark red clot, glistening.

We lost the baby.

Chapter Fourteen

Life went on, after a fashion. Every day I dragged myself out of bed and went to work as expected. Plagued by utter exhaustion, everything an effort, I could just about concentrate on my tasks in the laboratory but anything else, like reading a book of an evening, was beyond me.

At home I still cooked but only the least time-consuming meals, and cleaned when it was impossible to ignore the bits on the carpet, the dirt that ringed the washbasin. Sleep was hard to come by and I'd often go down to the kitchen and find something to eat while I waited for another dawn, another day, another night.

The worst of it was the voice in my head, bitter, carping, unkind, cold and full of loathing for myself, and others.

I'd give half a smile when someone cracked a joke or made a humorous comment but the soundtrack in my head rattled on: *Not even funny, pathetic. All of you with your smiley teeth and vapid little lives.* The vitriol appalled me and I disliked myself even more then. Thank God I hadn't stayed pregnant: I'd never deserved to. Who would want a vicious cow like me for a mother? The dark self-obsession filled my mind, no room for anything else.

Mac tried to reach me but whenever he wanted to talk I'd slap him down: 'It's hard enough without having to pick over it all.'

He rolled over to me one night in bed. I assumed he wanted sex and pulled away. We hadn't made love since the miscarriage. 'No, I can't,' I said.

'I don't know what you want any more,' he said.

'Me neither.'

'Are you depressed?'

'I'm fine, I just need some time,' I said.

'Maybe you could talk to the GP or see about therapy.'

'I'm fine.'

'Well, I'm not fine. This isn't fine.'

'Go, then,' I said. 'I won't blame you. Find someone who can have babies—'

'Don't! Don't you dare say that. I want you. I love you. But I think you need help.'

I didn't want help. I wanted my babies. And if I couldn't have them I really didn't give a shit any more.

'Lydia?' he said.

'I'm fine,' I said.

'Jaysus!' He threw back the covers and pulled on his clothes.

I didn't ask where he was going and he didn't say. I heard the front door slam, and after a few minutes I got up, put on my dressing-gown, went downstairs and made toast and Nutella. Ate it quickly, tears closing my throat, making it hard to swallow.

Mac hadn't come home by the time I left for work. Where had he slept? Perhaps there was someone else. Gina, his apprentice: she was sweet – foxy little face, slender frame. Or a customer? Someone baring their skin for more than just a tattoo. Face it, anything would be better than what I could offer him. I'd given him the option to go – he was taking it.

I broke down at work, making coffee.

It had been a stressful shift – one of the fridge alarms had gone off and we'd had to move everything out of there to make sure it didn't spoil. Then I'd had grief from two separate doctors who were waiting for results and hadn't received them.

Pattie, the one who'd had the baby, was asking me if we were doing anything for Valentine's Day and I began to sob, standing at the kitchen counter, coffee jar in one hand, spoon in the other.

71

She sent me home, even though I was senior. When she asked what was the matter I said only that I didn't feel well.

Walking out, I could feel the embarrassment thick in the room. I never made a fuss. I worked efficiently, rarely took sick days. I was the last person to lose control. No one knew how to react.

How would I ever go back? It would be excruciating.

Nice one, Lydia, the voice in my head crowed. *Losing your man and your job in twenty-four hours. Round of applause.*

But Mac came home that evening.

Unsmiling, he shed his coat and scarf, washed his hands and began making pasta. He didn't say a word.

A twist of fear gripped my spine. I'd never seen him like that, hard-faced. Had he learned it from his mother?

Eating, I could barely force the food down.

Afterwards he washed up, then stayed in the kitchen fixing a lamp that had broken. I sat in the lounge, the paper, headlines about the true cost of the foot-and-mouth epidemic, unread on my knees. *He hates you*, the voice said. *He's going to leave you. Just wait and see.*

I went through to him. 'I'm sorry, Mac. I'm so sorry.' I was crying.

He set down the screwdriver and got to his feet.

'I'll see the doctor tomorrow. Don't go. Please? I don't want you to go.'

'Hey, it's OK,' he said softly. He moved, arms enfolding me, his warmth an instant comfort. 'You'll not get rid of me that easy, missus. I'm in it for the long haul.'

I took time off work; a sick note from the GP for two weeks was extended twice. By then the antidepressants I'd been prescribed were helping. The sadness and flashes of anger were still there but muffled; the hateful thoughts gradually became less intrusive. There were some side effects: I put on more weight and had sweats at night. I was shaky too for the first month.

Like a sick person, I stayed in bed late, watching TV but avoiding the news or reading anything distressing. But as my mood settled and the four walls became constricting, I made myself leave the house every day to have a walk through Beckett Park or go swimming in the pool at the university.

My dreams were vivid, and I often remembered them, which I didn't usually. One recurring dream was seeing Bel in a crowd and trying to reach her, but people kept blocking my way. The next moment I was on the roof of a high building, impossibly high, and the crowds swarmed like ants far below. I'd never put myself in that situation in real life. I knew I had to jump. Was it to save Bel, or save myself? I could never work it out. I launched myself off the roof, terror flooding my bloodstream, and jolted awake, drenched in sweat.

Like a snail emerging from its shell, I slowly returned to normal life. One Friday night Mac and I went to see some local bands at the Cockpit in town. We ran into Colin and Javier. I had a moment's anxiety, worried that Bel might be there, still raw when I thought of her, but it was just the two of them.

Colin was pleased to see us and invited us to sit with them. The music began and talk was impossible until the break when Mac and Javier went to the bar and Colin asked me how I'd been.

'Not great. I've been off work, stress and depression. We had another go at IVF. I miscarried.'

'Oh, Lydia.'

'And with Bel . . . I can't—'

'I know.' He nodded. I didn't need to spell it out.

'But I'm much better. Back to work the week after next. And what are you up to?'

'New job! Design company in Huddersfield. And Javier is teaching at the uni there.'

'Brilliant. Will you move?'

'We're still talking about it. But I'd miss this.' He gestured at the room.

'They do have bands in Huddersfield, don't they?'

'In a manner of speaking.' He smiled.

I felt a rush of pleasure on Colin's behalf. He was such a nice bloke – he deserved all the happiness he got.

The others arrived back with drinks and I led the toast. 'New job, new beginning.'

Mac glanced my way and I could tell he was thinking, What's next for us? What happens now?

A week later, I'd just got in from shopping at the supermarket, late afternoon, and was putting everything away when there was knocking at the door.

Bel.

Shock rinsed through me. I wanted to close the door on her.

'You got a minute?' she said. She looked very pale, her face even thinner, sharper. But her eyes still had that brilliance. She wore a red swing coat that disguised the pregnancy.

'OK.' I didn't know how to refuse. 'Tea?'

'Thanks.'

She kept her coat on, leaned against the counter, hands in pockets, while I got out mugs and teabags and put the kettle on.

'Colin said you were off work,' she said.

'Yes.'

A pause. Then she said, 'This is stupid, Lydia. Maybe I should have told you but I didn't want you to get upset when you were in the middle of all that . . .'

I didn't say anything.

'Look, it doesn't have to be like this big nuclear war or something. You never used to be petty—'

'Petty! Shit, Bel, you have no idea—'

'Sorry. Sorry.' She held up her hands. 'You know what I mean.'

She stepped towards me and I caught a whiff of alcohol. 'You're drunk.'

'I'm not drunk,' she retorted.

'I can smell it.'

'I might have had a drink. Who are you anyway, the pregnancy police?'

'I know the advice,' I said.

74

'Yeah. Well, my mum drank herself catatonic both before and after I was born. It never did me any harm.'

I was surprised at the disclosure. 'I'd say you've been pretty messed up at times.'

She blinked. Opened her mouth, as if outraged.

'Why are you here?' I said.

She looked at me, closed her eyes for a moment. 'I never meant this to happen.'

'Another accident? Can you imagine how that makes me feel? When I've lost—' I swallowed.

'Tell me to fuck off and I will. I'll never darken your doorstep ever again.' She was arch, her default mode when things got too intense. 'But it's lonely. I miss you.'

'What about Philip?'

'Long gone,' she said. 'He wanted me to get rid of it. Prick. When that didn't happen straight away you couldn't see him for dust. Time went on and, I don't know, maybe the universe was trying to tell me something . . .'

And me? What's it telling me?

'When I said petty, I didn't mean it,' she said. 'It's just . . . We can decide how we do this, can't we? You only live once. Most people, a falling-out, they go their separate ways but we don't have to be like most people. Do what everyone expects. Stuck on a particular track. We're different.'

'Bel, this isn't about expectations or convention. I've not been coping. And being around you, with you having a baby, I can't do that. Not now, anyway.' My voice was halting, the tension gripping my neck, making my breath uneven. 'It's too much.'

'So that's a fuck-off, then? Don't bother with the tea.'

She stalked out. And I sat down, shaken and heartsore. Stunned to have had the courage to turn her down. Wondering if I'd done the right thing. Bel, who filled my dreams, who'd been part of my life for so long.

Chapter Fifteen

Finally I got to meet Mac's family. We flew to Dublin and Niall met us at the airport, then drove us to the family farm about ten miles from the Wicklow coast, where their dad Brendan still lived. Most of their land had been sold for development: new houses were being built, bungalows each bigger than the next.

Brendan and Niall were still in the building trade and times were busy enough for them to have all the work they could manage in Ireland and not have to travel to the UK.

On our first evening the whole family piled into the dining room. I was asked to call Mac in from the yard where he was playing some chase game with the kids, involving a lot of screaming and tickling.

His sisters, Terese and Angela, were in charge of the kitchen, producing dish after dish of food. There were twenty of us in all. The children were at their own table. Terese and Angela each had three children, Niall had one and the other brother, Luke, had two. Luke was a joiner, self-employed, Terese a stay-at-home mum, who'd trained as a solicitor and would go back when the kids were all at school. Angela ran a nursery, which she said was excellent for sorting out her own childcare.

The conversation at the main table was rapid and easy and, with so many of us present, soon divided into several smaller conversations between those people close to each other. There were jokes about Ireland's chances in the World Cup and talk of their recent election results, which had to be explained to me, though no one could really tell me the difference between the two main parties, Fianna Fáil and Fine Gael. And they all kept teasing Mac about his tattoos.

I joined in the banter as best I could and laughed at the antics of the children, especially the youngest, Terese's eighteen-month-old, Ewan, who was intent on doing everything for himself – with very messy consequences.

But beneath the surface I felt the swell of a sharp poignancy. It's not all happy families, I reminded myself. There'd been tensions between Mac and his mother about me, or our lifestyle, and there were bound to be other problems between the couples and among their children that wouldn't get any airing in so public a setting. But still . . . I wondered if they ever stopped to think how lucky they were.

The children were a lovely bunch and all shared the Kelly looks. Black hair and deep blue eyes. I tried to memorise all their names and whom they belonged to. They clearly adored their granddad and there was fierce competition for his attention. He was good with them, full of praise and encouragement. How he must miss his wife, I thought, but how lovely that he has so many people who love him, who are part of his life. It struck me how small my own family was.

Ewan took a shine to me and clambered up to sit on my knee after desserts had been polished off. I played 'One potato, two potato' with him, then sang 'Pop Goes The Weasel', tipping him over on each 'pop' until he made a grab for the bottle of red wine, drenched himself and was taken away for a clean-up.

After the meal the children performed their party pieces, songs from school, routines from dance class, magic tricks.

'It's an Irish thing,' Mac whispered in my ear. 'The TV reception was always crap so we had to make our own entertainment.' Then he and Niall played a duet on guitar and harmonica before the party broke up.

'Don't you miss it, the crowd?' I asked him, as we got ready for bed later.

'Not at all,' he said. 'It's here if I get homesick but it ain't happened yet.'

We all went to church the following morning. It was my first time at a Catholic Mass. The place was busy, most of the seats occupied. It smelt of beeswax. Perhaps that was the candles or the polish from the wooden pews. Rich stained-glass windows ringed the walls. There was a huge crucifix behind the altar, Jesus Christ dead on the cross. Blood trickled down his temples from the crown of thorns, and there was a gash in his side. It all seemed very graphic. The priest wore sumptuously coloured robes and all the props he used gleamed gold.

I followed the cues from everyone else about when to sit, kneel and stand.

After the service, people mingled outside, and I lost count of the number of people who came up to greet Mac and be introduced to me.

Back at the house we ate leftovers from the night before. I helped Terese to wash up. She talked about their home in Dublin where they were having an extension built. 'We need it done soon,' she said. 'We want to rent it out. John's being moved to York for work.'

'It'll help having builders in the family,' I said.

'No way. They're always too busy to do anything at home. That or too tired. You're not far from York, are you?'

'About an hour in the car,' I said.

'Grand. It'll be nice to have someone over there. We won't know a soul. And I'm sure Ewan would love to see you again.' She rinsed out the sink. 'I'd better round up the lads.' She folded the tea towel over the handle on the front of the range. 'You know, we were so sorry to hear about the IVF. My friend went through it too, in the early days. Four rounds she had before they stopped. It must be so hard.'

'Thanks,' I said.

'They adopted a little girl, from China. I'm her godmother.' She showed me a photograph. 'That's her at eighteen months, when they brought her back.' The child was beautiful, a beaming smile, shiny dark hair. 'She's fifteen now. She's brilliant. She wants to study medicine.'

'That's great,' I said.

'Right so. Soon as we have a date for moving I'll let Mac know. And you must come and help us give the place a housewarming.' Then she went off, calling for the children, and I took a moment to compose myself before joining them all.

* * *

Bel had a little girl, Freya. Colin called into the shop especially to let Mac know.

My heart clenched when I heard. 'What else did he say?'

'Nothing much. Just that it was weird having a baby in the house. Bel's OK, just very tired.' I couldn't imagine her as a mother. Breastfeeding, changing nappies. No doubt she'd find a way to do it all with panache.

I had a sleepless night deliberating over whether to send a gift or a card.

Or a poison-pen letter? Bel's dark wit in my head.

I didn't want to be churlish or unkind, but the way we'd left it, wasn't the friendship dead? How would Bel feel getting my congratulations when she knew I resented her so?

Perhaps if I just sent a small gift for Freya . . . but the child would never know me, so what was I trying to prove?

I never sent anything. But Bel and the baby intruded into my thoughts far more than I wanted.

I caught the beginning of a TV documentary about adoption and began to watch, promising I'd turn it off if it was too upsetting, but I was captivated by the stories: the couples like us, some of whom had been through cycles of IVF, the children in care who needed families.

Maybe we could do it.

I thought about the Chinese girl Terese had shown me. Remembered how Mac had raised the question of adoption but I'd shut it down at the time, too distressed by the failure of IVF.

I talked to Mac about it as we were getting ready for bed. 'I'm not sure what I think – someone else's child,' I said. 'I can't imagine what that would really be like. It's a nice idea but the reality . . .'

'One of my aunts adopted,' he said. 'They were fine. Two boys and a girl – all from different families. They were cousins to us, no different from any of the others.'

'One of my schoolfriends, Katy, she was adopted. We were all aware of it but it didn't come up much. It didn't seem like a big deal.

They'd all have been babies, Katy, your cousins?' I put my clothes in the laundry basket outside our bedroom door.

'Oh, yes. Unmarried mothers, that's all we were told.'

'It's different now,' I said, climbing into bed.

'Thank God.'

'But probably harder – adopting kids who've had to be taken into care.' I didn't like to think about the reasons behind that.

'We can always find out a bit more,' he said. 'We don't have to commit ourselves.'

'OK,' I said, a loop of excitement flipping my stomach.

'And knowledge is power,' he said, getting in beside me.

'Save that for the tattoos.'

It took me a few days to pluck up the courage but finally I went out into the hospital grounds during my morning break and used my mobile phone, the first I'd owned and a birthday present from Mac, to call the adoption and fostering department at the civic hall. They took our details and suggested we go along to one of their regular information sessions. It was a short, practical call but my stomach was churning by the time I hung up. I felt dizzy and agitated. This seemed like such a momentous thing to contemplate. How on earth could we tell if it was right for us?

The information evening was held at a family centre in east Leeds. There were seven other interested couples as well as a woman on her own.

A social worker gave a presentation about adoption, explaining why children came into care and what the local authority wanted for them. She took us through an outline of the whole process, saying that it would take several months to be assessed and approved as prospective adopters.

A parent, a woman who had adopted two sisters, talked about her experience. The younger daughter had moderate learning disabilities and both of them had found it hard to settle at first but she was very positive about the whole thing.

We were encouraged to ask questions and some chimed with the ones I had. How much would we learn about the child's background? How would we decide what sort of child we could cope with? Would they have contact with their birth family?

The social worker said there were no single answers, every case was different, but the preparation and assessment stages of the process would explore all those issues in depth.

We were given a pack to take away. Full of pictures of smiling 'for-ever families' in all shapes and sizes, quotes and statistics, diagrams outlining the stages involved.

The pack included a DVD of adoption stories. Simply filmed, mainly talking heads, but they had me weeping when we watched.

'I want this,' Mac said, when it ended. 'But only if you do. And if you decide you're not ready then we wait. We wait and see. And if it doesn't happen, then it doesn't happen.'

'How can you be so laid-back about it? Happy either way?'

'I want a child, Lydia. I'd love to be a dad. But I want you more. I want us to be happy. That comes first.'

'But you're making me decide,' I said.

'I guess I am. But if you can't say, "Yes, let's apply," then we go with that, go with your gut.'

The phone rang as he was speaking. There was no one there. I'd had a couple of calls like that. It wasn't a dead line – I could sense someone at the other end – but there was no heavy breathing. And after a couple of seconds, whether I spoke or not, the caller hung up.

'Silent call,' I said.

'You should whistle down the line, that'll put them off.'

'I can't whistle,' I said.

'Not you yerself. With a whistle like a gym whistle. Hey – how come you can't whistle? How come I never knew that?'

'It's just not come up.'

'I'm crushed,' Mac said. 'My woman and she can't whistle.'

'Give over.'

He blew a few notes in reply, some jaunty air, Irish no doubt.

On my way to bed I thought about the silent call. Why would

anyone do that? I dialled 1471, the service that identified the last caller's number. As the automated voice read out the digits, I felt a ripple of discomfort. It was Bel's number.

My mind circled round and round the possibility of adoption. One day imagining us as a threesome, a little boy in my arms, him racing round the park with Mac, the next deciding it was too demanding, the assessments, the references, seeking approval, and all with a huge unknown at the end of it.

What if I didn't love the child? A horrific prospect. Years of looking after a little boy or girl and feeling indifferent or resentful, disliking them perhaps. Pretending to be a happy family but empty at the core. Oh, God.

But then when I thought of Mac and me growing older, him at the shop, me in the lab, I couldn't see where our sense of purpose or adventure would come from. Would we travel, take a round-the-world trip? Emigrate, even? To do what, to be what? That future felt flat. I longed to be a mother. I wanted a child in my life. I wanted that special relationship.

'We should try,' I said eventually. 'If we don't try, I'll always wonder. I don't want to regret *not* doing something.'

Our adoption social worker was Janette, a petite British-Nigerian woman. 'One thing I want to be clear about from the start,' she said, when she made her initial home visit. 'Adoption is not for everybody. You'll probably find these next few months intrusive and intensive and emotionally draining. It's my role to make sure you have everything you need to decide if this path is for you. And to make sure we at the agency know everything we can to assess your potential as adoptive parents.'

'Do people get refused often?' I said.

'Not often but it does happen. I've been doing this job for twenty years and I've come across a handful of cases like that. Usually it's because information is withheld or there are questions about the motivation and the ability to commit of the adopters. There may be medical concerns. We don't want children who have already experienced significant loss to be in a situation where there is likely to be more. Most people discover for themselves whether or not they have the resources and qualities needed. A significant proportion withdraw.'

Janette asked us about our reasons for wanting to adopt.

I described our IVF troubles as baldly as possible and told her that we still wanted a family but not necessarily a biological child.

'That must have been very difficult, emotionally. Has either of you had any counselling around the issue?'

'No,' I said.

'It's crucial that you don't see an adopted child as a substitute for a biological child. It's different.'

'I know,' I said, thinking of the twins. And the miscarriage, which I had studiously avoided endowing with any sex or identity.

'It's something that will keep coming up throughout the process,' she said. 'Any grief you have from those losses needs acknowledging and processing.'

A flash of anger. How dare she tell me how to grieve? Of course the IVF had taken a huge toll. No one was denying that. I'd lain on this sofa hollow and haunted, staring at the pictures we'd chosen on the walls, and the curtains I'd made, and the honey-coloured wooden door that we'd had dipped and stripped, and not finding any pride or comfort in any of it. Seeing myself as worthless, barren. My body a traitor.

'I have grieved,' I said. 'I was depressed and took time off work. I was grieving. I'm back at work now.' The medical check – would my use of antidepressants count against me?

'And tell me what you expect from adoption,' she said.

Mac talked for a while about having a son or daughter or even more than one child, of creating a family.

'How many bedrooms have you here?' she said, suddenly practical, her eyes flicking round the room.

'Three. One's just a box room,' Mac said.

'And you own the house?'

'Mortgaged, yes,' he said.

'You're not married? How long have you been together?'

'Ten years,' I said.

'Do we have to be married?' Mac said.

'Marriage is still taken as a sign of stability and commitment. Of course, couples living together can have an equally strong relationship, but if a panel was looking to match children to adopters and all other factors were equal, the married couple would have the advantage. It's something to think about.'

She patted the papers on the table, the notes she'd been taking. 'Now, I can register your interest officially at this point and get your permission to carry out the various checks. Or you can think about what we've discussed. Put it on hold for now. If we do go ahead today and you change your minds, that's perfectly fine. Lots of people do. I'm not trying to put you off, just being realistic.'

We filled in the forms, signed our consent.

'Blimey,' I said, after she'd left. My shoulders were rigid, my mind noisy with chatter, some of it defensive. 'What do you think?'

Mac stretched his arms up, let them fall. He smiled. 'We'd best get married,' he said.

Chapter Sixteen

'Lydia? It's Colin. I didn't know who else to call.'

'Why? What's wrong?' I peered at the clock. Six thirty on a Sunday morning.

'It's Bel.'

My skin went cold.

'She's not – she's not coping,' he said.

'What d'you mean?'

'Could you come?' he said. 'I wouldn't ask but—' He sounded very upset. Sweet Colin, who had only ever shown me kindness. Loyal to his friends. Uncomplaining.

I felt trapped, resentful. But how could I say no? 'Yes. I'll be there soon.'

I roused Mac and told him what I was doing.

'Call if you need me,' he said.

I snatched a bowl of cereal, knowing I'd be useless if I was hungry whatever the situation.

It was just getting light as I left the house to drive to Hyde Park. The birds were singing, the sky a fragile blue, and I felt leaden with apprehension as I got closer.

Colin answered the door with the baby in his arms. He looked wiped out. 'Bel's upstairs. And this one's just gone off.' He nodded to the sleeping baby. It wore a lemon-coloured Babygro and had a muslin napkin, stained with yellow patches, tied like a bib around its chest.

Her chest.

Freya.

So tiny. She didn't look like Bel, apart from the dark hair.

Chubby-faced, a button nose, strong chin. I'd met Philip once or twice and thought she probably took after him.

'Come through,' Colin said.

The central heating was on, and the house was warm, muggy even.

Colin laid the baby on the sofa, then said to me, 'I need coffee. She'll be all right here.'

He talked to me as he made our drinks. Bel had been struggling with Freya and the lack of sleep. He and Javier had helped when they could but Bel seemed worse.

'Worse how?'

'She's so wound-up. Explodes at the slightest thing. Can't get the baby to settle and then she ends up screaming at her.'

The blood drained from my face. 'At the baby?'

He nodded. 'Or ignoring her. Javier's in Hebden this weekend and last night Bel wouldn't pick her up, so I'm trying –' he rubbed at his forehead '– to cover everything. All of it,' he blurted out. I'd never seen him so intense. 'The bottles and—' He broke off.

'What about the midwife or the health visitor?'

'She should have a six-week check with the health visitor in a couple of weeks but not before that unless Bel gets in touch. When I suggested that, she gave me a load of abuse. Said I wanted them to take the baby. I don't know what to do.'

I wanted to shout: Have you any idea of the pain I've been in? How bloody awful it's been trying for a baby? And you drag me here because Bel's too bloody self-centred to do what she should be doing! And you haven't got the guts to make her do it. The impulse to scream and turn away and leave them to it, to punish them, to punish Bel, was almost overwhelming. I closed my eyes. I could feel tremors of rage under my skin.

'I'm sorry, Lydia – after all you've been through. But I couldn't think who else to call. I just—' His eyes filled and his mouth was trembling, his long nose reddening. *Oh, Colin.*

'Hey, it's OK,' I said. 'Not ideal but I'll live. What about her mum?'

Colin looked taken aback. 'In Paris. They moved. I thought you knew.'

'When?' I said. Not that it mattered.

'Last year. If you could just talk to Bel. Get her to call the GP or whoever.' I remembered Mac insisting I do the same. My resistance, my fear.

I went upstairs, reluctance in every muscle, but determined to do my best if only to help Colin. To help the baby.

When I knocked on the door there was a moan from inside. She was awake then.

The room was lit by a bedside lamp, a dim bulb but it shed enough light for me to see Bel in the bed and the rest of the room. A tip. Clothes, baby paraphernalia and rubbish scattered about. A sickly smell of sweat and musk and cigarettes.

Bel scrambled up to a sitting position. 'What are you here for?' Mistrust plain in her expression.

'Colin called to see if I could help.'

'You needn't bother. I don't want your help. I don't need any help.'

'Look at the place, Bel.'

'Fuck off,' she said, but there were tears in her voice.

'I'll get you a cuppa,' I said. 'Do you want a shower?'

'Where's Freya?' she said urgently. 'Where is she?' I was shocked at the sudden switch, the panic that consumed her.

'She's asleep downstairs. Colin's there.'

'She never sleeps.'

I didn't know how to answer that. 'Have a shower,' I said. 'Have you any clean sheets?'

She didn't answer.

'Bel?'

'I don't know. There might be some in the cupboard on the landing.'

I went to look, praying she'd do as I asked. I could hardly force her to wash but if someone did make a house call it would be better to have cleared up a bit at least.

I found a sheet and a duvet cover, which I remembered from her old flat, grey leaf shapes on a cream background.

Where had they gone, those girls who whiled away the hours sprawled across her bed, sharing a spliff and cups of hot chocolate, or rum and Cokes, fantasising about what they'd make of their lives? The future had seemed so full of promise, an adventure we'd share together. We could go anywhere, do anything. And now? My nose prickled. I sniffed hard, no time to be maudlin.

Bel came out of her room, her face blank, and walked slowly to the bathroom. I heard the shower begin.

While she was occupied I turned the overhead light on and bundled together the old bedding, sour-smelling and bloodstained, along with the clothes that littered the floor. I took the lot downstairs.

Colin got out the washing powder and I put the first load into the machine, then went back up.

Used sanitary towels, nappies, tissues and baby wipes had been stuffed into carrier bags. I took them down and Colin put them out in the bins. I made another trip up and down for the crockery and overflowing ashtray, empty drinks cans and a bottle of baby milk that had rolled under the bed and was rancid, the contents separated into cloudy grey water and a cottage-cheese-like substance.

The baby's Moses basket, on the stand in one corner, seemed clean enough.

I made up Bel's bed with the fresh linen and was putting the duvet back, when she returned, draped in a towel, her hair dripping. Shoulders bony.

'When did you last eat?' I said.

'I don't know.' She looked around the room and shook her head but didn't say anything.

'I'll make some food. You get dressed.'

'I need to sleep.'

'Eat first.' I went before she could argue.

'Omelettes?' I suggested to Colin.

'She coming down?'

'I think so.'

'OK.' He got out eggs, butter and bread and, between us, we made the food and more coffee.

We heard footsteps on the stairs and she came into the kitchen, slid onto a chair, cigarettes and lighter in her hand, face pinched and wary.

'She took six ounces,' Colin said. He sounded nervous. Waiting for Bel to bite his head off, perhaps.

While we ate Colin and I exchanged small-talk about holidays, his and Javier's plans to travel round Spain.

Bel was silent. I noticed her hands trembled when she cut her toast. She didn't clear her plate but ate half of the food, then lit a cigarette, toying with her coffee cup between drags and flicking ash onto the congealing omelette. 'I'm going to bed.' She made to get up.

'You need to see a doctor,' I said.

'Why?' She gave a brittle laugh. 'Because I'm knackered?'

'Because you're not coping.'

'Who says?'

'It's obvious.'

'What will the doctor do? Clean up the sick and wipe her bum and stop her endless whining?' There was anger in her voice, and flecks of spit flew onto the table. Tears sprang into her eyes. 'Or maybe take her away. Give her to some perfect couple with a fat salary, vacant brains and an Ideal Home in some Godforsaken suburb?'

Her words stung.

'Why would they take her away?' I said.

'Because I'm crazy, aren't I? Going mad. That's what you all think. Or they could take *me* away, lock me up.'

'You're not crazy,' I said, trying to sound convinced. Was she? Was she having a breakdown? 'But carrying on like this won't help. It could be depression or anxiety but they can treat that.'

'And you'd know, wouldn't you?' she said.

'Bel!' Colin said.

'Yeah,' I said steadily. 'I would know. I've been there. And I hadn't got a baby to think about as well.'

Bel shook her head. Then she looked at Colin.

'I'm worried about you,' he said.

'I'll be all right if I can just sleep,' she said, her fingers working.

89

I jumped as a piercing wail rose from the living room.

Freya waking.

'Christ!' Bel said, and covered her eyes, weeping. The hostility was gone. I'd never seen Bel cry. Not in all the years I'd known her.

I sat and touched her arm.

Her hand sought mine. 'God, I'm so sorry. I'm such a bitch.'

'You'll be fine. I'm here and Colin's here.'

She looked at me, her eyes bright with anguish. 'I'm scared I might hurt her. I keep thinking – these horrible pictures— And what if I hurt her?'

My heart constricted. I shared her panic but kept my voice level. 'Ssh. It's going to be all right. But you must call the doctor. If you don't feel up to doing it yourself, then I will.'

'Don't let them take her!' she said. 'Please.'

'I don't think that'll happen,' I said. I put my arms round her. She was quaking, tears falling on my neck. 'I'm here,' I said.

Then I eased myself away and went to pick up the baby.

90

Chapter Seventeen

I shifted Freya higher against my shoulder, resumed pacing while Colin made her feed. She was so hot. Was that normal? What if she was ill? Did that account for her not sleeping?

'They'll send someone round tomorrow,' Bel said, appearing in the living-room doorway. 'I'm not mental enough for a weekend visit apparently.' I thought about Bel's fears that she might hurt Freya. Would she be all right for another night? Would I have to stay? Could Colin cope?

He came in then.

'I'm dead on my feet,' he said. 'If I show you . . . I could get my head down for a couple of hours? I'll be all right after that.'

'Sure. Why don't you both have a rest? I'll wake you if I can't manage.'

Bel watched from across the room as he showed me how to hold the baby and position the bottle. 'She'll stop sucking when she's had enough. Just put her upright, like you had her and she'll burp if she needs to.'

'Or throw up all over you,' Bel said.

'Like this.' He slid his little finger into the side of Freya's mouth and the bottle teat dislodged with a pop. He held her upright for a moment. 'You going to burp, eh? No? Fine by me.' He turned to me. 'You might need a nappy. The stuff's over there.' He pointed to the corner, a lemon changing mat dotted with coloured stars. 'She doesn't need a change yet but when she does—'

'How will I know?'

'The stench,' Bel said.

'Or the leakage,' Colin said. 'Look.' He grabbed the mat and laid

Freya on it. He showed me a clean nappy. 'Tabs here. Take the old one off, roll it up. Use warm water and cotton wool to clean her up. Wipe backwards.' He rolled his eyes. *How did I get here?* And I laughed.

Freya was crying again so I lifted her up and sat back on the sofa. I touched the bottle to her lips. She opened them and began to suck.

'OK?' Colin was still on his knees, Bel at the door, arms crossed, eyes drowsy.

'Go to bed,' I said to them both. 'You go.' Ignoring the anxiety that fizzed in my stomach.

Freya sucked away, her dark eyes locked on my face. There were movements overhead as the others went to their rooms, then quiet. Just the ticking of the house settling, the snuffling noises of the baby feeding and the drone of the washing-machine from the kitchen.

Freya's eyelids fluttered and closed. A few more sucks, then her mouth slackened, she gave a thready sigh and relinquished the bottle. Should I wind her now, even though she was asleep?

I put the bottle down and slowly moved her upright. She made a snorting sound but her eyes stayed closed. I held her almost vertical, one hand supporting her head as I'd been shown. After a few seconds she gave a hiccup and I moved her back to rest on my lap, with my arm for a pillow.

A baby! I'm holding a baby. She felt so precious. Humbling. The warmth of her, the weight of her against me. The way she'd surrendered in my arms.

Freya smelt sweet, almonds and perfume, perhaps from soap, or whatever they washed her clothes with. Her head, which looked overly large compared to her body, was covered with fine brown fuzz. When I looked closely I could see the beat of the pulse in the soft spot of her skull echoed at the side of her neck. Her legs were curled up. Hands so tiny, her fingernails reminded me of little snail shells. As a child I'd once kept snails in an old fish tank to 'study' them, watching their silver trails criss-cross the glass, the rippling motion of their foot moving, the two pairs of tentacles that grew and shrank back, the coils of dark waste from everything they ate.

Two table lamps lit the room. It was stuffy. The curtains were still drawn. Was it fine outside? The forecast had been for a warm summer's day. Could I take her out? Was she allowed out? I knew you had to keep puppies and kittens inside until they were a certain age, but babies? Was there a pram or anything? I'd not seen one in the hall. How little I knew about looking after a baby.

The twins hovered over my shoulders. They would have been six months old now. Why should Bel have a baby, one she couldn't even look after and had probably kept only to be bloody-minded because her boyfriend wanted her to have an abortion? The sense of injustice flashed hot and sharp.

We'd adopt it, Mac and I. Solving everybody's problems. A stupid fantasy. Then the sadness slipped through me, stinging my eyes and catching my throat.

I looked again at the sleeping infant and was almost relieved when I didn't feel any great pull or connection. She was small and vulnerable, so new. She needed my help and protection, my care temporarily, but that was all.

If Mac and I did eventually adopt, what if I felt the same with our child, that there wasn't any bond, any love? How could I raise a child feeling that distant? It wouldn't be fair to the child, would it? But it was the only way I might become a mother.

When my arm became numb I eased Freya onto the sofa. Colin had left her lying on her back so I did the same. I went to make a cup of tea and put the next load of washing on. There were photographs stuck to the fridge with magnets: Colin and Javier dressed for the millennium party where everyone had worn silver; Bel and I, arms round each other, some time just before I met Mac, judging by our haircuts; my postcard from Whitby. I would have expected Bel to tear up everything of me after I'd sent her packing.

I peered at a photo of Bel and Freya in hospital: Bel was smiling but I saw something frail in her eyes, a look of shock. I didn't know anything about the birth, how long it had taken, how painful it might have been, if she'd had any intervention. I hadn't wanted to.

My phone rang, startlingly loud, and I hurried to answer.

It was Mac.

'How you doing?' he said.

'Left holding the baby.' Freya began crying, the sound carrying from the other room.

'Seriously?' He sounded worried.

'It's OK. Can you hear that?' I tilted the handset to catch the noise.

'Anything I can do?' he said.

'A takeaway would be nice in a couple of hours. It's hungry work.'

'Curry?'

'Great.'

'How many?'

'Get four, different ones. Naan bread and chapattis. I'd better go. You can meet Freya.'

'She not a bit young for curry?'

'Funny.'

Between them Bel's GP and her health visitor were able to help. She was diagnosed as suffering from post-natal anxiety and was prescribed meds. She found a local childminder, paid for by her parents, to take Freya three afternoons a week. Bel drew the line at joining the mother-and-baby group who met at the local community centre. 'I want to get away from all that, not wallow in it,' she said.

'But maybe if you try it—' I'd said.

'No,' she interrupted. 'Non-negotiable.'

After I'd talked about it with Mac, we offered to look after Freya on alternate Sundays. Janette had said we needed experience of looking after children. We were already seeing Terese and family regularly, now they were living in York. We took turns, every few weeks, getting together at our house or theirs on a Saturday evening and staying overnight, with a trip out on the Sunday to a gallery or museum or a walk somewhere.

'They want walking every day, like dogs,' Terese said of her kids. Ewan and I had become firm friends. He called me Diddy – he couldn't say Lydia. He had a fascination with everything so walking anywhere at his pace took for ever as he stopped to examine each stick, stone and blade of grass. He was too young to join in some of his older brothers' games and we would often be left to our own devices.

Freya was so easy, a pleasure to look after. She was a quick learner, and as long as she was fed and clean, she was happy.

One day when she was five months old Mac and I took her to the park. She was blowing raspberries and making little sounds, trying to copy our talking. I held her on my lap, sat on a swing and moved to and fro. She chortled, her legs pumping in delight.

Mac took photos, for us and for Bel. Then he held Freya and droned some old Irish song and she gurgled back at him.

We can do this, I thought. We'll be good parents.

Mac went to fetch coffee and I sat with Freya at the picnic table.

'You are such a lovely girl,' I said to Freya, and rubbed my nose on hers.

She burbled back at me. 'Clever girl.' I kissed her cheek and swung her onto my lap.

I got out the little snacks I'd brought. Put them on the table with my keys.

Freya reached for the keys.

An older woman, grey-haired, a grandma, I guessed, who'd been in the playground with twins in a double-buggy, stopped to talk.

'How old?' she said.

'Five months,' I said.

'She's so like you,' she said. 'You make a lovely family.'

I wanted to say, 'She's not mine. I can't have children. We don't have any.' But I just smiled, thanked her and asked her about the twins, who, she said, were a handful and didn't know the meaning of sleep. Then she said goodbye.

And I went back to sorting out the cheese sandwiches and Freya's mashed banana.

'Can I talk to you?' Mac said, one evening after tea, when we'd seen off Terese and family.

His face was solemn and I had a flashback to the night he'd

walked out, the same sense of the ground shifting. Falling. The blood drained from my face.

'What is it?'

'I love you, Lydia. I want to be with you. We're talking about getting married, about adopting a child. I want all that.'

I waited for the but. And it came.

'But we're not together any more.'

'What d'you mean?' I said, stalling. I knew full well. Sex. Whenever Mac made any bid for intimacy, I found excuses. He was frustrated, and I felt guilty and defensive about my lack of interest. The awkwardness had increased so I was avoiding any physical contact, not wanting to send mixed messages.

'You won't let me near you. I can guess why it's difficult. Sex was all about getting pregnant for so long . . . Maybe it'll get better in time, but what if it doesn't? Don't you miss it at all?'

'Not really,' I said. Mac had been an enthusiastic lover, sometimes noisy, energetic, vocal, and I used to love the sensation of being caught up in his fervour. He would shower me with kisses, my eyelids, shoulders, belly, fingertips. There was often laughter. Or, at least, that was how it had been before we started trying to conceive.

'You don't want me any more?' His face was solemn.

'I do, but . . . not at the moment.'

'You don't want me as a lover?' His face tightened.

I looked away. 'It's not that . . .'

'How can we try and adopt when we're not even a proper couple? Don't you think they'll find that out?'

'I don't think our sex life will be a criterion. We can be together without it all being based on that.'

'Really?' He stared at me intently. 'Isn't "that" part of a healthy relationship? Isn't "that" why we first got together?'

I didn't answer.

'I want us to be happy again.' He was equating sex with happiness. How did he expect me to change? Just flick a switch?

'There's a place does counselling,' he said. 'Sexual therapy. I want us to go.'

I wanted to die. The thought of talking to someone . . . 'And if I don't want to?'

'Why would you not want to try? This stuff helps people.'

I sniffed hard, my nose stung.

Across from me, Mac's hands were tight fists, his knuckles white. I could lose him. And what if it didn't work? How could you force someone to feel something they didn't? And then what?

I was cornered. 'OK,' I said.

The introductory session was just as embarrassing as I'd expected. We talked about our prior sexual experiences, our habits and preferences, and used little models to represent our network of relationships.

I was surprised when the therapist told us to abstain from sex initially, only doing the exercises she set us.

That first week we took an hour out of our schedules, made the room warm and comfortable, and Mac began to touch me, avoiding my genitals and breasts, stroking and massaging and caressing me everywhere, varying the pressure and speed and type of touch. We weren't to talk, apart from me saying if I particularly liked or didn't like anything he did.

As Mac stroked the length of my spine, held my shoulders and cupped my head in his hands, I came undone, weeping quietly at my love for him and his for me.

A couple of days later it was his turn. I straddled him, pressing and kneading, running my hands over his shoulders and down his spine. I was discovering Mac all over again with fresh eyes, with curious hands. His broad back, the heft of his bones, the mass of his glossy dark hair, starting to grey at the edges. Asking him to turn over, tracing the ink on his arms and the bow shape of his clavicle, the rim of his jaw. Reawakening a hunger for him that I had to wait to satisfy. Craving that falling sensation when he would part my legs and touch me.

Over the weeks it was a revelation to find that spontaneity no longer worked, not for me. Instead anticipation, knowing sex was on the agenda, meant I looked forward to it. It was like when we were

97

first dating, when we knew getting together meant sex, but the sex was even better. Slow, enticing, more sensuous, headier.

We had also agreed with Janette to use contraception while we were applying to adopt as our adoption would be put on hold if I got pregnant. Sex wasn't about babies any more. It was about love and passion and each other.

Chapter Eighteen

'I don't know how anyone does this full-time,' Bel said, one Sunday morning, as Mac and I arrived to collect Freya and stop for a coffee. 'Women do it till the kids start school, or secondary school, even. It's either killing me with boredom or it's like being put through a mincer. Chewed up and spat out. How can anything so small be that powerful?' She nodded at Freya, who was dozing in her car seat. 'Anyway . . .' She lit a cigarette and edged the back door open, a token to not smoking in the house any more. Mac and I exchanged a look. The draught only served to blow the smoke back into the room. '. . . I go back to work next month.'

'The Playhouse?' I said.

'Yes. But they've moved me into an admin job, office hours, so she can go to Carol's full-time.' Carol was the childminder.

A handful of times I'd seen Bel being affectionate, kissing Freya when I took her or brought her back, a kiss on either cheek, one, two, three times, talking to the baby in French as she fed her, reminding me that Bel had spent much of her childhood in France. But mostly Bel regarded her as a chore, a burden she wanted to escape from. Would I be the same?

Colin came downstairs then, looking pretty wasted.

'Good night?' Mac said.

'Brutal,' Colin said. He poured himself a glass of water. 'What've I missed?'

'I've had my medical for the adoption,' I said. 'Mac's got his tomorrow. Next, they want all our bank records, proof of income, that sort of thing.'

'Bit cheeky, isn't it?' Bel said.

'They want to make sure we can feed and clothe someone. Not up to our necks in debt.'

'Isn't everyone drowning in debt, these days?' Colin said. 'My credit cards – I daren't look.'

'Also . . .' I said, glancing at Mac, who winked at me, '. . . we're getting married, register office do at the town hall, next Friday.'

'Oh, my God,' said Bel, whirling round. Her face alive.

'You kept that quiet,' Colin said.

'Marriage of convenience,' Mac said.

'We'd like you to be witnesses,' I said.

'Can we dress up?' Bel said.

'Wear anything you like.'

Bel pumped her fist. 'Whoo-hoo! Where's the party?' Freya started at the shout but slept on.

I thought of all those nights out we'd had in pubs and parks, at clubs and house parties. The anticipation while we were getting ready in my bedroom or at her bedsit. The joy of it. 'We're not having a party. Just a meal,' I said.

'We can always go on somewhere,' Bel said, still animated.

'Aren't you forgetting something?' Colin said. 'Someone?'

'I'll figure something out. Carol might keep her if I pay her enough. How can you not have a party?' Bel complained.

My parents had been disappointed, too, that we weren't doing the whole thing 'properly', and that so few people would be there, but my dad had offered to pay for the meal afterwards and eventually we agreed to go halves with them.

Terese had refused point blank to keep it quiet, and nothing Mac or I said persuaded her otherwise, so in the end all Mac's siblings and partners were coming, as well as Brendan. Which at least meant that our parents would get to meet.

The day went fine: no one got too drunk, though Bel came close; no fights broke out; no feuds erupted. It all felt slightly odd – the combination of people from disparate parts of our lives, the off-the-peg service, the snapshot photos on the town-hall steps taken by Javier and my dad. But that was fine. It was a means to an end, that was all, a possible advantage in our adoption stakes.

The first of our training and preparation days began with coffee and biscuits served by the two social workers running the course: an older woman who told us she was retiring soon and a younger one in training. There were also two adoptive parents who would be contributing.

They'd arranged a dozen chairs in a large circle with tables in the centre, and once we were all seated, we made introductions: we gave our names and occupations, and said what we had hoped to be when we were children. A zoo-keeper was my answer (preceding my vet days).

Then the senior social worker asked us to help ourselves to a piece of flip-chart paper from the sheets on the table. 'I want you to think about your life when you were three years old. Use the big felt-tip markers and draw yourself, aged three, at the centre of the page. Stick figures are fine.' People made jokes about not being able to draw or wanting wax crayons and glitter glue but the room gradually quietened.

'Next put around you the people you live with. Then add grandparents and other relatives, neighbours, family friends. Write the name beside each person. Draw any pets.'

I had the sensation of being back at school as I drew my father and mother, my grandparents – the ones who lived in Scotland and my grandma who lived in Bradford – Steven as a baby, Pixie, the cat we'd had before Harvey.

Beside me I saw Mac sketching a large dog, then he scrawled lots of horns and wrote 'cows'.

'Cheat,' I whispered. He could have drawn a herd of cows in his sleep, he was a wonderful artist, but this probably wasn't the time or the place. Someone complained they were running out of space.

'No worries. Here's more paper.'

When we'd finished, the workshop leader, her colleague and the two adoptive parents collected up our papers. There was a collective gasp as they slashed through the sheets with large scissors, cutting them to shreds. I felt insulted, stung, watching them crumple the paper into balls and drop them on the floor.

They handed us back just the figure of ourselves from the centre, a little scrap of paper daubed with colour.

'Think about what you're feeling now. Any responses?'

She wrote our replies on a whiteboard. *Angry. Sad. Cross. Upset. Pissed off. Lost. Violated. Abandoned.*

'Now imagine what a child in care feels when it loses its family and everything familiar.'

I smoothed the fragment of paper in my hand, the stick figure in her red skirt and green top, hair in bunches. All alone.

The social worker pointed to the board. 'Lost. Let's think about being lost. Did you ever get lost as a child?'

The memory rushed over me, like a freak wave, knocking me down, chilling my skin. I'd been five, a hot day, the beach crowded with families. I'd padded out across the hard sand, where the waves had left ridges that hurt my feet, in search of mussel shells. Near the water's edge I found a starfish. When I touched it, it felt crunchy, stiff and muscular. Eager to show my parents I ran back up the beach with it.

All the people shimmered in the heat haze. I couldn't see them, Mummy and Daddy. Panic ripped through me and I dropped the starfish. I ran on, crying, my heart banging. Then I saw her! She was towelling herself dry, her back to me. I ran to her. 'Mummy!'

She turned. It was a stranger. 'Are you all right?' the woman said.

I cried louder. Barely able to speak I sobbed that I'd lost my mummy and she asked me lots of questions. But I didn't know where we had been sitting, what colour our towels were, how far we'd walked. She took my hand and together we combed the sands. What if we never found them? There was a hole inside me, a pit of terror and desolation. Then I heard my name and my father was calling and I was found.

'Think about what that felt like,' the social worker said. 'Think about how it might be if you'd never been safely reunited with your family. A child removed from its birth-family carries that sense of abandonment, of loss and anxiety. It's important to recognise that and not pretend that everything is perfectly fine. All of you will have experienced some loss, the loss of bereavement, the loss of not having the children you wanted, the loss of infertility and miscarriage. Adoption is your chance to create a family but it will not be the same as having a birth-child, just as for the children themselves, having you as parents will not be the same as having their birth-parents. Every adopted child has four parents. Embracing that is the best possible approach.'

'You're saying we have to be willing for contact?' one of the other prospective adopters asked.

'Not necessarily. Contact will vary depending on what's judged to be in the best interests of the child. In most cases there will be letterbox contact with letters exchanged through us between the birth- and adoptive-parents, once or twice a year. But whether contact remains or not you can't take a child's identity away.'

I looked at Mac's drawing of himself, only a few marks on paper but it was unmistakably Mac. I imagined him on the farm, in that big, boisterous family.

I'd missed some of what was being said and tuned back in. '. . . even though they will be living with a new mum and dad. Tom or Ayesha comes from that birth-family, from that mother and that father. That is part of who they are, of their life-story. It always will be. It's not helpful or healthy to ignore that, or deny it. Honesty, openness, the truth appropriate to the age and understanding of the child is the best approach.'

I tried to imagine talking to a child about the parents who had given them up or, more likely, the parents who could not be trusted. It made me uneasy. What if the parents had been cruel or abused them? Wouldn't I want to forget about them? Wouldn't the children?

Next we had to pair up with someone we didn't know and talk about our earliest memories and how they made us feel. I spoke to a woman called Erica, whose memory was more traumatic than mine. About a dog barking and knocking her down. She'd been frightened of dogs for years but her partner had had one when she'd met him and gradually she had overcome that fear.

By comparison my earliest memories were bathed in warm affection. I was sledging in the snow with my dad. Sensations of speed and being jolted and bumped. My fingers burning with cold. I think I was about two.

There was another, falling and skinning my chin and hands, sitting on my mum's knee. Her singing to me. The smell of pink ointment.

'I felt safe,' I said, suddenly realising it. 'Even though I'd fallen and got hurt, on my mum's knee I was OK. And on the sledge, it was fast, a bit scary, but I knew I could trust my dad.'

Over a lunch of sandwiches and cakes we were able to chat. Mac and I spent most of the time talking to a lesbian woman, who had been adopted. 'Very different back then,' she said. 'My birth-mother wasn't married, so having me adopted was her only option. But I was never neglected or anything.'

'Have you met her?' I asked.

'Yes,' she said, and her eyes fell, 'a couple of times, but she can't really cope with it. She never told her husband. He's ill now and she doesn't want to bring it up. I've two half-brothers who don't know I exist.'

'That must be hard. What did your adoptive-parents think about your meeting?' I said.

'They were great. They're amazing.'

Would someone say that about us one day? That we were amazing parents?

In the afternoon we looked at case studies of children placed for adoption, their early lives and how that might affect their development. One baby had been removed from a drug-addicted mother who had already lost two children. Three siblings had experienced neglect. A child with learning disabilities was relinquished by a mother who couldn't cope. A boy had been treated with cruelty and physically abused by his stepfather. And two sisters had been sexually abused by their father.

In most cases the parents had been subject to poor parenting themselves and had deep-seated problems of their own. One surprise to me was how frequently some children were moved, staying with a number of temporary foster-carers, every move a reminder of that break with their family. A freshly opened wound.

'How might these children behave after trauma like that?' the senior social worker said.

We filled another large sheet of paper with suggestions: *anger, hoarding food, acting out, disobedience, bedwetting, soiling, stealing, withdrawal, aggression, psychological problems, destructive tendencies, trouble bonding, crying, clinging, biting, anxiety, self-harm, sexualised behaviour.*

Some of the examples seemed so extreme, they repulsed me. How would we ever cope with that? We weren't trained or qualified to deal with that sort of damage. What if we responded the wrong way, made things worse?

'Anyone feel like leaving now?' The social worker's joke punctured the atmosphere. 'It's a daunting list but we know that providing children with love, stability and routine gives them the best chance to overcome these problems.'

The adoptive-parents each gave a potted history of their experience. The man had adopted siblings aged three and four, now teenagers, and the woman had adopted a five-year-old Down's syndrome boy three years ago. Both of them said the same thing: adoption had been hard and there had been times when they'd found themselves close to breaking point, but it was the best thing they'd ever done.

We were invited to ask questions.

'Did you love them straight away?' I asked.

'Yes,' the man said. 'I didn't expect to – you don't really know what to expect. But our first meeting, the pair of them were giddy, clambering all over the place, and I couldn't take my eyes off them. It was really hard to leave after an hour. We just couldn't wait to bring them home. We were euphoric.'

'Not for me,' the adoptive-mother said. 'I liked Ben. He made me smile and he was really sweet, but loving him came gradually as we got to know each other. He was always pleased to see me, even if I'd just been in the other room, and hearing him call me "Mummy" – that was amazing. The bond just got stronger over a few months and now I can't imagine life without him. He's my boy, my son. I'd do anything for him. I love him completely.'

I swallowed, moved by her testimony. But what if we didn't like the child, couldn't love it? Surely there were some people who adopted and never found the love. Maybe biological parents asked themselves the same thing, but wouldn't there be some instinctive recognition with a biological child, a bond based on genetic factors, a pull hardwired into us? Then I thought of Bel and Freya, Bel's ambivalence about being a mother.

Coming away I felt shattered, as if I'd been travelling overnight or survived some accident. We heated up pizza for tea and opened some wine.

'That was pretty full on,' I said.

'Has it put you off?' Mac said.

'I don't know. It's daunting but I don't think so. You?'

'No.'

I put down my glass. 'Something shifted. Today. For the first time it wasn't about us, was it? It was all about the kids. Those stories . . .' I shook my head. I imagined a little boy, sometimes a girl but mostly a boy, afraid and lonely and hurt, and him coming to us, and soon his laughter ringing round the house, his hand plump in mine, his arms about my neck. Happy and safe.

Chapter Nineteen

Bel's parents were coming to visit before the Christmas break, and Bel asked Mac and me to join them for Sunday lunch at a restaurant in town. We were due to see Terese and family but Bel pleaded with me. 'They're here for a week. I'll end up sticking a fork into one of them. Or worse.'

'They can't be that bad.'

'Not with other people around.' She grabbed my hand and squeezed. 'You could bring Terese and her lot. That'd be fine.'

'We were going to them in York,' I said, 'but I'll see if we can swap dates.'

On the surface the meal was entirely pleasant but I could feel the tension that crackled between Bel and her father. I knew he worked for a bank at a pretty high level and had lived abroad, but he affected a sort of bluff, blustery style, a mix of bonhomie and crabbiness, like the stereotype of a blunt-speaking Yorkshireman. I pictured him kitted out like John Bull, roaring for his pipe and ale, beating his horse.

A jovial smile on his face, he referred to Bel as 'the thorn in our side' and 'determined to swim upstream', adding 'she was born awkward.' The fact that Bel had struggled on becoming a mother was never acknowledged.

Bel's smile was too bright, and when she glanced my way I saw her eyes were lanced with anger. We talked about safe subjects, new films we'd seen, like *The Pianist*, the vagaries of home internet access, the success of the Commonwealth Games in Manchester earlier in the year.

Bel's mother said little. She had stick-like wrists and a scrawny neck but an incongruous pot-belly. Her hair was brittle, sprayed in place. She wore heavy eye make-up that reminded me of Tim Burton animations. She drank steadily and her movements were slow and studied, as if she were having to be extra careful. I remembered Bel's description of her as a heavy drinker.

Freya, in her car seat by our table, woke partway through the meal when her grandfather insisted on holding her.

'No gadding about the globe now,' he said to Bel. 'Not with little missy here. Have to knuckle down. Start acting like a grown-up.'

Bel got up so abruptly she almost knocked over her chair. I left it a minute, then followed her into the toilets. She came out of the stall sniffing. Was she crying? Then I saw the dusting of white under her nose.

I pointed at my own nose. 'Christ, Bel. Here? Couldn't you wait?'

She threw back her head, eyes closed, and groaned aloud as she wiped her nose.

'Mother's little helper,' she said. 'No . . .' She pressed a hand to her chest. 'Daughter's little helper. I'd like to tell them to fuck off but they're giving me a deposit for a house here. They've been trying to talk me into going over there. Can you imagine it? Being stuck with Fuck-face and Gin-tits.'

'Bel!' I couldn't help but laugh. How much of Bel's recklessness had been shaped by her parents? How much was just her personality?

'D'you want some?'

'No.'

'Oh, Lydia.' She put her palm to my cheek, cupping my chin. 'What would I do without you? I'm so glad you're here.' Her eyes glistened, the pupils changing size with the effects of the cocaine. 'Whooo!' She shook her head. 'Right. Up and at 'em. Roll on tomorrow morning. Adieu. And good riddance.'

'It's nice of them to help with the deposit,' I said.

'Yeah, well, money costs nothing,' she said, then giggled. 'They think they can keep me in line if they own the roof over my head. We'll see. "Once more unto the breach, dear friend . . ."' And off she went, high as a kite.

* * *

108

Janette met and interviewed our referees – my mum, Mac's sister Terese, and Bel – and told us that they had all given glowing reports. With the checks in place and preparation sessions complete, we started the second stage of the process. Assessment and home study. At the end of this, Janette would put forward our application to be considered as adopters to a formal panel.

'People worry a lot about this stage,' she said. 'You've heard talk about the F form?'

'Yes,' Mac said. 'It's like a job application for the job of parent.'

She smiled. 'It can feel very intrusive. You'll share things that many couples would never dream of sharing and consider questions that most people starting a family wouldn't need to think about. To start off I want you to write down your life story, include all the key events, everything that made you into the person you are today.'

'Whoa,' Mac said.

'Yes,' said Janette. 'Along with that, fill in this information form and find a recent photo that you'd like to use for your profile.'

After work each night I returned to the task. We had no indication of how much or how little we should include, and at first I thought I had hardly anything to write. My life had been stable, unremarkable, but gradually I fleshed it out, remembering things I hadn't thought of in years. My mum going into hospital, when I was ten and Steven six, and being sent to stay with my grandma for several weeks. I had a stomach-ache all the time. I couldn't sleep, missing my mum, my home. She'd had a hysterectomy, I found out when I was older.

Steven breaking his wrist at the park, the horrible screaming sound he made, and me running for help. Pixie the cat getting run over. The fox breaking into my rabbit hutch and savaging my beloved Moppet.

We each met with Janette separately to talk about ourselves, how we dealt with conflict and rejection, our prior relationships, our fears, weaknesses and vulnerabilities, our childhoods.

After that we had to talk about ourselves as a couple. It felt strange, trying to analyse how we worked. 'Mac is the one who puts it into words. When there's a problem, he makes us face it,' I said. 'And we don't row, do we, not really? Is that weird?'

She shook her head. 'Did your parents?'

'No, not really. They'd sulk a bit, my mum would get snappy with us, but I never heard them shouting.'

'And yours?' she asked Mac.

'Oh, my mother had a temper. She'd kick my father out of the house every so often. Till bedtime. Dishes were thrown.'

Christ! Would this count as violence? Would it be held against us?

'Luckily she had a terrible aim, missed every time.' He grinned.

'What did they argue about?' Janette said.

'Money, mainly,' he said.

Brendan had seemed so calm, so settled. Had those outbursts been hard for him? Now he was a widower, was that one thing he didn't miss?

'I don't like conflict, not shouting and chucking stuff,' Mac said. 'I guess that's why.'

'What about house rules?' Janette said. 'What were the rules for each of you growing up? What will your house rules be?' She encouraged us to look beyond the obvious – set bedtimes or no shoes in the house – to those unspoken rules we'd learned: listening to others, greeting people when we came home, looking after people's possessions, sharing food.

We also looked at the logistical aspects of becoming parents. Where would a child or children eat and sleep? What nurseries and schools were in the area? Where were the outdoor play facilities? The house was checked for any health and safety issues. We'd already child-proofed much of it for Freya: at nine months old she was pulling herself up on furniture, crawling at a fast sprint, fingers into everything.

It was made clear that I'd have to take a year's leave and be a full-time carer. We'd have to manage on a lower income. And stability was paramount. 'Moving house won't be an option,' Janette said, 'not for some considerable time. You'll need to create and stick to routines, minimise any change in your circumstances. New situations reawaken a sense of dislocation and trauma in looked-after children.' Looked-after children – the term was used a lot by the professionals we met, interchangeable with 'children in care'.

We kept a diary for a week, our times at work, at home, what we were doing when. Then Janette talked us through it. 'You'll probably be getting up an hour or two earlier. You might have been up in the night. A child will want to eat before seven in the evening and we've looked at how important mealtimes together are. How can that be managed with Mac still at work?'

One of the last things we had to do was fill in the check-list covering what type of children we would consider adopting.

'I don't know where to start,' I said to Mac. 'Look.' I jumped through the sections. 'Female or male, number of children . . . bi-racial . . . Would you consider a child with cerebral palsy . . . limited life expectancy . . . foetal alcohol syndrome . . . blindness . . . delayed development . . . epilepsy . . . autism?'

'Boy or girl's easy,' Mac said. 'If it was a birth-child we wouldn't get to pick.'

'Fair enough. I'm happy with that.'

'We'd likely be matched more quickly if we went for a sibling group rather than a single child,' he said. 'I think of having a crowd of them, two or three. They'd have each other. I like that idea.'

It overwhelmed me. Slightly panicked, I said, 'I don't know. Isn't one enough? And wouldn't one child be easier to manage? Wouldn't they settle more quickly if they had all our attention?' I looked back at the form. 'How on earth are we going to decide about all these?'

'We just work through it. Talk about it. It'll take some time.'

'You're not kidding.'

'I feel guilty saying no,' I told Mac, as we rejected various options. 'But I think it'll be hard enough without taking on a child with any special needs.'

We finally settled on a boy or girl under four, of any racial background, and would consider minor hearing or visual impairments and allergies. Our application went to the local authority. Now we waited for an adoption panel date.

Chapter Twenty

I was so nervous. My stomach was in knots and my armpits prickled with sweat as we sat in the waiting room. Mac was drumming his fingers on the arm of his chair.

We would be called into the panel meeting after they'd examined our application so we could answer any questions that had arisen and raise anything we wanted to.

'What do we wear?' I'd asked Mac the night before. 'Do we dress up?'

'Sure, as long as we look clean, I don't think they'll care at all.'

Now, I tried to distract myself, looking at the old paintings of aldermen and mayors on the walls, then wandering over to stare out of the window at the crowds crossing the square below, many holding umbrellas. A drizzly March day.

The country was at war: UK troops had invaded Iraq. It was hard to comprehend. Here we all were, going about our business, while thousands of miles away bombs were falling. But even thinking about that gravest of news couldn't divert me for long.

If we weren't approved, if they said no . . . But why would they? We were settled, educated, financially solvent. We had a lovely home. We could offer love and safety and comfort. If they said no . . .

My phone pinged. A text from my mum. *Thinking of you today x*. She'd taken to mobile technology with aplomb and, in her retirement, had joined a computer class at the library.

Then Janette was at the door, asking us to come.

There were nine other people in the room. They introduced themselves but I forgot immediately who was who and what their role was. I was close to tears with the stress.

The chair thanked us for coming and said they had a couple of questions for us.

One of the women asked how I would cope with being at home for a year after working full-time.

'I'll have to adjust,' I said. 'It'll be a big change.'

'It could be very difficult?' she said.

I floundered. 'Well, yes. I won't know until I've done it.' *Shit.* Did I sound too defensive? Hostile?

A woman with grey hair, who I realised must be the doctor on the panel, brought up my depression. Would I be able to recognise the symptoms if there was any recurrence and seek help?

I could feel my cheeks blazing. 'Yes, I think so, now I've been through it. And I'm sure Mac would tell me if he had any concerns.'

Someone else wanted to know how we'd found the whole process, and Mac talked about it being hard work and emotionally demanding but said we'd learned a lot.

He was asked to elaborate and I wondered if they were trying to trip him up but he didn't hesitate or fumble his reply. 'We know so much more about the needs of children in care and our own skills and strengths as a couple.'

'What are you most scared of if you do get a match?' said a young woman, with huge tortoiseshell glasses and hair that flicked up at the ends.

That I won't love the child. I didn't say it aloud, and Mac said, 'That the child won't settle, we won't be able to make them happy.'

'Lydia?' the woman said.

'The same, I think. That the placement will break down. That we'll lose the child.' I felt a swoop of light-headedness, the sickening sensation of being somewhere high up. I gripped my hands on my lap and locked my eyes on the water jug they had beside the bowl of grapes and plate of biscuits.

Mac said my name. Someone else had been speaking. A young man with a pointy face.

'Sorry?' I said.

'Lydia, your medical was generally good but your overall BMI puts you well into the overweight category. Could you tell us a bit about your diet and whether you have any concerns about it?'

I felt as if I'd been slapped. I cleared my throat. 'I've always had a big appetite,' I said. 'And a sweet tooth. I comfort-eat at times, I'm aware of that, but my weight hasn't changed a great deal over the past few years. It's pretty stable.'

'And in terms of feeding a child, of setting an example?' he said, tapping his pen on the table.

'I know nutrition is very important for children, a good balanced diet, with plenty of good fats, vitamins, proteins for growth. We'd do that. We'd eat together, and most of the food we'd have would be home-cooked.'

No one nodded or smiled or seemed to appreciate my answer. I wanted to shrink away. The pointy man spoke again: 'A child might be physically demanding. Will you be able to deal with that? Running around, outdoor activity, exercise?' He waved the pen in the air.

'Yes, of course.' My voice shook. 'We often go walking. I swim too.' I wanted to say more, to object to the questions but these people had our fate in their hands. They had all the power.

We were asked to return to the waiting room while they finished their discussion, and Janette showed us through, putting out her hand to touch my arm. 'You did fine, it's going well,' she said. 'We shouldn't be much longer.'

'What a dick!' Mac said, about the man who'd queried my fitness.

'We can't all be fucking stick insects,' I said.

'And I'd never want you to be.' Mac hugged me. 'Soon be over.'

But what if it *was* over? What if this was the end of our 'adoption journey', as the jargon went? If we were refused here, would we have a chance anywhere else? With a private agency, or abroad, like Terese's friend?

The chair of the panel came out after a few minutes and asked us to join them.

With a thumping heart I followed Mac into the room and we took our seats. My ears whined and my skull buzzed. I felt sick. What if I was sick in front of everybody?

I heard individual words: pleased, recommend, subject to final approval, decision maker.

'Thank you!' Mac said, laughing. He pulled me to him, one arm around my shoulders. 'Thank you so much. That's just brilliant!'

Ten days later I was in the lab. Pattie and I had been for lunch. I'd had a prawn-salad sandwich and a granola bar. Pattie and I had got to know each other since I'd come back to work after my sick leave. Her baby was teething and she had been up half the night. 'It's the one thing I miss more than anything else – sleep, proper sleep,' she said. Then yawned and apologised.

Everyone in my department knew Mac and I were hoping to adopt, now waiting for final confirmation that we could go ahead.

The phone rang at my desk, and when I answered, Janette said, 'Congratulations, Lydia, you've got final approval, you and Mac.'

I couldn't talk. My eyes filled with tears and I pressed my hand to my mouth, trying to keep control. Even though I'd washed my hands there was the smell of prawns.

'Lydia?'

'Thank you,' I squeaked.

Across the room Pattie was on her feet, eager for news. I nodded to her and she grinned, turning to the others.

'I'll ring you later,' Janette said. 'It's fantastic news. Well done.'

'Thank you so much,' I managed, between sobs. 'Thank you for everything.' I put the phone down and the room burst into applause.

We'd done it. The last day of March 2003. Four years after we'd first started trying for a family, we were formally approved to adopt.

Now we had to wait for a match. A son or a daughter to call our own.

Chapter Twenty-one

'Let's see, then.' Bel sat beside me on the bench.

Freya was driving the playground train, twisting the steering wheel and chattering to herself.

I opened my bag and pulled out the photograph of Chloë.

Bel held the hair out of her eyes. It was a gusty November day, bright and chilly, the leaves skittering around, swirling in circles and clustering in heaps against the fence and the foot of the trees. 'She's lovely.'

'Yes.' My heart rose every time I looked at her. In the picture she was sitting on the floor, soft toys scattered around, a baby-walker to one side. She was looking up at the camera, the smallest of smiles on her face. Delicate features, not baby-like, really, a heart-shaped face and short, wispy blonde hair. She was wearing a pink top with a silver star appliquéd to the chest. Matching pink trousers. Would she be a girly girl? Would she want pink and princess dresses and Barbie dolls? I'd pored over every inch of the photograph, as if I could find more clues as to who Chloë was.

I carried it with me. Mac had made a copy for himself.

'It's a bit like people do with scans,' I'd said to Pattie. 'That first glimpse.'

'She's gorgeous,' Pattie said. 'We'll have to get together when you're on leave. It'll be weird, you know, you not being here.'

'If,' I said, 'if . . .'

She smiled, inclined her head. 'OK, if . . .'

Mac's sister Angela had wanted to send us some of her kids' clothes when she'd heard it was a girl, but we'd turned her down. Not yet. We didn't want anything, didn't even dare to start preparing a room, until it was more definite. I was poised on a cliff edge, the uncertainty reminding me of having IVF, that same balancing act between hope and fear.

'She's two months older than Freya, nineteen months now,' I said to Bel. 'Born in April last year.'

'Have you said yes?' Bel asked.

'Yes.' I wanted to cry. The enormity of it all. *Chloë. Chloë.* 'Now we have to wait for the matching panel.'

'So they decide who gets who before you've even met?' Bel said.

'That's right.'

'Weird.'

'Mama!' Freya called.

Bel waved at her and shouted, 'Ring the bell.'

Freya nodded enthusiastically and reached to tug the rope. The bell clanged. A dog on the perimeter path barked in response.

'If they think we're not right for her, they could backtrack, say no. I don't think I could bear that.'

'You'll be fine.' Bel flicked her lighter, cigarette in her mouth. The wind snatched the flame. She tried again, stooping lower, *snick, snick*, and it caught. 'They'd be insane to turn you two down. Do you know why she's in care?'

Freya jangled the bell again and again.

'Neglected. Her mother's a drug-user – she's not been able to look after her. That's about all we know so far. She's been in foster-care since she was thirteen months. We don't know anything about the father. I don't think he's on the scene.'

'I wouldn't worry about that,' Bel said drily.

'What will you tell Freya?' I said. 'When she starts asking about her dad.'

'That he's dead.'

'Bel!'

'What?' She blew a stream of smoke. 'Freya! Enough with the bell. Stop it.'

'You can't tell her he's dead,' I said. 'She'll need to know the truth.'

117

'What – that he's a dick who didn't give a shit? Didn't even want to meet her?' she said.

'And if he turns up in the future and wants to get to know her? You hear stories like that all the time. You'd be lying to her for years.'

Freya shrieked for me: 'Lydia. Me go on a swing. Go on a swing.'

'In a minute,' I called back. 'She has a right to know,' I said to Bel.

Bel gave a little shake of her head, as if annoyed. She stared at her cigarette, then took another drag. 'Maybe. But what is he to us? A sperm donor.'

'*Unwitting* sperm donor. Listen, he's half of her genetic make-up. And what about other relatives? She might have half-sisters or -brothers eventually. She's got another set of grandparents.'

'God forbid,' Bel said crisply.

I giggled despite myself. 'I just don't think you should be lying. He's her father. You can't keep that from her. It's part of her identity.'

'Yeah. I see that every time I look at her,' Bel grumbled.

'She's got your hair, similar,' I said.

'It's dark,' Bel allowed. 'But the rest of her . . .' She pulled a face. Freya was sturdy, stocky, full-faced. More my build than Bel's. I felt defensive on her behalf.

Freya had moved to the top of the small chute that led from the train to the ground. She slid down.

I got to my feet. 'Look at her. She's brilliant,' I said. 'And you should be straight with her.'

'OK,' Bel said impatiently.

'Swing!' Freya yelled.

'I'm coming,' I said. 'Hold your horses.'

'Not horses,' Freya scoffed. 'Swing.'

In early December Janette phoned to tell us that the matching panel wouldn't meet until mid-January. I thought I'd explode. 'Seven weeks! What are we going to do for seven weeks?'

'There is Christmas,' Janette said. 'New Year's.'

I sighed.

'My advice? Have fun. Get away, if you can take the time, go out and socialise, stay up late. Do all the things that you won't be able to do as new parents.'

'I can probably use up my annual leave and take a bit unpaid, scrape together ten days,' I said to Mac that evening.

'I'd rather work Christmas week. We're always rammed and I've already a lot of people booked in. So maybe after Christmas,' he said.

'Where can we go this time of year?'

'Skiing?' he said.

I shuddered. 'You'll not get me climbing up any mountains.'

'They have ski lifts.'

I felt sick. 'Don't.'

'Australia will be warm,' he said.

'It's so far. What about Thailand? Bel loved it. Or Vietnam?' I said.

'Jabs, visas. Not sure whether we'd need visas but jabs for definite.'

'It's not going to be cheap, anywhere hot,' I said. 'And it's last minute. Can we afford it?'

Mac shrugged. 'Might be the last chance for a while. Let's see if there's any offers on the web.'

While I cleared out the fridge, ready for a shopping trip, Mac browsed deals on his laptop, calling out possibilities. 'Dubai?' he said.

'No, don't fancy that.'

'Gambia, not bad . . . Ah, dates don't work.'

I emptied a bag of peppers, turned to mush, into the bin. 'Why do we buy peppers? Do you like peppers?'

'I'd say I like the idea of them more than the actual thing.'

'The idea?' I said.

'The look. The colours,' he said.

'We're just throwing them away.'

'Moratorium on peppers. How about St Lucia? Now that looks gorgeous. We could do . . . nine days. Have to fly from Liverpool, though. No . . . New Year's Day out of Manchester. There we go.'

* * *

119

And there we went.

It was idyllic. Horrendously expensive but beautiful. Fine white sand on the beach, turquoise water, and palm trees rippling in the wind, just like the pictures on the website.

The first night we sat out on the veranda. The sky glittered with a frosting of stars. The moon was almost full: it cast a light over the water, catching the white of the foam. We could hear the waves and the clatter of palms in the breeze. The air was alive with the shrill cries of tree frogs and the whistling of crickets.

Mac winced and slapped his cheek, leaving a smear of blood. 'They never mentioned the mozzies in the blurb.'

'Do you think she'll need a bed or a cot?' I said. We couldn't go more than a couple of hours without talking about Chloë.

'They'll tell us,' Mac said.

'Someone in the adoption chatroom said they got to the matching panel and were told there were concerns. The children's social worker didn't think they were properly prepared. And that was it.'

'Hey.' Mac stroked my arm. 'We've done everything we can. It's out of our hands. But Janette thinks it's a good match and so does Chloë's social worker.'

'If that pointy-nosed prat is there again . . .' I said.

'Well, what you said last time worked. Just repeat it.' Mac slapped at his arm. 'Ah! I'm being eaten alive.'

'I'm boiling. I thought it might cool down when it got dark. We'll have to run the air-conditioning all night. But it's good that it's not all perfect here.'

'How's that work, then?' he said.

'I don't know. Like if this is too perfect maybe something will go wrong with the adoption.'

'That sounds awfully like magical thinking to me.' Mac pulled the wine from the ice bucket. 'I'm shocked, a scientist like you.'

'Shut up. Shall we book a day trip while we're here? Scuba-diving maybe,' I said.

'No,' he said quickly.

'No? Because of the money?'

He took a swallow of his drink. 'It gives me the heebie-jeebies.'

'Why? You're a good swimmer.'

'Not the swimming. The oxygen mask, that yoke.' He'd gone more Irish with the emotion. 'Yoke', I knew, meant 'thing'. 'Suffocating.'

'You never said.'

'It's never come up. And I might not either,' he said darkly.

I laughed then, at the worry on his face, at the notion that this big, brawny bloke was frightened of scuba-diving.

'Hey.' He nudged me. 'I've never laughed at you being scared of heights. You could at least show a fella a bit of sympathy.'

I stifled my laughter. 'OK.' I took a deep breath. 'No scuba-diving.'

'There is another sort of diving I could do,' he said. And winked. It took me a moment to cotton on. 'Is there now?'

'If you fancy it.'

'I just might.'

'We'll go in, then, shall we?' He lifted the wine up.

'We shall.'

Chapter Twenty-two

When I drew back the curtains on the day of the matching panel everything was coated in a blanket of snow six inches deep. The trees on the street, the parked cars, the hedges and fences all smothered, their shapes rounded and blunt.

'Mac, it snowed. What if they cancel? What if people can't make it?'

There was a grunt from the bed.

'Mac?'

'Yes. I'm awake.'

'Up. Now. Look. Snow.'

'Grand. We should get a sledge.'

'Idiot.'

I went to make breakfast. Ate my porridge and banana in front of the television watching weather porn, with images of abandoned vehicles and gritting lorries and children building snowmen.

We set off early to allow for the conditions but the main roads were already clear, the snow now dark grey slush melting in the gutters.

We were the first to arrive, but soon Janette came in and then Chloë's social worker, Adrian.

Janette offered us a drink but I didn't want anything, close to nauseous again. 'It's going to be OK,' she said. 'You know Adrian and I think this will be an excellent match.'

'They'll probably have a few questions for us,' Adrian said, 'based on our reports.'

'And you chip in if you want,' Janette said.

The sky grew dark as we waited and it began to snow again, fat white flakes. I went to look out of the window at it, following flakes as they spiralled down. Every one individual. One of the first times I used a microscope we looked at snowflakes. The teacher had frozen them in slides. I remembered the excitement of peering down the lens, a porthole into a hidden world.

'Just be honest,' Janette was saying.

The chair of the panel knocked on the door and invited us all through.

Most of the people were familiar but the pointy-faced man wasn't there.

Once everyone had been introduced, the chair asked Adrian to talk about the question of contact between Chloë and her birth-mother.

'Chloë has had supervised contact with her birth-mother, though birth-mum has not always attended.' I thought of the child waiting, the social workers watching the clock. Would Chloë have understood anything of that?

'If a placement was approved we would be looking for a farewell visit and then letterbox contact,' Adrian said.

The chair looked at me. 'And, Lydia and Mac, have you discussed meeting with the birth-mother?'

I dreaded the thought. I couldn't imagine how painful, how awkward it would be for everyone concerned. 'It's something we'd be open to,' I said. 'It would probably be good for Chloë in the future, to know we'd met.'

The woman with the tortoiseshell specs, the one who'd asked about our fears last time, said, 'Why this child?'

Janette had briefed us that this question often came up.

'We've not met Chloë,' I said, 'so all we can go on is the photo, and what we've heard about her in the report and from Adrian, but it feels right. She looks lovely and we can't stop thinking about her. We can give her a home, a new family and all our love.'

'Mac?' the woman said.

'It feels right, like Lydia says. Just a gut instinct. We want to be her parents.'

123

'And if there's trouble bonding?' she said.

'We know that can happen,' I said. 'We have to be aware of it. All we can do is provide a home and security, show her our love and hope she'll respond.'

'We know it won't be easy,' Mac said. 'None of this has been easy. But it's what we want.'

A man spoke, an older man with a rugged face: 'Janette, you've highlighted that Lydia will be at home with Chloë for the first year, and that while she has a relatively good support network, most of those friends and family won't be available during the weekdays – either they live at some distance or are in full-time work. There could be a problem with isolation.'

'Yes, we have discussed that,' Janette said. 'And Lydia has made it clear that she will build up new networks.'

I nodded. 'There are two mother-and-toddler groups we can go to nearby, and my mum has retired now so she'll be around to help as much as I want.'

'Thank you,' the man said.

The chair looked round at his colleagues. 'I think that's all we had.'

We were only back in the waiting area for five minutes before we were asked to return to the panel. Everyone was smiling. I had a lump in my throat.

'Congratulations,' the chair said.

I nodded, my hand over my mouth, blinking back the tears, while Mac thanked everyone profusely.

Chloë would be ours. Our daughter. Our little girl. We were finally going to be parents.

Chapter Twenty-three

Adrian and Janette drew up an introductions and placement plan with us and I notified work of my intention to take adoption leave. We had two weeks before our first meeting with Chloë, then we'd spend increasing amounts of time with her at her foster-home and after that at ours until she moved in with us full-time.

My friends from work took me for a goodbye meal.

'We got you this,' Pattie said. One of the others helped her to lift a large box onto an empty chair. I tore off the wrapping-paper. It was a microwave oven.

'I know you've not got one but, believe me, it's a lifesaver. You can heat up all those cold cups of coffee you're too busy to drink. Saves on washing-up, too, if you do soup or beans – no need for pans.'

'Speech,' someone shouted. And the others clapped.

'OK.' I held up my hands. 'Thank you so much for this, and for everything else. I really will miss you lot. But I'll be back. It's just a year. I've left my mug in the kitchen at work. And anyone can borrow it – as long as they *wash it up*!' Jeers and cheers greeted the long-standing gripe. 'But honestly, thanks.'

Pattie led the hip-hip-hoorays.

The taxi driver helped me carry the box into the house.

Mac was in bed but still awake. 'They got us a microwave,' I said, getting undressed.

'You're slurring,' he said. 'Are you drunk?'

'Very.'

'I heard from Luke. He says don't buy a bed.'

'They're getting us a bed?'

'Don't know. Maybe they've a spare.'

Luke turned up that Sunday driving a van.

Terese and crew were visiting so we had a mini Kelly reunion at ours.

Mac made roast leg of lamb, but before we ate everyone helped bring in the bed and swap it for the double mattress we used for visitors. Terese and John would take that back to York with them.

'It extends,' Luke said. 'You can fold out the base section here to make it a full-size single once she's big enough. Then you'll need a new mattress. And the guard rail comes off when you're ready.'

'It's beautiful,' I said. The pine frame and headboard gleamed like syrup.

Terese looked around the room. 'Are you keeping it white?'

'We want to find out if she has any favourite colours,' I said.

'New drawers?' She nodded. 'They're gorgeous.'

'Got them on Gumtree. Just tidied them up.'

'God, it's so exciting,' Terese said. 'Does it seem real to you?'

'No. Not one bit. I can't imagine it.' Chloë here. Sleeping, waking up here, eating with us. It seemed preposterous.

Ewan wanted to try out the bed.

'He can have a nap, Lydia. He'll be cranky otherwise,' Terese said.

'Should we have a story?' Ewan nodded at me. We had a few storybooks already, for Freya.

The others left the room and I spread our spare duvet on top of the mattress.

I sat on the bed, knees bent and he leaned back between my legs while I read to him.

'You have a little rest now.' I lifted him off me and laid him down. He felt heavier with sleep, limbs loose, eyes shut.

We crowded round our table for the meal, some people using plastic garden chairs.

The lamb was cooked to perfection, smothered with rosemary and spiked with garlic. The roast potatoes were crunchy on the outside and fluffy within. Mac had also made a selection of vegetables and a rich gravy.

When everyone had loaded their plates and filled their glasses, Luke led a toast. 'To Mac and Lydia and their new arrival, Chloë.'

'I remember when you came along, Mac,' Terese said. 'Niall had his nose put way out of joint. He was so bold, he kept bringing the cat in and dropping her in your cradle. Mammy lost the rag. He reckoned he was giving you the cat to play with when he really wanted to suffocate you.'

'You weren't much better, Terese,' Luke said. 'You dragged his cradle out into the yard one day because his crying was so loud.'

'I got clobbered for that,' Terese said.

'And the day Mac climbed on the roof,' Luke said.

'Oh, don't,' Terese said. She wagged her finger at her older boys. 'Don't you lads go getting any ideas.'

Mac told the tale and said, 'And Dad had done the exact same thing as a wee fella.'

Chloë would have none of this, family stories shared with brothers and sisters, anecdotes passed down the generations. The child torn from everything familiar, like those sorry scraps of paper, the little drawings, at our preparation day. But she'll learn new stories, I thought, our stories. And the ones we make together.

'Lydia?' Terese said. 'You and Steven, did you get on?'

'Until I was a teenager. Then we just wound each other up.'

'I'm dreading that,' she said.

'What, Mammy?' her eldest son, Joshua, piped up.

'When you're all teenagers, giving cheek and banging doors and staying out too late.'

'And getting piercings and tattoos,' Luke added.

'Nothing wrong with that,' Mac said.

'Says the fella who wore long sleeves every time he came home so Mammy wouldn't see his arms,' Terese said.

The table erupted.

'Ah,' Mac said, 'you're jealous, lads. Art, that is. Unique. People pay hundreds for work like it.'

'How old do I have to be to get a tattoo?' said Joshua.

'Now see what you've done,' Terese said.

'How old?'

'Eighteen,' Mac said. 'That's the law.'

'Even if you know me, like, if I'm a relative?'

'Ah, no, now,' Mac said. 'Then it'd be twenty-one.'

Adrian came to tell us more about Chloë. 'She's been with Rita and Gerry, her foster-parents, for six months. Before that, she was in emergency foster-care for eight weeks after removal from birth-mum. This is Chloë's life story book, which you will be adding to.' He held out a colourful binder, each page laminated.

I opened the cover. A blurry photograph, Chloë asleep, wrapped in a pale blue and pink blanket. She had almost no hair. The large type read, *Chloë was born on Wednesday, 3 April 2002.*

'We're not sure who took that,' Adrian said.

I turned the page. *And this is your birth-mother, Debbie.*

'Oh, God,' I said. She was so like the photo of Chloë, the same shape face and colouring. And she looked so young. She was smiling into the camera. Long white blonde hair, frosted eye make-up and lipstick. She had a ring through her nostril, silver chains around her neck.

Debbie had you in hospital and took you home. A photograph of a newish-looking estate, social housing. No street name or house numbers.

Your birth-daddy is called Neville. Neville lived in another town but he visited you and Debbie.

Debbie loved you very much but she didn't feel very well sometimes, so she found it hard to look after you.

'You could put in more detail here as Chloë gets older. About the drug abuse and the violence.'

'Won't that be hard for her?' I said.

'Chloë needs her story to be honest and clear. You can judge how much you share and when.'

'How do you put something like that?' Mac said.

'There are templates you can look at online,' Adrian told us. 'I'd say something like "Debbie took drugs to try to make herself feel happy but then she didn't have money for food and clothes and to keep the house warm. When Neville visited he and Debbie would argue. Sometimes Neville hit Debbie." It's factual but it's not using emotive language.'

'How old would she be, when she could hear that?' I said.

'Take a lead from her. But I'd say by the age of six or seven.'

'Seven! Really? It seems so brutal.'

'From the outside it can seem that way but, remember, Chloë has lived all this. It's already happened to her. All the research shows that hiding past trauma, denying the facts of life with the first family, keeping it a secret from the child, causes even more emotional damage in the long run.'

I returned to the book. *Sometimes Neville and Debbie went out and left you on your own. Babies don't like to be left on their own. They need someone there all the time to look after them.* It was like a grotesque bedtime story.

This is Adrian, your social worker. Adrian wanted you to be looked after all the time. He took you somewhere safe. First you lived here with Maxine. A terraced house, no picture of Maxine. *And then you went to live with Rita and Gerry, your foster-carers. Here are Rita and Gerry.* An older couple, both with grey hair; she wore hers in a long ponytail, and had apple cheeks. He had a moustache and beard, a pot belly.

Here are your foster-brothers, Sam and Joe, and your foster-sister, Ella-Mae. The children were together on a roundabout. *Here is Bingo the rabbit.* Chloë standing by the rabbit's cage. *You like to stroke Bingo and help Rita feed him.*

Adrian looked for a for-ever family for you. Here are your new mummy and daddy, Lydia and Mac.

Here is their house. It felt strange to think of Chloë being told that we were her new parents before she'd set eyes on us.

'Has Neville been in touch?' Mac said.

'No. He's not registered on the birth certificate so he has no parental rights. He spent some time in jail for affray around the time Chloë was born. Given the violence involved in the relationship, and the lack of any involvement since Chloë's removal, we won't be recommending any letterbox contact between you and him.'

I handed him back the book.

'Now, Friday,' he said, 'the meeting with Debbie. I thought it would be useful to go over what you might expect. Areas to talk about and what to avoid. You can ask Janette if you think of anything else before then.'

'I just want this to be over,' I said to Mac, on the drive to the family centre to meet Debbie. 'We're taking the woman's child.'

My legs felt unsteady, my mouth chalky as we walked up to the building.

This is what Chloë will look like when she's a woman, I thought, when we were introduced. Debbie was only nineteen, barely an adult herself. Thin as a rake. I felt huge compared to her.

Janette sat to one side and the three of us were in easy chairs around a low table.

Debbie was clearly nervous, her hands shaking, her voice too, when she said in a broad Yorkshire accent, 'I wanted to see you and give you this for her.' A pink teddy bear.

'Thanks,' I said. 'We hope she'll be happy with us – and we'll be able to tell her that we met you and talked.'

'Yeah, right.' She coughed. Her lips were dry and cracked.

Mac said, 'Are there any things we can tell her about the family, any hobbies or talents that got passed on?'

'You're Irish?' she said.

'That's right. Been over here a long time now.'

'My granny, she were Irish. She were a singer, with a dance band and that. They all liked to sing. I like singing.' She darted glances around the room as she talked but didn't look at either of us directly.

'That's nice,' I said. We knew that Debbie's mother had left Debbie to be looked after by her grandma, and Debbie had gone into care herself at the age of eleven when her grandma had had a stroke and died.

'What music do you like?' I said.

'All sorts. Britney, Westlife, Craig David.'

'What about TV?' Mac said.

'*Big Brother*, *EastEnders*, *Trisha*. Watch owt, really.' She scratched at her arm and coughed.

'Why did you choose Chloë as a name?' I said.

'I liked it, that's all. I decided before she were born. And if it was a boy then Cody.'

'What was the birth like?' I said.

'It were hard. They give us an epidural but it still hurt. She were born at midnight, near enough. I'd been going all day. On us own. Her dad, he were inside then. Didn't know if I'd see him again.'

'Is there anything you can tell us about Neville that Chloë might want to know?'

'Not really.' Her face closed down.

'Did he work?' I said.

'He did tiling for a bit. What d'you do?' she said.

'I work in health care,' I said.

'And I'm an illustrator,' Mac said. We had to be careful not to give any information that might help identify us.

'Drawing and that?'

'Yes.'

'That's good. I like drawing. She'll like drawing.' She started to cry, saying, 'Sorry, sorry,' and wiping at her face. I felt myself choke up too. She was wearing mascara and eyeliner and it began to streak.

Mac cleared his throat.

'We'll write every year,' I said, 'let you know how she's doing.'

'Right.'

Debbie would visit Chloë one last time to say goodbye and then she wouldn't be allowed to see her again until Chloë reached eighteen and could decide for herself if she wanted any contact.

'We thought we could get Janette to take a photo of us all, for Chloë,' I said.

'Yeah. That'd be good.'

'Your mascara . . . you might want to . . .' I said.

131

'Fuck!' she said. 'It's supposed to be waterproof.' We both laughed. A moment's connection, and I wanted to comfort her, to reassure her, but I couldn't, not beyond saying, 'We'll look after her, we'll give her everything we can. We'll love her and keep her safe.'

Keep her safe? Was it arrogance or naivety on my part?

Chapter Twenty-four

The day we were introduced to Chloë we met first with her foster-carer and Adrian at a family centre in Bradford.

'I've brought some photos for you to keep,' Rita said. 'We take them regularly. Lot easier now it's all digital.'

'You've been fostering a long time?'

'Twenty-three years,' she said.

Rita was clearly a heavy smoker. I could smell it on her and the first fingers on her right hand were stained conker brown. I imagined what she did was so full on and stressful that smoking would be a relief.

'What can you tell Lydia and Mac about Chloë?' Adrian said.

'She's quiet. Hangs back. Cautious, you know,' Rita said.

'Frightened?' Mac said, concerned.

'More wary. Weighs it all up, you know. She's a bit behind with her speech and language. She's not one for cuddles. Doesn't like being held or touched. It makes her anxious.' How sad that was. And why? Had she been sexually abused? Or beaten? There was nothing about that in the reports, and Mac and I had said we wouldn't consider a child with that background. There must be some other reason. But I'd have all the time in the world to reassure her, to coax her to trust me, like taming a shy, wild creature. Take it gently and slowly until she'd come to snuggle up with me, making up for all the loving hugs she'd missed.

Rita said, 'And it makes getting her dressed and stuff like that harder.'

'Is she in nappies?' Mac said.

'No. Toilet-trained. She was really quick with that. She doesn't wet the bed either. Which is practically unheard-of.' She rolled her eyes. 'What else? We've had some tantrums, rages. It's impossible to tell what sets her off.'

'Has she got a favourite colour?' I said.

'No, don't think so,' Rita said.

'What about food?' Mac said. 'What does she like?'

'Toast, bananas, cereal – the more sugar the better. Fish fingers. Won't touch anything green or anything she doesn't recognise.'

'What does she like to play with?' I said.

'She's got a Snoopy Dog that goes everywhere. She likes most of the toys,' Rita said.

'OK,' Adrian said. 'Shall we make a move?'

'Yes,' I said. But suddenly the enormity of what was happening hit me. I was about to meet my daughter. It was too much, too immense. It was like looking over a precipice. My nerves jangled, the hairs on my neck lifted. I couldn't do this. It was all a mistake.

Mac looked at me, raised his eyebrows, held out his hand. I don't know if he sensed that I needed reassurance or if he was after some for himself.

Rita's husband Gerry was at home with Chloë; the other foster-children were at nursery. We saw him at the window as we arrived, kneeling up on the sofa. Standing beside him, her face just visible, was Chloë. He said something and she slipped from sight.

Inside, wet clothes were draped on the radiators and the smell of fabric conditioner was heavy in the air, sickly and chemical. Rita took us straight into the living room. The house was a similar size to ours but their living room and dining room were knocked through.

Chloë was sitting on the floor, her back to us, her fine blonde hair a puff of bright colour. She was playing with a toy farm set, pushing buttons that opened gates or made sounds. A cow mooed.

'Give her a minute,' Rita said. 'Let me take your coats.'

'Here, I'll do it.' Gerry took them out.

Adrian sat next to Chloë. 'Hello, we've brought someone to see you. Someone very special. Your new mummy and new daddy.'

Chloë pressed a button. *Baaa*. How much did she understand? She wasn't even two years old.

'They've come to say hello. Can you see them on the sofa?'

She pressed a button, jabbed at it three times. *Woof woof woof.*

'Shall we show your new mummy and new daddy this game?'

A twitch of her shoulder and she scooted a little further away from Adrian.

'OK. In a minute, yes?'

I could feel the tension building across my shoulders and my stomach churning.

Rita spoke: 'I think we'll take your new mummy and daddy to see Bingo. And you can give him some dinner.'

Chloë dipped her head, swivelled round and stood. She bobbed down and picked up her Snoopy toy to bring with her. She glanced up at Rita briefly but didn't look at either of us.

My heart turned over. I wanted to touch her, hug her, pull her close. She was tiny. Two months older than Freya but she looked half the size. So skinny. She was beautiful. I couldn't take my eyes off her. I was besotted, and scared, and euphoric, and sick. All the things love brings.

She ran into the hall and we filed out after her, first Rita, then me and Mac.

The back garden was a muddy lawn with a small trampoline on it, a Wendy house and one of those rockers made of moulded plastic. At the far end was the rabbit hutch. I could see the black rabbit.

'He likes these leaves,' Rita said. She picked some cabbage from a box beside the hutch. She passed me a piece and stepped aside so I was immediately behind Chloë.

'He likes cabbage, does he, Chloë?' I said.

No reply.

The smell of hay and rabbit pee hit me. I remembered arguments with my mum about cleaning out the hutch. And the awful morning when I saw the hutch door had been ripped open.

I crouched down beside Chloë. 'I had a rabbit called Moppet when I was a little girl.' I held the cabbage out to her. 'Will you give it to him?'

She didn't respond. I glanced up at Rita.

'Your new mummy can feed him,' she said.

I pressed the cabbage to the chicken wire.

The rabbit came and tugged at it, nose and whiskers twitching. 'He loves that,' I said.

'Let's go in,' Rita said.

Chloë ran up the path.

I looked at Mac. Was she going to ignore us completely? He gave a rueful smile.

While Rita and Gerry made tea, the rest of us went back into the living room.

'Where's the bricks?' Adrian said.

Chloë moved to the corner and pulled a plastic box on wheels into the centre of the room.

Mac and I got down on the floor. Chloë picked out Stickle Bricks.

'Can I have some?' Mac said. When she didn't respond he put his hands in and got a pile. 'Some for you.' He passed me a handful. 'Some for me.'

Mac fixed his pieces together, rummaged in the box for more. 'There, a doggy.' He put it down in front of Chloë and she pushed it over.

'OK,' Mac said. 'Has he fallen over? Or is he going to sleep? Night night.'

Chloë pressed some Stickle Bricks together.

'What's that, Chloë?' Adrian said.

'Bricks.'

I laughed. It was impossible not to stare at her. I wanted to drink her in, capture everything about her. My daughter.

Rita and Gerry brought our drinks in and a plate of biscuits.

'Chloë, will you help me share out the biscuits?' Rita said. 'Give one to Adrian.'

Chloë took the small plate to him.

'Now one for your new daddy.' She did the same.

'And one for your new mummy.'

Chloë hesitated. Shy? Rebellious? Confused?

'That looks yummy,' I said.

But Chloë moved to Rita and held out the plate. 'Oh, OK, one for me first,' Rita said. 'Thank you. One for New Mummy now.'

I wanted Rita to stop. I didn't want Chloë's reluctance to acknowledge me highlighted any more. I looked at Adrian, hoping he'd pick up on my discomfort, but before he could register it, Chloë came to me and thrust out the plate so fast that both biscuits slid off into my lap. 'Whoops, never mind.' I returned one to the plate. 'Thank you. That's lovely,' I said. I took a bite.

Chloë tilted her face up and met my gaze. Her eyes were greeny-grey. She looked guarded, suspicious. I smiled and said, 'Thank you,' again and she turned away.

When we left, Chloë didn't say goodbye. I hoped she might look out of the window, show some interest, but there was no sign of her, just a blank black rectangle reflecting the street.

Chapter Twenty-five

'Last night of freedom.' Bel raised her glass to toast us. We'd all met up for drinks in the Fenton.

'How's it gone so far?' Colin said.

'We're knackered already,' Mac said. He had been charging about from the shop to our meetings with Chloë, taking on evening appointments to make up for lost time.

I nodded. 'She was with us all afternoon yesterday. Brought some of her toys and clothes over. She's very reserved. It's going to take time.'

'When do we get to meet her?' Javier said.

'Not yet,' I said. 'We have a couple of weeks just settling her in. Her social worker thinks that's best. No visitors. My mum and dad are itching to come.'

'I shan't be surprised if we find my lot camping out in the alley,' Mac said.

'What surname are you going to give her?' Colin said.

'Kelly-Ross, hyphenated,' I said. 'Chloë Kelly-Ross.'

'They've had you practising it all, then?' Bel said.

'Yes. Doing stuff at the foster-carers' first. Giving her a bath, making meals. Putting her to bed. She hates having her hair washed.'

'Didn't we all?' Colin said. 'I screamed the place down.'

'You still do,' Javier said.

'Once! Once I got shampoo in my eyes and you thought it was funny.'

Javier grinned.

'It's unreal,' I said to Bel, when we went to the bar, 'that she's coming tomorrow and staying. Not just overnight but for ever.'

'No going back now,' Bel said.

'I know. It's scary. I can't get my head round it. That we've got her, that she's ours.' I raised my hand to try to catch the bar staff's attention. 'And what if I get it wrong? What if something goes wrong?'

'You'll be great. We all make mistakes – fuck knows I do. Cos we're learning on the job. They'll all need therapy when they're grown-up. Like the poet said, they fuck you up.' She leaned forward and gave our order.

'Bye-bye, Chloë. You get in the car now. Your bag's there and Snoopy's waiting for you,' Rita said.

Chloë stood unmoving, feet planted firmly on the ground, head lowered. Studiously avoiding eye contact. A frown wrinkled her brow.

Rita looked across the roof of the car to Mac, then at me. Pulled a face. Rita was upset, I could tell from her voice, brighter and more brittle than usual. She'd confided in us that it was a real wrench to say goodbye, especially to a child like Chloë, whom she had become very fond of. 'We even talked about adopting her ourselves a while back,' she'd said, 'but we're too old. It wouldn't be fair on her even if we could get them to bend the rules.'

Rita stooped down. 'You want me to lift you in, Chloë?'

Chloë's shoulders rippled, a shrug of rejection.

'You climb in, then.'

I hated the stand-off.

'Mummy and Daddy are getting in,' Rita said.

'Yes,' I said. I climbed in to demonstrate. So did Mac.

'Now Chloë,' Rita said.

I held my breath. Would she kick off? I glanced at Mac. His face was drawn, worried. We'd witnessed one of Chloë's rages when we'd taken her out to the park near Rita's house.

She'd been climbing on the jungle gym.

'We're going to go back and see Rita,' I'd told her.

She came down one of the ladders, lost her footing near the bottom and fell.

I dashed to pick her up. She screamed, arching her back, thrashing

139

her arms. She flung her head back, clouting me on the nose. Pain exploded through me, and a hot anger at being hurt.

Rita had told us the only way to deal with an outburst was to give her space and wait it out.

Flustered, I tried to sit Chloë in the pushchair but her spine was rigid.

'Put her on the grass,' Mac said. 'You're bleeding.'

I sniffed and tasted copper in the back of my throat.

I walked to the grass and laid her down. It was horrible watching her smack her head on the ground, hearing her scream and scream. Two women and their children were watching us from across the play park.

Freya had tantrums when she'd stomp and wail but they usually dissolved into crying jags. She could cry for a long time, a whining, grizzling sort of crying. Bel would snap at her, 'For Chrissake, Freya, give it a bloody rest. You're driving me insane.' And when that didn't work Bel would try bribery.

We had crouched at either side of Chloë, not too close to be oppressive, and waited. Now and then I said quietly, 'It's OK, Chloë, we're here.'

Gradually the bucking and the head-banging slowed, then stopped. The screams dwindled into cries. A few spasms shook her.

'Here's Snoopy.' I handed her the stuffed toy. 'We'll go back to Rita's now.'

She didn't answer but got upright and went to stand beside the pushchair.

'Are you going to push?' Mac said. 'You going to push Snoopy?'

She climbed into the pushchair, the toy on her lap.

'Right, then,' Mac had said. 'Off we go.'

Now Chloë clambered into our car and plumped herself into her car seat. Rita leaned in to fasten the straps.

'Bye-bye,' Rita said briskly, and shut the door. Watching in the wing mirror, I saw her turn and walk away, hands in her pockets, shoulders slumped.

* * *

140

At home we tried to keep things calm, very low key, knowing the experience of leaving her foster-home and joining us would be overwhelming enough for Chloë.

'You hungry?' I said, once we got in. 'Let's make you some toast.'

A nod.

'Good. Here's the kitchen again. Here's your chair. We'll have some toast, then put your things in your room. And we've got *The Tigger Movie* to watch.' We had the whole day planned out, a routine as similar as possible to the one she'd been used to. We'd brought Chloë's pillow from Rita's as well as her clothes. They all smelt strongly of that fabric conditioner. The familiarity might help her settle in so we wouldn't wash anything until it really needed it.

I cut the toast into fingers as we'd done at Rita's. It had been strange, strained, doing those tasks in someone else's house, with them offering advice and comments.

Chloë took a bite of toast from one finger and left the rest. She drank her milk.

She was silent throughout the film, though she reacted to the rhymes by nodding. Mac sat sketching some designs for work. Once or twice I saw her peeping at him.

After tea, I ran her bath. We'd bought bath toys for her but I just got one out, a soft squashy turtle that made a whistling sound when you squeezed it.

While Mac showed her that, I tried to get her undressed as efficiently as I could with as little touching as possible. She was tense, flinching each time I put my hands on her.

'We need to lift you in now,' I said. She took a step away, her back to me. I saw the wings of her shoulder blades, the little knots of her spine.

'Shall I just go for it?' I said to Mac.

'Hang on.' In the corner of the room there was a wooden box where we kept hot-water bottles. 'This can be a step,' Mac said.

He pulled the box in front of the bath. Quick as a flash, Chloë stepped up and climbed into the bubbles.

141

I knelt on the floor, reached into the bath and gave the turtle a squeeze. 'It's nice and warm in there,' I said.

She just sat there, showed no sign of wanting to play. Her face was grubby, smeared with food. 'Chloë, here's a little sponge, you wipe your face. Like this.' I rubbed it on my own. 'Wipe your nose and mouth.'

She did, after a fashion, a dab here and there.

'Well done. That's very clever. Good girl. Nice clean face. That's lovely. Out you come.'

It was harder for her to climb out, she couldn't raise her leg high enough.

I put my hands out. 'You hold my hands and I'll swing you up and out.'

She didn't move. Would it be easier if I lifted her under her arms? Would she freak out? 'Let's count – one, two, three – and then I'll lift you onto the box.'

She gave a shiver. I could see her ribs, the veins that traced blue over her neck and shoulders.

'Pass the towel,' I said to Mac. I took it from him and draped it over my hands then said, 'Here we go.' Quickly I picked her up and swung her over the edge of the bath onto the box, then wrapped the towel all round her. 'Let's go find your pyjamas.'

Once she was dressed, she got into bed. There was just room for me to sit next to her on top of the covers, Snoopy acting as an additional buffer between us.

I read to her, *Where's Spot?* Chloë looked absolutely shattered, her eyes hollowed out, daubs of blue beneath them, face pale.

'You lie down now. We'll leave the light on and the door open,' I said. Chloë lay flat on her back, her hands clasped together under her chin.

'I'm going to be downstairs with Daddy, and then we'll go to sleep in our bed. If you want me you can come and find me or you can call me. Call Mummy and I'll come. I'll put your songs on, now.' She had a CD of lullabies.

'Night night, lovely girl,' I said. 'See you in the morning.'

Downstairs Mac and I hugged wordlessly.

'Wine?' he said, when I pulled away. 'Food?'

'Oh, yes.'

We'd made several meals to freeze ahead of time. Mac reheated a lamb and turnip dish in the microwave. While we ate we picked over the day, interpreting every incident, measuring it against our expectations and our fears.

Mac showed me a sketch he'd done. 'She's like a little dandelion,' he said. 'Her hair all fluffed up.'

He had captured perfectly that elfin face and tentative smile. He'd dressed her in a tawny gown with draped sleeves and fur around the cuffs. 'That is gorgeous,' I said. 'I'm going to see if she's asleep.'

She was in the same position, eyes closed, breathing so softly I had to watch intently to see if she was moving. The CD had finished and I switched the player off.

I watched her for a little while. *My daughter.*

I really hadn't expected to sleep that first night but I did drift off and started awake to the sound of Chloë crying.

'I'll go,' I said to Mac, who was stirring. I was the primary caregiver now. I had to be there whenever she needed me.

She had turned onto her side and was pressed up against the wall.

'Chloë, I'm here,' I said. 'It's all right. Mummy's here. You sound sad. I'll stay with you.' She kept crying, a deep, desolate weeping.

I sat on the bed beside her, longing to hold her, to cradle her, to stroke her back and rock her in my arms. None of these things would comfort her so I sat and listened as she wept, my heart aching. And I wondered how I could ever show my love for her if I couldn't cuddle her.

Chapter Twenty-six

Adrian came to see how things were going. I told him about the crying.

'She's mourning,' he told us. 'I know it's hard to hear but, if you think about it, it's a natural response to what's happening.'

'And the touching. I can't comfort her. Was she . . . was there any abuse?'

'No. Not that we can establish.'

'So there might have been?' I was dismayed.

'We don't think so. Physical anxiety is also a sign of neglect, and we do know Chloë was neglected. All those normal developmental stages of bonding, of communicating and getting needs met, physical contact, eye contact, talking, singing – because they didn't happen, her emotional wiring didn't develop as it would for a baby who was properly parented. It'll take time for your parenting and your love to help her heal. It's early days, but she's very young, young enough to learn all those things she missed out on.'

While he talked, Chloë lay on her stomach on the floor, watching television. She had ignored Adrian, which made me feel slightly better. *Not just me, then.* A twinge of guilt followed the thought. It wasn't about me, none of this was supposed to be about me, but it was hard to hold onto that at times.

'To some degree it's also about control,' Adrian said. 'Chloë had no control over anything. She was completely helpless so anything that threatens her sense of being in control is very frightening for her.'

When he left, Chloë ran into the hall and sat by the door.

'I think she wants to go with him,' I said to Mac. 'She probably thinks he'll take her back to Rita.'

I tried to explain: 'Adrian has gone back to work. You're staying here with Mummy and Daddy. We'll have some dinner soon, watch *The Tigger Movie* again after.' She kept her vigil for over an hour, rocking a little, Snoopy at her side. I kept the kitchen door open so I could see her and she could see me while I tidied round.

Mac had gone upstairs, taking the opportunity to shower and shave.

There was knocking at the front door and Chloë scrambled to her feet.

It was a delivery, a huge bouquet. I took the flowers, closed the door and Chloë screamed. She flung herself down, her face reddening and furrowed. She hit her head against the skirting board. I was terrified she'd crack her skull. I felt hot and sick. I dropped the flowers and grabbed her feet, pulling her away from the wall. She kept screaming and banging her head.

Mac appeared at the top of the stairs in a towel. 'You OK?'

I waved him away. I sat on the floor and leaned back against the wall, saying, 'I'm here. Mummy's here,' every so often.

My teeth were forced together, my jaw aching. A voice in my head was willing her to shut up. I yearned to walk out, to escape, just wanting it to stop.

When the screams weakened and the thump of her head on the carpet stopped, I said, 'Time for dinner, Chloë. We've got some chocolate pudding, too, for afters.'

She sat up, her eyes swimming with tears, snot thick under her nose.

'Wipe your nose.' I reached out with a tissue.

She jerked away.

'Can you do it?' I held out the tissue. She wouldn't take it, just wiped the back of her hand across her face smearing the mucus over her cheek and her hair.

I wanted to laugh. Or weep. 'You're a funny little thing. Come on, then.' She trotted into the kitchen and climbed up into her chair.

'Hello, Dandelion,' Mac said. 'Toast coming up and we have jam or honey. Have a taste?' He put a smidge of jam on a spoon. 'Try that, Chloë.'

I sat down, my stomach gurgling with hunger.

'What do you fancy?' Mac said to me. 'Soup? Cream of chicken?'

'Great,' I said, trying to keep the exhaustion and tension out of my voice. Was that right? I knew keeping calm was important, but hiding my own feelings?

'And this is honey.' Mac passed another spoon to Chloë.

'Who sent flowers?' he said.

'Oh.' They were still in the hall. I went to fetch them. It was a luxurious bunch. White roses and stiff stems of lilac sea lavender, sweet-smelling purple stocks, some sort of thistles, pink daisies, ferns and grasses.

I opened the card, read aloud: '"Congratulations and welcome to little Chloë. Love from Bel and Freya. PS Stock up on the Calpol and gin. You're going to need it."'

'Make a change from a Bloody Mary,' Mac said, buttering the toast. 'I'm not sure Calpol works as well as tonic water, mind. Now, Chloë, jam or honey?'

She nodded.

'Both. Grand. Half and half.'

It was only day two. It was just midday. And I felt like weeping with tiredness. I looked at her, the tear-streaked face, a patch of hair stuck with snot, holding the toast in her fine little fingers. Looking sideways at me, like some wild creature. Her eyes haunted. My daughter.

When Chloë had been with us for three months we applied to get an adoption court order. It would make the adoption legal, permanent, giving us all the rights and responsibilities of parents.

Adrian came to meet me at the community farm where I took Chloë every Tuesday morning with my mum. 'I wanted to tell you in person,' he said. 'Debbie's contesting the adoption.'

I felt a jolt of alarm, like electricity under my skin. 'No!'

146

'It's not uncommon,' Adrian said. 'Birth-parents want to show they're doing all they can to keep the child, fighting for them, even if everyone accepts that adoption is the best option.'

We were sitting on a bench in the sunshine, an Indian summer. I watched Chloë follow a hen that was foraging for food. She was fascinated by the animals, the pigs particularly, wrinkling her nose at the smell, even tolerating being picked up to see over the wall into the sty.

Tuesday was the quietest time. Chloë couldn't cope well with crowds, with strangers and unpredictability. Sometimes I wouldn't realise how much stress she had been in until we got home and then she'd explode. At others the meltdown came in public. The shrieking, the head-banging, the rolling on the floor. Some people mistook it for a fit, asked if it was epilepsy.

'Could Debbie win?' I said.

'Surely not,' my mum said.

'Extremely unlikely,' Adrian said. 'It will delay things while there's a reassessment by her social worker but you really needn't worry.'

Adrian asked about the tantrums.

'I'm getting a bit better at spotting when she's overloaded. She becomes frozen, a blank expression. Like she's shutting down. But she's actually building up to an outburst. And I'm better at avoiding difficult situations but we're still having rages almost every day.'

'And the crying?'

'Most nights. Sometimes she'll wake and come into our room. We've a cot mattress on the floor there now. She comes in and she'll go to sleep but often she wakes again and cries. Not for as long.'

The hen flapped its wings and flew up onto the fence. Chloë watched it from a distance.

'None of them get any sleep,' my mum said.

'Mac does, if he goes and sleeps on the floor in her room. We've a mattress there too.' I shook my head.

'It's worth one of you getting some rest,' Adrian said. 'It can grind you down.'

'I wait for him to get in from work, I watch the clock. He comes in the door and he knows the rest of the evening he's in charge,' I said.

With the hen out of the way, a pair of sparrows alighted, pecking at the ground, cocking their heads at each sound or vibration, taking flight as Chloë turned back to watch them. She's like the sparrows, I thought, needing space, everything a threat. On high alert all the time, hyper-tense, heart beating fast and light like theirs.

'You're making progress,' Adrian said. 'I know you probably feel it never gets any easier but baby steps are all we can hope for.'

'She sat on my knee last week,' I said. 'I couldn't believe it. I think she'd almost forgotten it was me, just treated me like a chair. She was busy playing this little harmonica and she just hauled herself up on me. I didn't move an inch.' I knew if I put my arms round or shuffled her closer or anything she might throw a tantrum. 'She blew some notes and slid off. I keep waiting for it to happen again.'

'It will,' he said.

Adrian went over to say goodbye to Chloë. He held his hand out flat, sometimes she would pat an open palm. Today she ignored him.

'I'll be in touch,' he said as he left us. 'As soon as we hear. And, honestly, there is nothing to worry about.'

A mother with a baby in a buggy and a toddler at her side, a boy who looked a year or so older than Chloë, came into the farmyard.

The boy ran up to Chloë, shouting something, some game he was playing. Chloë stilled. I went over as quickly as I could. 'Come on, Chloë, time for dinner.' I smiled at the mother, who looked a little affronted but I didn't have time to explain – if we don't go now my daughter just might destroy your morning.

'Chloë. Come on, Grandma's waiting. Chloë.'

She ran then, over to my mum, and got into the pushchair. Crisis averted.

'How is she with Bel's little one?' my mum asked.

'It's like that.' I nodded back towards the boy. 'They won't play together. Freya's very keen. Too keen sometimes. She doesn't understand.'

'Ah, they're still very young. I remember Steven was very much off on his own, till school really. Then he was thick as thieves with Matthew. Do you remember Matthew Ollershaw?'

'No.' The comparison really didn't help. I'm sure it was intended to reassure, finding parallels, but it actually annoyed me. I'd noticed it with other people too, with Bel and Pattie. Why couldn't they see that Chloë's rages were not the same as the tantrums Freya had, that her crying at night couldn't be equated to Pattie's son teething?

Look at her, I wanted to say. She was left in a cot in a cold room on her own for hours on end. When she cried, no one came. When she was hungry, no one fed her. When she was dirty, she was left like that. Then she's taken away from everything she knows and moved to foster-care. She's getting used to that and we take her away again. She's lost everything. She can't trust anyone. When she cries or screams now, she has all that to cry about.

I bent over the pushchair. 'What shall we have to eat?'

''Getti,' she said.

'That is a great idea,' I said. 'And Grandma's bought buns.'

Chloë kicked her feet, a little one-two motion, a sign that she was happy. And my heart lifted.

Part Two

2013–17

Chapter Twenty-seven

'Just leave your bags in the living room,' I said to Bel and Freya. 'We've put you in there. God, they're enormous.'

'They're American. Everything's enormous,' Bel said.

'Where's Mac?' He'd collected them from the airport.

'Gone to the corner shop.'

'For milk,' Freya added.

'Look at you!' I gave Freya a hug. 'How tall are you?'

'Five foot one.'

'She's catching me up,' Bel said. 'Ten years old and we're shopping in the women's section now.'

'Come through,' I said. 'Tea, coffee, food? Or do you want to sleep?'

'I could eat,' Freya said. 'I'm hungry.'

'You're always hungry,' Bel said.

'Same as me,' I said. 'Like a gannet, that's what my mum says. We've got some chilli – I've done a veggie one too.'

'Cool. Thanks,' Freya said.

'Bel?'

'Just a drink. Red, if you've got some.'

'When did you set off?' I asked Bel.

'Eleven this morning.' She yawned and pulled out a chair.

'Twenty-three hours with stops and all,' Freya said.

'Three flights, LA to Vancouver, then Heathrow, then Leeds-Bradford,' Bel said. 'Town's still booming, then, I see. More luxury flats for young professionals, office blocks going up.'

'Yes, the bigger the better. You should see what they've done around the docks,' I said.

'Money coming in,' Bel said.

'In certain places. Not much sign of it filtering down to anyone who really needs it.'

Mac came in with the milk.

'Where's Chloë?' Freya said.

'In her room,' I said. I exchanged a glance with Bel. 'She had some food earlier. I'll fetch her when we've eaten, if she's still awake.'

'Is that right?' Freya pointed to the wall clock. Eight-thirty in the evening.

'Yes,' Mac said.

'Santa Monica is what?' I said.

'Like eight hours behind. We flew through five different time zones,' Freya said.

I passed over a bottle of wine and took out glasses.

'You've got a right Yankee accent,' Mac said to Freya.

'Have not.'

'Yes, you have,' I said.

'Not according to the Yanks,' Bel said. 'They're always taking the piss.'

'They do not!' Freya said crossly. 'They're nuts for my accent. They think I'm like a lady or royalty or something. They think it's all like the olden days over here.'

'Whatever.' Bel poured the wine. She looked amazing. Her dark hair was cut short and choppy and she had bleached the tips. She was tanned. I thought back to that summer all those years earlier, sunbathing topless on my parents' lawn.

I put the serving dishes in the middle of the table and let people help themselves.

Bel's phone buzzed. She glanced at it. 'Wank-face.' Ethan, I guessed, the man she'd followed to America four years ago.

'Mom!' Freya protested. 'Quit the swearing.'

'Sometimes only swearing will do,' Bel said.

'You swear all the time. You do it to bug me.'

'Freya, it's not about you.'

'There's more chilli,' I interrupted their bickering.

Bel sighed theatrically. She held up a packet of fags.

154

Freya opened her mouth.

'Don't.' Bel pointed a finger at her.

'Backyard,' I said.

'You jet-lagged?' Mac said to Freya.

'Kinda.' She nodded. 'You can like dehydrate on a plane. And people have these DVTs, like when you don't move and you get a blood clot and drop down dead when you get off the plane. So you have to move your feet, and keep getting up, and do all these exercises.' The same old Freya, bright and precocious. She must be more than just jet-lagged, I thought. Wrenched away from her school friends so suddenly. Her life disrupted yet again by one of Bel's moves.

The first I'd heard of the break-up was a Skype video call from Bel asking to stay for a few days until they could sort out somewhere to live.

'What happened?'

'He wants to get married.'

'So you're fleeing the country?'

'If he'd asked me three years ago I might have gone for it. But he's getting like some old fart. We don't do anything, we don't see anyone.'

Was she exaggerating? Ethan was a respected choreographer, who'd worked in London's West End, Hollywood, and on Broadway. When Bel had first gone out there she was full of stories about fascinating people and the buzz of something new every day. She'd worked as his PA.

'He's toxic. His last show bombed and now he wants to retreat. Hide away and start some academy. Anyway, it's over.'

'Sorry.'

'No.' She'd waved a hand at me. 'Narrow escape. I can't stay on here without a job. He's my sponsor. So, time to come back. Green and pleasant land and all that.'

'Have you seen any news recently? They've opened a food bank down the road. Cutting everything to the bone. Half the country's snowed in, power cuts, no trains, nothing.'

155

'Home, sweet home.'

Now Bel came back in. 'It's freezing.' She shuddered.

'You've gone soft,' I said. 'Too much sunshine. Did you hear back from any schools?'

'A couple replied. Where's Chloë going?'

'Lawnswood. It's the nearest.'

'Mom wants to send me to Cardinal Heenan, which is so totally wrong,' Freya said. 'Like, I'm not Catholic. I'm not even baptised. They won't let me in.'

'I don't *want* to send you there. We'll go with anyone who'll have you. Everyone else has already got their places,' Bel said.

'I'll see if Chloë's coming down,' I said.

Upstairs I knocked on her door and went in. Bracing myself as I always did in case she'd done something stupid. Gone too far and hurt herself really badly this time. The blade too deep.

She was sitting on her bed and the small TV was on, *Casualty* just finishing.

'Bel and Freya are here. You going to say hello?'

She gave a small sigh, pressed the remote and pulled on her slipper boots.

Downstairs she slid onto one of the chairs and replied to Bel's hello with a quiet 'Hi.' She got out her phone and put it on the table.

'Is it a smartphone?' Freya said.

Chloë shook her head.

'I'm getting a smartphone for my birthday,' Freya said.

'You hope,' Bel said.

'You promised!'

'I did not.'

'You did so. That is so typical, Mom. You promise things and then—'

'Chill!' Bel held up her hands. 'Be nice.'

'What – like you?' Freya spat.

The spiky atmosphere made me uneasy, and it wasn't good for Chloë.

I'd always found Bel's attitude to Freya difficult. 'Be kind,' I'd told her once.

Freya was seven and wanting to make her own birthday cake. Bel had ridiculed the idea. 'I've better things to do, and it'll cost twice as much and probably taste revolting anyway.'

'You treat her like shit sometimes,' I said.

'Don't tell me how to be a mother,' Bel said sharply. 'I don't go in for the self-sacrificing, martyr act. I'm honest with her.'

'Listen to yourself. She's seven. That girl didn't ask to be born. However tedious you find it, it's your job to care for her. To make her feel good about herself, not rubbish her when you're feeling fed up.'

'Spare me the preaching. She's fine! It's just how we are with each other. She doesn't need special handling, like Chloë.'

I had stared at her, furious. She still needs love, I thought, your approval, your praise. But before I could continue my arguments Freya had come back into the room with a recipe she had printed off for a cake, clearly determined to prove Bel wrong.

Now I made an effort to separate them. 'You want a shower, Freya? Before bed?'

'Sure. Yeah. OK. Thanks.'

'Remember the way?' I said.

'I'll get my PJs.'

Chloë stayed with us for a few more minutes, making herself as invisible as possible. Replying to any questions with a monosyllable or a nod. On edge.

'You want to go up?' I said.

She nodded. Stood up. I went and kissed the top of her head. 'Night-night.'

'Hey,' Mac called, as she turned to go. He proffered a fist and Chloë touched knuckles with him. A tentative hand jive.

'She been any better?' Bel asked, when she was out of earshot.

'Not really,' I said. 'We've got a referral from the GP. On the waiting list to see someone at CAMHS – child mental health. School – they just don't get it. She did see an educational psychologist but they'd had no training in adoption, didn't know anything about attachment issues or any of that. They just didn't understand.'

Plenty of adoptions went well. The kids settled in without problems. They were happy, loving families, like the ones in the adverts and the brochures. How I envied them. But that's what people expected, wanted to see. Not us, failing, aberrant, not up to the task.

'And social services?'

I laughed. 'Same as ever. Social services washed their hands of us as soon as the ink was dry. You remember how I used to ring them, leave messages begging for help? No one ever rang back. Nothing's changed. Occasionally there's some waffle about doing more to support families in crisis, but when you actually ask for anything, forget it.' I could feel my throat tightening with the frustration of it. 'They won't even give us a week's respite, a weekend. Nothing.'

'I don't know how you do it,' Bel said.

'What choice do we have? You just keep going. You have to.'

I left the rest of them sleeping to start my shift, earlies, six-till-twelve. Mac would take Chloë to school on his way to work, and I planned to get more food for our visitors and call at the post office to renew the car tax before I picked her up.

Dealing with transfusions, work was steady at first, but at eight o'clock we were notified of a seven-vehicle pile-up on the M62. As we were a major-trauma centre, the injured were coming to us. Everyone wanted cross-match supplies at the same time. The phone was ringing off the hook.

I was in the middle of logging the latest requisition I'd fulfilled when my screen went blank. I tried rebooting but nothing worked. The screen was unresponsive. The Telepath system refused to load.

I checked with Clotting and Coagulation: the same with theirs. I rang through to A and E and told them our computers had crashed.

'It's the whole hospital. Everything is going to have to be done manually,' they said.

Jesus Christ! 'How can the whole system fail?' I said.

'Don't ask. It's old, it needs replacing. Should have been updated years back.'

Even with extra staff being pulled in from the main lab, and others coming from home, we were stretched to the limit, porters rushing in bearing handwritten notes for bloods and plasma, requesting tests, and us having to manually double-check patient ID, date of birth, and the request against the product before signing it over. We had to keep written records of every transaction and photocopies of all the blood units issued so that the system could be updated if and when it was revived. A queue was waiting at Reception to rally the bloods to Intensive Care and Theatre.

In the middle of it all a doctor rang me, insisting on a whole bevy of tests for a patient whose surgery wasn't due until the day after tomorrow.

'It'll have to wait,' I said. 'We're up to our necks here – the Telepath's down.'

He swore at me. 'Fucking pathetic. I need those results now.'

Prat. I hung up and returned to the crisis.

Snippets of news about the incident filtered through to us. A family of six en route to the airport had been involved, only one survivor. An HGV had mounted the central reservation. Five fire tenders were in attendance at the scene. The motorway was still closed.

All those lives, I thought, most of them on the morning commute, the same old routine, radio or CD on to stave off boredom, mind circling on their work ahead or looking forward to the end of the day, worrying about troubles at home, or remembering last night's television. Then bang.

I cleared my last two requests, bags of A positive and some platelets, and handed them through to reception. It was twelve-fifty-five.

My head felt spacey from the adrenalin buzz and the lack of food or drink. So before leaving I called at the café for a portion of fish and chips. Ravenous, I rushed to eat it and burned the roof of my mouth on a chip. A blister formed. I kept running my tongue over it.

The sky was overcast; clouds threatened rain. Another unwelcome reminder for Bel and Freya.

I'd only just begun shopping, was picking up a bag of potatoes to add to the onions in the trolley, when my phone rang. *School.*

'Mrs Kelly? Bev here. I'm afraid Chloë's left school. I wanted to check that you or your husband haven't collected her without us realising.'

The skin on my scalp tightened. 'What? No. When did she go?'

'She wasn't here for afternoon registration. We think she must have left during lunchtime play. We've made a complete search of the whole school.'

'Oh, Christ. I'll go and check at home. And I'll ring her dad. I'll call you back straight away.'

'Yes. Thank you.'

I realised I wouldn't need to drive home if Bel was still there. I abandoned the trolley and rang her as I hurried out of the store. It was spitting rain.

'Has Chloë come home?'

'No. Why?'

'Can you just double-check? Look in her room. And the garden.'

'Sure. What happened?' I could hear her breath change as she took the stairs.

'She's walked out of school.'

'Shit. No sign here. Hang on.'

'What's wrong?' Freya in the background.

'Chloë's gone missing,' Bel said.

There was the sound of Bel unlocking the back door. 'No. She's not out the back.'

'Thanks. Can you stay there for now?'

'Sure. Have you asked her friends?'

'Chloë doesn't have any friends,' I said. I pressed my tongue hard against the roof of my mouth. Felt the sting. 'I've got to go.'

School didn't allow phones but I tried ringing Chloë's – she might have sneaked hers in. It went to voicemail.

'Chloë, we don't know where you've gone. We're very worried. If you get this please call me. I'll come and pick you up. You're not in any trouble. We just want you home safe.'

Mac took time to answer my call. I pictured him bent over someone, inking a petal, a Gothic letter or a tiger's tooth. 'Lydia?'

'Chloë's left school, and no one knows where she is.'

'Aw, fuck.'

'I'm going there now. Bel's staying at the house just in case.'

'I can be with you in fifteen minutes,' he said.

'No, stay where you are. She might be on her way to you.'

'Ring me.'

'Yes.'

In the car, I called school and asked them to go ahead and alert the police. Then I started the engine and left the supermarket.

My heart was beating too fast and my mouth was parched. Where would she be? Had she any money? She usually had a couple of pounds on her. Not enough to get far. She was ten years old and looked younger. The thought of her wandering around on her own . . .

Chloë hadn't run away from school before. But there had been several occasions when she'd disappeared on us. I'd been half mad with fear, especially the first time, when we were on a day out to try canoeing. I was close to exploding when I spotted her on the riverbank half a mile from where we'd been. She was just sitting there, hugging her knees, and I wanted to yank her upright and shake her.

On another occasion we'd been visiting Terese's lot in York. We were packing up the car ready to drive back and Chloë was nowhere to be found. That time Mac discovered her about a quarter of a mile from their house near a row of shops. She was sitting on a bench outside the post office.

We'd never worked out why she did it, whether there was a trigger.

My phone rang and I slammed on the brakes. The car behind screeched to a halt. The driver sounded her horn and mouthed obscenities, her face a mask of rage.

Cheeks hot, I inched my car forward to park, ignoring the double yellow lines.

'Mac?' I said.

'I'm thinking, could she have gone to your mum's?'

'I don't know. I'd rather not worry her.' My mum was ill with breast cancer and had recently finished a course of chemotherapy.

'But it's a possibility and if Chloë is headed there . . .' he said.

'I'll ring her.' My mum was someone Chloë was close to. As close as she ever got to anyone. There was no answer. The voicemail kicked in. I explained that Chloë had left school, trying my best to sound calm, not wanting to panic her. Phrases of reassurance ran through my head, *She can't be far away . . . probably on her way home . . .* but they were tempting Fate. Instead I said, 'I'll let you know as soon as we've found her.'

At school, I was shown into the office. The head, Sandra Kent, was there with Chloë's teacher, Lisa Hathaway, and a police officer, who introduced herself as PC Ingle.

'We've notified the neighbourhood team and I'm going to get out there and help the search,' PC Ingle said. 'We're starting with main roads and sectors off them. Does Chloë have a mobile?'

'I've tried it, left a message.'

'Any upset this morning, any arguments?'

'No.' Mac would have said if there had been.

'The description we have for her is white, four foot three inches tall, shoulder-length blonde hair, wearing a navy school jumper and trousers, and a navy and red hooded coat.'

'She's taken her coat?' I asked Lisa.

'Yes.'

'Any bag?' PC Ingle said.

'Red backpack,' I said.

'Have you a recent photo?'

'Yes, on my phone.'

'Can you email it to me?' She gave me her address.

Once I'd done that, she said, 'Any idea where she might be headed?'

'No.' I told her who I'd already contacted.

I pressed my hand to the top of my chest, made small circles, trying to ease the crushing pressure there.

'Has she done this before?' PC Ingle said.

'Not from school. She's gone missing from us a few times,' I said.

'Did she come back on her own then?'

'No. But we found her.'

'Sandra says she's not registered with any special needs.'

'That's right. But she's vulnerable,' I said.

'Of course any child—'

'No. She's been referred to CAMHS.'

'Right.'

'She self-harms,' I said.

PC Ingle blinked, gave a nod.

'And she can get very agitated, angry,' I said.

'Is she any danger to others?' she said.

'No.' My voice broke. I cleared my throat. 'She has issues. She likes her own space. If she's crowded, she gets overwhelmed and she can react badly.'

'Violently?'

'She's only trying to get away from the situation. She can't help it,' I said. 'It's just how she is.'

'Let's swap numbers and I'll pass on what you've told me.'

When she'd gone, Sandra offered me a cup of tea.

'Thanks, no, but if I could just use the loo? Then I want to go looking for her.'

I chose to walk in the direction of our house first, along the main road. It was twenty minutes away. I checked each side street and looked down the alleys and cul-de-sacs.

What had made her leave? An argument? Some nasty game in the playground or had she simply found the prospect of another two and a half hours in the place intolerable?

Was she running away from something? Or in search of something?

Chloë was isolated in school: regarded as disruptive or sometimes plain weird, she was given a wide berth by her classmates. There was a boy in the year above her who was also adopted. I'd talked to his mother a couple of times in the past, hoping to find common ground, someone who would understand what we were going through, but

163

our experience of parenting diverged so much. 'We've been lucky,' she'd said. 'Wesley's such a sweetie. Just a joy.' I'd felt inadequate in the face of their contentment.

Whenever I met anyone I asked if they'd seen a little girl in a red and navy coat, showed them the photo on my phone, shielding it against the rain, and indicated her height with my hand. I had looks of concern and sympathy but no sightings.

At the crossroads I went into the park. The rain was heavier now, the playground deserted.

I spoke to a dog-walker and to a man on a bike, but they'd not seen her. I was cold and sick and shivery. Nightmares crowded my head. Chloë hurt. Chloë snatched, screaming. Chloë hanging.

A splash of red caught my eye as I turned into one road and my heart thudded but it was only the postman.

My phone rang. It was PC Ingle. 'We've found her. She's fine.'

I broke into a sweat. Felt dizzy.

'We're bringing her home now. Are you at home?'

'Almost, yes,' I said. 'Where was she?'

'At a bus shelter on Otley Road.'

'Thank you. Thank you so much.'

I called Mac immediately and told him the news. As soon as I was home I left a new message for my mum. Bel and Freya, coming through from the living room, heard me talking.

'Where was she going?' Bel said.

'I don't know. She'll be back soon. Maybe if you could give us some space? I'm sorry, but it'll be easier . . .'

'It's fine,' Bel said. 'We were going to have a look round Cardinal Heenan's, anyway. We can get a cab. Or take your car?'

'Shit. It's at school.' Suddenly the fact that I'd left the car seemed an enormous hassle. 'Shit. I just left it. I walked back.'

'We can fetch it,' Bel said.

'You aren't insured. Third party only,' I said. The last thing we needed was Bel writing off our car on top of everything else.

'Fine,' Bel said shortly. 'Come on, get your coat.' She beckoned to Freya.

Moments after, PC Ingle arrived with Chloë and another police officer.

Chloë came in, eyes averted. She was soaked, her hair all rats' tails, her lips tinged blue.

'Are you OK?' I said gently.

A nod.

'Take your coat off, and your shoes. I'll make you some hot chocolate.'

I asked the officers, 'Would you like a drink?'

'Coffee'd be great, thanks, two sugars,' PC Ingle said.

Her colleague shook his head. 'No, thanks.'

Chloë's shoes had leaked: the toes of her socks were wet. She sat down, tense, unmoving, her head tilted to one side and down, as if braced for a blow, trembling.

'I was saying to Chloë in the car, if anything's wrong at school she should tell you about it, or a teacher, not just go running off,' said PC Ingle.

'Yes,' I said. 'Did something happen at school?'

Chloë shook her head.

'Where were you going?' I said.

'Nowhere,' she said quietly.

'Why were you at the bus stop then?'

'It was raining.'

'Can you tell us why you left school like that?' PC Ingle said.

Silence.

'Chloë?' I said.

A shrug.

I put the drinks down.

PC Ingle shifted in her chair. 'You see, you've caused a lot of worry, for your family and your teachers. Not only that but it's my job to protect the community, to keep people safe. If all the other police officers and I are looking for you, and someone else needs us and they're in real danger, we can't be there to help them. Do you understand what I'm saying?'

'Yes,' Chloë said.

'She does,' I said. 'And you're sorry, aren't you, Chloë?'

'Yes,' she said. She shivered.

'You go and get changed,' I said.

Chloë got up and moved to the door.

'You just think, next time,' PC Ingle said, 'if you feel like running away, you talk to someone. Someone your age shouldn't be off on your own when you should be in school. It's not safe.'

'I'm sorry,' I said to the police officer, when Chloë had gone. 'Thank you.'

'I hope she's learned her lesson,' she said, getting up.

I hadn't the heart to set her straight. It seemed impossible for Chloë to learn from bad experiences, like most other kids might. Star charts, rewards and punishments, none of that could help. She was stuck, trapped in patterns of reaction, of flight, of constant anxiety and self-doubt.

The few books I'd been able to find on adoption, the ones that actually acknowledged the scale of trauma and loss involved, had given me some guidance on how to deal with Chloë's anxiety and her outbursts, to understand how fundamental her fears and sense of abandonment were, how her start in life had programmed her to fear trust and love, to believe that she didn't deserve any happiness. The authors also suggested that reunion with the birth-family was one way for the adoptee to heal. But it wasn't an option until Chloë was eighteen.

We didn't know how to make it any better for her. We'd asked for help time and again but there was nothing. She didn't meet the criteria; there weren't enough resources; there wasn't anything suitable in the area.

We were howling for the moon.

Chapter Twenty-eight

By May 2015 my mum's health had deteriorated so much that the only treatment left was palliative care and she had been moved into a hospice.

'It's just a question of time,' the nurse had said, the evening before, to Steven, his wife and me. 'Could be hours, could be days.'

'Would you like to come with me to see Grandma?' I asked Chloë.

'I don't know.' She'd taken some bubble-wrap off a handbag I'd had delivered and was popping the blisters with her thumbs.

'It'll be a chance to say goodbye. I think you should. She'll be asleep mostly. Chloë?'

She continued pressing the plastic.

I bit back my irritation. I remembered the first time I'd seen her, how she'd kept her back to me and pressed the buttons on the farm-yard toy. She was thirteen years old now but still so much like that toddler.

'I'm leaving in twenty minutes. I'd like you to come, but it's up to you.'

I went up to brush my teeth and get ready. When I came down Chloë was outside, smoking. Another battle I'd lost. 'Are you coming?'

'Yes.' She squashed her cigarette on the top of the wheelie bin then put it inside. It was May, still light at eight o'clock. The garden was neglected, last season's plants withered and brown, the shrubs desiccated, clumps of couch grass and dock leaves the only things thriving. With all the hospital visiting on top of work and dealing with Chloë, I'd not had time to plant anything or water what was there.

She pulled the headphones from her coat pocket, effectively ruling out any conversation on the drive over.

When we reached the car park I signalled to Chloë to remove her headphones. 'She looks a bit strange,' I said. 'So it might be a bit of a shock.'

Chloë gave a nod.

Once we'd signed in we went straight through to her room. A nurse there greeted us and said, 'We've just turned her and she's got a new nightie on.'

Chloë made a sound in her throat.

'You all right?' I said. 'She does look different, doesn't she?'

My mum's face was waxy, grey, gaunt, her cheekbones protruding and her eyes sunken. Her mouth was open. She looked smaller in the bed, shrunken, not that she'd ever been overweight, like me.

'Her breathing's changed,' I said to the nurse. The rhythm was erratic, a hoarse rasping and gurgling, then a long pause.

'Yes, we call that Cheyne-Stokes. It's a sign that she's getting closer.' The nurse stroked my mum's cheek. 'She's not in any pain, are you, my love?'

I got a tissue from the box on the side and wiped my eyes.

'Cup of tea, juice, anything?' the nurse said.

'No, thanks, we're fine,' I said.

'Call me if you need anything.'

'You can sit there,' I said to Chloë, pointing to the nearest chair. 'I'll go round the other side.'

Standing at the bedside I took my mum's hand. It was warm and limp, blotched with bruises from the cannula.

'I do bruise easily,' she'd said one time, when I was still at home.

'Like a peach,' my dad had said, and kissed her. They'd laughed.

I missed my dad but I was glad he'd died first and hadn't had to cope on his own without my mum.

When I trusted myself to talk I said, 'Hello, Mum. I'm here and Chloë's here too. It's been a lovely day. Sunny and breezy. Getting windy now. They reckon there's a storm on the way.'

I looked over at Chloë. 'They say it's good to talk, though we don't know whether she can really hear.'

'Because she's asleep?'

'She's unconscious. We can't wake her up. Chloë's here,' I said again.

'Hi, Grandma.' She looked uncomfortable.

'They've got Wi-Fi,' I said. 'We can play some music. She loved Petula Clark, and Dionne Warwick. See if you can find something on your phone.'

We listened to 'Walk On By' while I sat and held my mum's hand. After a while I said, 'Chloë, I'm going to stay here tonight so I'll see how your dad's doing and if he can pick you up. If not then I'll get you a cab.'

Mac was working late at the shop.

I stepped out into the corridor and rang him. He was just locking up. 'Sure, I'll swing by.'

I rang Steven next, the strains of 'This Girl's In Love With You' faint from the room behind me.

'Her breathing's more laboured. They reckon that means she's closer to the end. I thought you'd want to know. They can't say how long. But I'm going to stay over.'

'We'll come down first thing. Sevenish. But ring me.'

'Of course.'

Back in the room, I saw that Chloë had her hand over my mum's. I felt a lump in my throat. 'Dad won't be long,' I said.

The song ended.

'Where will you sleep?' Chloë said.

'I'll sit up. I might doze. She loved to knit, didn't she?' I said, wanting to revive some good memories for Chloë. To remind her there was so much more to my mum than the frail body in the bed. 'She could follow any pattern.'

'Like those gloves,' Chloë said.

'The fingerless ones. You wore them till they dropped to bits. And the puddings she made.'

'That white one.'

'Pavlova,' I said. 'You always cleared your plate at Grandma's. She loved you so much.'

'Can I wait for Dad outside?'

'Sure. Tell you what, I need to go to the loo so how about you stay here while I go, say your goodbyes, and then you can go down to Reception?'

'OK,' she said, rocking lightly on her feet, eager to get away. Anxious again.

Chloë's eyes were bright, glassy when I got back. Perhaps she'd cried. It was hard to tell.

'I'll see you later,' I said, kissing the top of her head.

Mac popped in a few minutes later. 'Everything all right?'

'Yes. She's getting weaker.'

He nodded.

'I'll see you in the morning,' I said.

Once he'd gone, I made myself as comfortable as I could and sat, held my mum's hand and listened to her breathe. When the nurse called in again, I took a cup of tea and some biscuits.

The building was quiet, just the occasional snatches of sound, voices from the corridor, the squeak of a trolley, then the bang of a door, an engine starting outside.

There were some foam lollipops in a tray of water and I used one to moisten her lips, which were peeling and crusty, gummy at the corners.

I grew tired but not enough to sleep. Several times the pause between her breaths stretched out, but then came the creak and draw of another. Heart still beating, blood still pumping.

I opened the curtains and turned out the lights. The moon had risen high and bright, and the branches were silhouetted in front of it, buffeted by the wind. I liked the dance of the trees. The simple beauty of it.

Later I tried to sing to her, 'You Are My Sunshine', one of the songs she used to sing me to sleep with, one that I'd sung to Chloë, but tears robbed my voice.

'We'll be all right,' I told her. 'Mac and me and Chloë, Steven and

Kim. We'll look after each other, love each other. You can rest now, Mum. You can go.'

The night deepened. I closed my eyes and let my thoughts wander: Freya's birthday soon . . . How long would it take to sort out my mum's estate? Six months? A year? Must get our boiler serviced. Cancel Bel and Thomas – whatever happens we won't be having people round to dinner on Saturday . . . Nice guy, Thomas, rides a horse . . . Chloë used to love riding at the community farm. Would she go again?

I shifted position. And stared out into the dark, the silver shafts of light, the boughs dipping and swaying. The wind calling her on.

I listened for her breath. And waited. I held my own. And she was gone.

Chapter Twenty-nine

'Chloë, we want you to stay here. These eejits, you don't know them. They don't care about you.' Mac was furious, flinging up his hands as he spoke.

'Fuck off.' Chloë's face was screwed up, head thrust forward as if she'd charge. 'They're my friends.'

'Get them to come round, then,' I said. 'Let's meet them.'

She sneered. 'No. That's weird.'

'You're only thirteen. How old are they? The drugs, the drinking – it's not safe,' I said.

'You can't keep me locked up. Fuck you!' She kicked at the table. A glass rolled off and smashed on the floor. She gave a little laugh.

I looked at the glass. Shards glinting. Dangerous. Thought of the lattice of scars on her belly, legs and arms.

'If you leave this house now,' Mac said, 'I'll report you missing and the police will get involved.'

Chloë was balancing on the balls of her feet, buzzing with energy. Her eyes fixed on mine for a moment, a blaze of rage making them greener. Then she turned and ran upstairs.

I put my head into my hands. 'God. I don't know what else we can do.' I opened my eyes and looked at Mac. 'What can we do?'

I went to fetch the dustpan and brush from under the sink.

There was an enormous thump from upstairs and the whole house shook. Then crashing and more thumps.

'Jaysus!' Mac got to his feet.

'Leave her,' I said.

'She's trashing the place,' he yelled.

'And how will you stop her?' I shouted back.

'Christ!'

Another crash, then several bangs. I could feel the vibrations through my legs into my stomach.

'We could ask for respite,' I said. 'If we keep asking, surely they'll have to try to find something. Get the funding somehow.'

'We need it now. It's not going to happen. We're fucking kidding ourselves. How bad does it have to get before they listen? Unless we put the ball in their court. Tell them she needs to go back into care.'

My knees went weak. He didn't mean it, did he?

A volley of bangs. What was she doing? Kicking the drawers? Booting the door in? At least if she was destroying some inanimate object she wasn't attacking herself.

'That's exactly what she's expecting, isn't it?' I said. 'That if she's foul enough we'll walk away, abandon her like everyone else did. Prove to her that she really is worthless.'

'And if we carry on?' he said, holding his hands out for answers. 'All of this? Fights at school? Another exclusion and she'll be sent to a pupil referral unit.' He jabbed a finger towards the window. 'She's doing God knows what with those scumbags out there. They could be grooming her.'

'Do you think I don't know that?' I rounded on him. 'But I can't give up on her. I couldn't live with myself.' I didn't know how else to explain it. We were all she had. Adopting her had been a lifelong commitment, a promise. Not one I could possibly break. Yes, she was wild and uncontrollable, difficult and angry, but she was also that lost little girl. Edgy and scared and so very hurt. I couldn't add to that hurt. 'I can't put her back in care. I won't. She's our daughter. I'm her mother. I won't do that.'

'Well, I can't do this any more.' His face worked with emotion. 'This is killing us, Lydia.'

Ice water flooded my guts. Was he leaving us? Leaving me?

'I can't breathe. You know?' he said. 'It's hell. Day after fucking day. I love her, Christ, I love her but she—' He sat down. He rubbed at his face and groaned.

'What if we move?' I said quickly. 'Move somewhere else? I could give up work, home-school her. Get her away from these people. From the bullying at school.'

'Move where?' he said.

'I have no idea.'

'How would we manage?'

'I've the money coming through from my mum's house.'

'And what about the parlour?' he said.

'You said yourself the lease is going to cost double. We could find somewhere cheaper. Or go mobile. Less overheads.'

'What happened to *no big changes*?' He made quote marks with his fingers.

'That's working out really well, isn't it?'

We laughed, an abrupt release.

I looked up to the ceiling, listened. All quiet. 'I think she's finished. When's the lease up?'

'July.'

'Will you think about it? Please?'

'OK.' But he sounded defeated. Had he already reached the end of the road, made up his mind? It was not an unfamiliar story. People who'd adopted, struggling with kids who were disturbed and out of control. I'd caught a radio documentary about it: 'Children like this split couples apart,' the narrator had said. 'They destroy families.' It seemed such a brutal view. But painfully true.

I bent to sweep up the glass, tipped it away and got out the bin bags. 'Better go and see the damage.'

Mac pushed his chair away from the table to come with me.

There was a sick feeling inside me, the hollow fizzy nausea of stress. How could I cope if Mac said no? Would I have to choose: my marriage or my daughter? It was hard enough for me to manage with Mac at my side. But without him?

Chapter Thirty

Bel and I had a table in the window. The waiter brought our drinks and took our orders.

'I just wish it wasn't Whitby,' Bel said, for the umpteenth time. 'There isn't even a direct train service.'

'Yeah, well, it's the only option.' I looked out of the window at the pedestrianised area, the planter full of grasses and herbs. A young lad, homeless, sitting on a sleeping bag, a can of lager in his hand, his eyes red and feverish-looking.

'You'll go mad.'

'We're all mad as it is. And a bit of support would be a refreshing change.'

She pulled a face.

'If we stay here, things will just carry on getting more and more bloody disastrous. We can't say no. Niall's letting us stay there rent-free while we do the place up. When it sells we get a share of the profit.'

'Don't fancy taking Freya, too, do you?'

You don't know you've been born. I looked at her. 'Freya is a good kid.'

'She's so uptight, you know what she's like. It's like living with my mum. Well, not my mum,' she corrected herself, 'the lifestyle police. Holier than fucking thou. Every little thing is an argument. Fourteen units a week, air travel's killing the planet, bacon gives you cancer.'

It was true that Freya could be bossy and opinionated, every-thing was black or white, and she'd leap to judgement. But she'd just become a teenager: of course she knew the answer to everything.

'She cares about stuff. That's a good thing,' I said. 'And she worries about you.'

'No. She just likes feeling superior. She and her little gang of acolytes.' Was Bel's prickly response to Freya bound up with her relationship with her own mother, cold and distant, or perhaps to Bel's struggles when Freya was small? Whenever I did try to unpick it more, Bel clammed up or changed the subject. She lacked the ability or the willingness to look dispassionately at her own behaviour. Mac and I had had to reveal ourselves to each other, excavate and analyse our family dynamics, our emotional make-up, as we'd prepared to adopt, but Bel had no such understanding.

'And Thomas encourages her,' Bel said. 'You know what he came out with the other day? I swear too much.'

'Fucking liberty.'

She laughed. 'More or less what I said. He went into a strop for days. Radio silence. I was thinking about asking him to move in. But . . .'

'Let me guess, you're going to get rid. You don't think there might be some sort of pattern developing?'

'Shut up.'

'He's a nice guy. Can't you work something out?' I said.

'Maybe that's it. Too nice.'

'You'd rather have a bastard who messes you about?' I said.

'No. It's just that tipping point. Everything was exciting and fun at the start, and I liked his company. We had actual conversations about stuff and the sex was fucking amazing. See what I did there?'

'I did.'

'And then . . .' She levelled her hands like scales, then tilted one up, one down. 'He's predictable and he's always snapping or moaning at me, and he makes this humming sound when he's getting excited which is just—'

'Enough!' I said.

'Freya won't approve. Something else for her to hate about me.' She took a drink. 'I do love her, you know,' she said. She turned to stare out of the window. 'I just don't like her. Never have. She gets

176

under my skin. You're not supposed to say that, are you? That's me. Shit mother. Shit friend.'

'Hey.' I pointed to her and back to myself. 'I'm still here.'

'Except you're fucking off to Whitby,' she said.

'Two words: Santa Monica.'

Our meals arrived. I leaned over and breathed in the scent of coconut and lemongrass. The prawns were plump, the rice colourful. I bit into a prawn and savoured the taste. 'It's good Freya's got friends,' I said. 'These days . . . they've all got so much more to deal with, all the stuff going on . . .' I trailed off, blew out my cheeks.

'Chloë still being bullied?'

'I think so. She was barely at school this last term. Getting her there, getting her to stay was hard enough, and zero-tolerance policies don't work so well with someone like Chloë. But bullying's everywhere. Out there on social media. She's a freak. She's a psycho. She should kill herself. Her birth-parents were serial killers and paedos.'

Bel winced.

'You take stuff down but it's done the rounds. Chloë doesn't always tell us. If those parents knew what their kids were saying . . . but then they all think Chloë's the problem, that she's disturbed and causing all the trouble, she's the threat. Because she can't control her reactions.' I put down my fork. 'Sometimes I just freak out. It feels like there's some self-fulfilling prophecy – that whatever we do she's still heading for disaster. Her dad was violent, he was in prison when she was born, her mum was a drug-user, their lives were a total fuck-up, and she seems hell-bent on heading in the same direction. I know that's not fair. I hate thinking like that.'

'Then don't.'

Bel's phone rang. 'Hi . . . Where from? . . . Isn't there a bus? OK . . . Well, I'll be about forty minutes.' Shook her head at me. 'When can they learn to drive?'

'Not for a while. You going to be OK?' I nodded to her glass. Her third.

'Don't you start! The curry will have soaked it up. So, we'll come and visit, eh?'

'Oh, we'll be back here now and again. The place will be a building-site for the next year, I guess.'

'Fine, you come here,' she said. 'To pastures new!' She raised her glass. 'And roll on empty nests!'

It was dusk when we arrived in Whitby, and there was a sea fret coming in over the land.

I pulled up in the car, Mac behind us in the van he'd bought to use as a mobile tattoo parlour.

The cottage, two knocked together, was caught in the glare of the headlights. Huddled low to the ground, single-storey, built in big blocks of dun-coloured stone, with a tiled roof, small windows and low doors. It looked as if it had grown there.

'It's creepy,' Chloë said.

'Looks better in daylight,' I said. Niall had already repaired the cottage roof, had it insulated, and installed triple-glazed windows throughout. The rest of the renovation was up to us either to do or to organise. 'Let's get our stuff into the caravan.'

We'd hired a two-bedroom caravan to live in until the house was habitable.

Mac unlocked it and put the lights on.

It looked clean and fresh. The couches were upholstered in golden velvet, and yellow curtains decorated with sprigs of flowers hung at the windows. But it felt damp and smelt musty. There were dehumidi-fier traps on the windowsill and in each bedroom.

I switched on the heaters.

The three of us ferried bedding, suitcases, boxes of groceries and toiletries, pots and pans from Mac's van.

'Water?' I said to Mac.

'There should be a container under the van. Tap's by the house. You want to come, Chloë?'

'OK.'

He had a torch and I watched the beam flash across the yard to the cottage.

Once they'd loaded the drum and hooked it up, I filled the kettle.

With cups of tea and drinking chocolate made, I put on the stew I'd brought to heat up.

Chloë played with the TV, surfing channels. 'No Netflix,' she said.

'Only Freeview,' I said.

'We'll have to use the laptops for anything else,' Mac said, 'but the Wi-Fi should be working.'

Chloë snapped off the set, threw the remote onto the couch at her side. Face miserable.

'It will feel strange at first,' I said, 'for all of us. Take time to settle in.'

'It's horrible. What if I want to go home?' she said.

'This is home now,' Mac said.

'We talked about this,' I said.

'*You've* talked about it,' Chloë said.

The muscles in my back tightened. I stirred the pan. 'Just give it time,' I said. 'And we can find out about the stables in the morning.'

I'd promised Chloë she could go riding as much as she wanted. 'Maybe they'll let you volunteer,' I'd said. 'Mucking out and grooming and looking after the animals.' She'd been keen on that idea.

I hoped the horses were a way of rekindling an interest that might eventually give Chloë a direction in life and a route into work. We'd agreed it would be asking for trouble to try to enrol her in a new school after the problems, the bullying, the fights, the exclusions she'd had at her old one. So I'd home-school her.

Chloë wasn't academic. She was so different intellectually from either of us. The fantasies I'd had of helping my child with special projects at home, of glowing school reports and after-school science clubs, of eventual visits to university open days had evaporated when she was still small.

Once we'd eaten, Chloë went to her room. Mac and I had a beer and watched *Doctor Foster* on TV, a new drama about a cheating husband and his vengeful wife.

We were ready to turn in early. I took a breath, knocked on Chloë's door and went in. She was sitting up in bed and using her phone. She glowered at me. I ignored her expression.

'Try to get some sleep,' I said. 'If you want anything, give us a knock.'

She didn't look at me. Her thumbs flicked over the phone.

'Who are you texting?'

Silence.

'Right, we're off to bed. Night-night.'

I couldn't think of anything to say to her about the situation that I hadn't already told her.

'I love you,' I said. 'See you in the morning.'

I fell asleep reasonably easily but woke in the night. I thought I heard crying and held my breath to listen. But there was only the faint sound of the wind outside, Mac's breathing, and an occasional chinking noise, which must have been something knocking against the caravan. Perhaps the cry had been the sound of trees in the wind or a gate creaking or the bark of a fox.

Mac and I spent the next day working out what we needed to do in the cottages. They were still cluttered with pieces of old furniture, sagging couches, bedsteads, broken drawers. One bedroom had an old wardrobe that almost reached the ceiling. It was burled walnut, heavy and ornately carved, frosted with white mould. I wondered who had brought it there, what lives had gone on before us.

The new window frames in their protective wrapping looked out of place next to the rotting carpets and rickety chairs.

A look around confirmed that there was nothing salvageable or saleable in the contents. We needed to rip out and remove everything we could. Mac phoned for skip hire. The whole place reeked of mildew, and black mould bloomed in the kitchen and bathrooms. Great grey swags of cobweb festooned every corner: large hairy spiders scuttled for cover as we shifted pieces, and woodlice nested under the carpets. Everything was thick with dust and I sneezed repeatedly.

I persuaded Chloë to give us a hand in the kitchen. The wall had been knocked through between the two original kitchens so they could be merged into one. The back doors had been removed and the stonework between them replaced with wide patio doors. But the remaining walls still had old fitted cupboards and cabinets. Chloë helped to prise them off the kitchen walls and break them up with a lump hammer.

Then she complained that it smelt rank and went back to the caravan.

We stopped for tea and bacon butties at midday. I rang the stables and arranged to call round with Chloë that afternoon.

The owner, Barbara, was tall and thin, stooped, with a raw, weather-beaten complexion and a warm smile. I guessed she was in her late sixties but she could have been older. She sized Chloë up and asked about her experience.

'She was riding once a week until a couple of years ago, then lost the habit,' I said. 'She's home-schooled so it doesn't have to be evenings or weekends for sessions.'

'We have classes, if she'd like to get to know some of the other girls,' Barbara said.

'We'll think about that,' I said. 'But for now can we book some solo lessons?'

We negotiated three afternoons that worked. 'Wednesday's tricky,' Barbara said. 'We have special groups then, autistic children – we do a trek with them – but the other weekdays are fine.'

There had been times when we thought Chloë might be autistic, or on the spectrum. The rages, the lack of eye contact, the physical anxiety. But when she was tested they said not.

'Oh, and we've not got a hat – she grew out of it,' I said.

'Should be able to sort you one out. Now, I think you should start on Brandy.' She led Chloë over to the stalls and I followed them. 'She's a very placid horse. And Pippin, next door but one. She's taller, friskier. You could move onto her once you're comfortable back in the saddle. You can try Brandy in the arena now, if you've time.'

'Can I?' A moment of eagerness, so rare.

'Shall I stay?' I said.

'I'm fine,' Chloë said.

I left my number with Barbara and arranged to go back in forty-five minutes.

I drove into town and called at the dentist's where I registered the three of us, then did the same for the GP. I also made enquiries about getting Chloë some help from CAMHS and found out that the waiting list in the area was approximately ten months, unless the young person was suicidal. Ten months.

Our experience in Leeds had been disappointing. Chloë had attended twice: she had been restless and uncooperative, then refused to go again. Still, I had to try to get her some help so I asked them to go ahead and make an appointment for her to see the GP and hopefully get a referral.

I arrived back early and sat on one of the benches in the stable-yard. The autumn sun was golden, warm on my face.

A female blackbird flew down to a stone bird-bath built on a pedestal. She drank and then splashed about in the water, splaying her wing feathers. Other smaller birds I couldn't name were busy in the beech hedge.

Chloë and Barbara came trotting in from the arena. 'She's got a good seat,' Barbara called. 'She's a natural.'

And I dared to hope that we'd made the right decision in coming here. That things really were going to get better.

Chapter Thirty-one

Living where we were meant it was difficult but not impossible for Chloë to get into Whitby on her own. It would take an hour and three-quarters to walk. There was a local bus service up on the main road but they only ran every two hours. With the car we could be there in twenty minutes.

That first week, I took her to explore our new town. I parked in the centre and we walked up the winding streets and through the avenues full of large guesthouses to the top of the west cliff, to Captain Cook's statue and the whalebone arch.

'Now you can smell fish and chips,' I said to Chloë. 'Back then it would have stunk – they'd boil up whale blubber in factories all along the edge of the harbour.'

She curled her lip. 'What for?'

'To make oil for all sorts – lamps, margarine, soap.' I pointed out the Spa Pavilion, an entertainment complex. It included the old Victorian cinema. They ran a programme of new films, only one at a time, but they had matinees, which I thought we might enjoy together.

We took selfies in the arch, the abbey, our next destination, visible across the estuary behind the smaller church of St Mary, with its square tower and crenellated walls.

There are steep steps up to the top, 199 of them. I couldn't face making that climb or, more accurately, having to come down from the dizzy heights, but Chloë wanted to so I pointed her in the right direction, then drove myself across the swing bridge and up to the car park on the top.

She'd have to walk through the church graveyard to reach the abbey itself and I went to meet her. The large gravestones stood in ranks across the sloping site. Many were tilted at treacherous angles, some completely fallen, and most were gnawed by the weather, the inscriptions eaten away. The church tower looked crooked, as though it might topple over and tumble down into the town.

There were notices about respecting the churchyard and the burial ground. On the perimeter fences at the top I saw bunches of old flowers in cellophane, memorials to the people who had lost their lives there. Who had jumped.

Looking across the jumble of red-tiled roofs to the harbour below, I could see cormorants ranged in a row on the breakwater, funereal with their dense black feathers. The sun danced silver on the iron-grey waves. Above me, gulls wheeled and shrieked.

Chloë arrived, hair blowing in the wind.

The abbey ruins were vast: soaring arches, enormous windows three storeys high. The huge sandstone columns were corroded by wind and salt, honeycombed in places. They looked like they were melting, like sandcastles in the rain.

No wonder Bram Stoker had been inspired: the drama of the plundered abbey, its carcass dominating the skyline, the graveyard, close by, sinking on the crumbling cliffs, the treacherous seas below – all rich material for his horror story.

The next day I downloaded the film, the Bela Lugosi classic, which Chloë said was lame because it was in black-and-white, and then we tried the Keanu Reeves version, which she preferred, though I couldn't stand his mangling of an English accent.

'Buffy's better,' she said. 'I'll watch some of those again.'

We developed a routine, working on the house every morning, then Mac would continue on his own while I took Chloë to the stables, or organised something educational, letting her set the direction for that, seizing on any expression of interest, any curiosity or idle question as the basis for study.

A comment from her that the house was probably haunted led us to the local-history section at the library, down near the marina. We searched old maps and books of photographs, then went online to check the census for 1851.

William Holt, head of household, was an alum worker.

I got Chloë to google 'alum'.

'See?' I said. 'Used to help dye wool and preserve leather. They dug shale out of the cliffs, burned it for months in great pyramids, soaked it and sent the liquid to the alum works.' I scanned the next paragraph. 'They added urine.'

'Eww. That is skanky.' She wrinkled her nose.

'They needed tons of it, had it shipped in from all round the country, collected it in buckets on street corners.'

'That is so gross.'

'I think it's amazing.'

'Well, you're weird,' she said. But I saw a small smile.

Dinosaurs had lived in the area and the coast was rich with bones and fossils. We went fossil hunting one day on the beach below the east cliff and actually found a small ammonite in the shingle.

'Is it a snail?' she said.

'More like a squid or an octopus.'

I bought a second-hand microscope in one of the antiques shops in the town and showed her how to take specimens. Disappointed when her initial fascination evaporated.

When I was helping her research the local geology, we found a website all about jet. My eyes snagged on the opening text. *A mourning stone*. And I felt my stomach tighten. Of course, *black* jet. That was why it was so popular with the Victorians. I still wore my jet pendant sometimes, the cluster of grapes I'd bought in the middle of our IVF misery. I'd imagined it was a fertility symbol but jet was used to mark a death.

In late October I went into town, to the chemist and the newsagent's, and found myself in the middle of a carnival. It was the Goth weekend, the second in the year, when hundreds of fans came together to celebrate all things Gothic. Families, pensioners, couples, bikers, wearing fabulous Goth costumes, steam punk, Victoriana, macabre make-up and outrageous hats. It was as if I'd time-travelled to an alternative Victorian age where the division between the real world and fiction and fantasy had dissolved.

'We could go in and try the market if you'd like,' I said to Chloë, when I got back. 'There are stalls up at the Pavilion. There'll be all sorts on sale. You can see the costumes.'

'Goths,' she said, with a sneer. Chloë would only wear sports clothes, tracksuits, sweatpants and hoodies, trainers. She'd never shown any interest in fashion or the various subcultures that her schoolmates had signed up to.

'Here.' I gave Chloë the cigarettes I'd got in town. When we lived in Leeds she'd found a shop where they would sell them to her, even though she was under age, and sometimes her so-called friends gave them to her. Now I was buying them for her. I hated it. But if I didn't, she threatened to steal them.

'What about trying Nicorette?' I said. 'I'm sure the GP would see the sense of it.'

'What are we doing for Christmas?' She changed the subject.

'What would you like to do?'

'Not stay here. Go home.'

'We can't do that. There are other people living there.'

She slammed her hands on the table.

I kept talking, hoping to calm her down. 'Maybe we can go to Bel's. I could talk to her and see what they're up to.' I didn't really want to go back to Leeds and risk her running off to find the crowd she'd been hanging around with.

And we couldn't stay with Terese and family in York. They'd moved back to Ireland and they'd be spending Christmas at Brendan's. The whole gang would be there. Taking Chloë into a situation like that, crowded, busy, would almost guarantee she'd get stressed out and have a meltdown.

'If we did go to Bel's you'd have to stay with us all the time,' I said.

'You could chain me up,' she said. 'Handcuff me.'

186

'That wouldn't be very practical. Look, I don't want to lock you away or stop you doing things but I'm not going to put you at risk. That's why we're here.'

'I hate it here. I fucking hate it.' She banged her head with her fists, tears of anger in her eyes.

'I know it's hard but—'

'I don't care,' she yelled. She swept her arm across the counter next to the sink, flinging cups and cutlery, a coffee jar and a colander of apples to smash on the floor. An avalanche of broken crockery. Then she slammed out of the caravan, which shook in her wake. I stood and braced my hands against the table and breathed, resisting the surge of adrenalin that made me want to charge after her and yell.

Gregory Davis, I reminded myself. Light at the end of the tunnel. He was a private therapist, who had experience of working with traumatised and adopted children. Based in Newcastle he had an opening for a new patient in March. That prospect, of someone who really understood the issue trying to help Chloë, of being able to get a proper diagnosis and appropriate treatment, felt like a lifeline. Only four months till March.

We spent Christmas in Whitby. We bought Chloë new riding boots and a tablet. We did our best to make it cosy and festive.

Together she and I made paper trimmings and I decorated the caravan.

Mac dug up and potted a small fir tree and it filled the caravan with the smell of pine.

We ate a traditional Christmas dinner: I just managed to fit a turkey crown and roast potatoes into the small oven, and we watched *Doctor Who* and *Downton Abbey*.

And that night she set her bedroom on fire.

Later she claimed it was an accident, that she'd been playing with a lighter and it had caught on a fleece throw, then spread to the curtains. I didn't know whether or not to believe her.

Waking in panic, my heart banging, I could hear her yelping and the shriek of the smoke alarm.

Mac was out of bed before me, yanking open her bedroom door and pulling her out, smoke choking the air. I grabbed the fire extinguisher from the kitchen wall, fumbled to release the safety catch, then aimed it at the flames dancing around the room. Drenched everything with bursts of foam.

The room was sodden, daubed with thick black marks and reeking of burning plastics. I put the extinguisher down. I could barely get my breath, my pulse too fast, my chest hurting. I shut the bedroom door and opened the outside one to get rid of the smoke.

'You all right?' I said to Chloë. She was standing next to Mac, her hands clutched at her throat. I saw the red along the edge of her palm. 'You burned your hand? Show me.'

She held it out. The shiny skin was beginning to blister.

'Under the tap,' I said. Had she intended to burn herself? Was this a new weapon in the self-harm arsenal?

'What the fuck, Chloë?' Mac said. 'You could have killed us all!'

'Mac.' I tried to caution him.

He was furious. 'Are you insane?' he said to her.

'It was an accident,' she said.

'Was it?' Mac said, voicing the doubts I had.

'I was playing with my lighter. You won't believe me. You never believe me.'

'Did it not occur to you that that might be beyond stupid?'

'Mac, please,' I said.

'So she's just going to get away with it?'

'No one's getting away with anything. We'll talk about this later. Calmly.'

He grabbed his coat

'Where are you going? It's the middle of the night. It's freezing out there.'

He didn't answer. Pulled on his boots. 'Mac?'

'I'll sleep in the van,' he said.

188

'Don't be daft,' I said. 'We can put a sleeping bag on the floor here for one of us.'

'Leave it,' he said. He got the torch and a rug from the cupboard and went out, shutting the door behind him.

Chloë shivered.

'That's enough.' I turned the tap off. 'It's going to hurt a lot. We'll put some Germolene on, take the sting away.'

'It's OK,' she said.

Yet more chaos and destruction. Anger seethed inside me as we got into bed. That suppressed fury, the acrid burned smell and my worries about Mac stopped me sleeping. 'You could have killed us all.' Mac's words and the anguish with which he'd shouted them tolled like a bell in my head.

I'd been angry before, so many times, Chloë's rage igniting my own. I'd learned to control my response, knowing it didn't solve anything. I'd been frightened for her before, when we'd discovered the cutting, when she'd run away from school, when she'd slammed her head so hard against the walls I'd thought her skull would crack. But now for the first time I felt something new. I wasn't frightened for her. I was frightened of her. And of what she might do.

Chapter Thirty-two

Our insurance claim for damage to the caravan was refused so a chunk of my mum's money went on paying for the damage and sorting out a replacement. It was identical, right down to the yellow curtains and golden couches.

Mac had set up a website for his mobile tattoo business and there was a slow trickle of enquiries, which occasionally took him away for a few hours, but as we carried on with the renovations there was a desperate, dogged atmosphere to our lives and the work. The same claustrophobic feel of us all being cooped up together in the caravan that I'd had as a teenager on family holidays. The sooner we could move into the house the better.

Chloë went back to riding after the Christmas break and that continued to be a positive. She'd graduated to the larger horse and was doing longer rides with Barbara.

Barbara was happy for her to help with the animals so Chloë did that every weekday morning. It meant early starts, waking to frost in the air and the bite of the bitter east wind. Scraping ice off the windscreen and driving over there in the dark, the headlights picking out the winding roads and the blunt thorn hedges.

By the end of January we'd had the heating installed and the rewiring done. Together, Mac and I laid wooden floors. The bathrooms went in in mid-February – we had consultations every day with the plumber.

Niall wanted to retain some of the original features, such as the exposed thick stone walls and the beams, so we only needed to re-plaster and paint the ceilings between the beams. But that was back-breaking work. Every bone in my body ached from the labour of it all. My hands were covered with cuts and my knees were two balls of bruises. I'd pulled a muscle in my shoulder that hurt day and night.

'I'm having a bath this evening,' I told Mac, the day the plumbing was connected. 'A bath and a bottle of wine. Five months with only showers. You could join me later?'

He looked at me, his gaze softening. 'I might do that.'

The claw-foot tub was enormous, like a boat, taking central stage in the bathroom. I brought in a stool to balance my glass on and dimmed the lights.

The water was deep and hot, and I let myself melt into it. With that release I had an urge to cry. It was all so hard, too hard. I was so very tired of the struggle to cope with Chloë. I needed a break – we all did. But it was impossible. We couldn't leave her with anyone. Perhaps Mac and I could get away individually. It'd be better than nothing.

Mac came in, carrying a tumbler of whiskey, and used the toilet lid as a seat. 'Good?' he said.

'Brilliant. It's looking amazing, isn't it?' I surveyed the bathroom. The raw stone walls, the solid black beams and freshly painted plaster, the wooden shelves glowing in the light.

'It is,' he said, staring at me.

'Are you leering?'

'Most definitely.'

I took a drink. 'I've been thinking. We could move in here even before the kitchen's done. We can cook in the caravan, eat there, but do everything else here.'

'Yeah, sure.'

'We'll need some furniture, beds, couch, chairs, table. We could try on eBay – see if there's anything in driving distance. Get new mattresses. Or use the ones from the van until we let that go.'

'Get a telly, too,' he said.

I told him my thoughts on us each getting away for just a couple of nights.

'Sounds like a plan.'

'You want to get in?' I said, swishing the water.

'Thought you'd never ask,' he said, standing and stripping off his top.

191

Chapter Thirty-three

One day when I went to pick Chloë up, she was still busy grooming Pippin. Barbara asked again if she might want to join any of the groups that trekked at weekends.

'Chloë finds groups hard,' I said. 'She's better one-to-one or on her own.'

'That's fine,' Barbara said. I sensed she understood, that she didn't need any more details. That just as she could read her animals she could read their riders.

'We've been talking about jumping,' she said. 'It would make a change for her, be a challenge.'

'What did Chloë say?'

'Keen on the idea. Is it all right with you?'

'Yes, sure. Thank you.'

She beamed, a kind smile that made me glow.

Chloë came over, mud-spattered, hat swinging from her hand, colour in her face. Close to happy.

When Chloë heard that we were going to sleep in the house she was angry. 'I want to sleep in the caravan.'

'We've moved the mattresses,' I said.

'Move mine back,' she shouted.

'Chloë, are you sure? Your dad and I are staying in the house tonight. You'll be on your own.'

'Move it back,' she shouted again, shaking.

'Help me, then.' I challenged her. 'Come on.' Physical activity might derail the coming explosion. I didn't want her alone in the caravan. I couldn't imagine she'd sleep easily on her own, but I couldn't force her to move.

Turning to go across the yard to the house, I hoped she'd follow. And I released my breath when I heard her footsteps scuffing behind me.

We had set up both bedrooms in the right-hand side of the cottage, reasoning that after eleven years of sleeping in close proximity it'd be best to carry on that way. That it would reassure her, but now I stripped her bed.

Chloë was still slight but she was strong for her size, though a mattress isn't an easy shape to shift. We lugged it out and bumped it over the yard, luckily the ground was dry, and put it back in place in the caravan.

'Now the bedding,' I said.

While we made the bed, I told her I'd leave a key for the cottage in case she changed her mind. She could always come in and sleep on the sofa.

When Mac got back from a job in Filey, I was putting our clothes away. He swore when I told him what Chloë had decided. 'It's never-ending,' he said.

'Look, it's not perfect,' I tried to reason with him, 'but it's not a catastrophe either. We know she wants to feel in control. This is one way she can. We have to pick our battles.'

'And if she sets the place on fire again?'

'Mac, if she wanted to do that, then us being in the next room isn't going to stop her.'

'And what happens when the kitchen's in and we have to return the caravan? What then?'

'I don't know. We'll have to work something out with her.'

He looked sick of it all.

'What else can we do?' I said. 'You go over there now, scream and shout or even try to talk to her about it, and she'll just dig her heels in further. We should let it go,' I said. Practice had taught me that Chloë wanted us to react, to be angry with her, to shout back and push her away when she acted out. To confirm that she was 'bad', to echo the loss and neglect she'd experienced as a baby.

She was constantly testing me but for Mac it was worse. The common ground they'd shared, a love of drawing, had gone as Chloë had lost interest. His gentle resilience had been eaten away by the increasing vitriol of her outbursts. Her emerging womanhood made it harder to know how to deal with her and he was left perplexed and frustrated.

He sighed, covered his eyes.

'Mac?'

'I need a drink. Be back in an hour.'

There was a pub in town where Mac had found a home, got to know some of the regulars, had a game of darts (arrows or 'arrers', they called them, in true Yorkshire tradition). He was able to escape for a while. Have a pint and a laugh, a bit of the craic in his terms. It was helping him cope. But I wasn't sure how long it would be enough for him. I didn't have an equivalent but I could keep going while I had Mac to support me. And I was determined to do everything possible to make this work, to prove to him that he didn't need to give up on Chloë, that however hard it was we would get through it.

'Listen,' I said. 'What we were talking about before, getting away, why don't you sort out a break for yourself soon? There's no point putting it off.'

'And what about you?'

'I'll do the same after you're back.'

He gave a nod and moved to go. I could feel the antagonism, the weariness, in him but I didn't want us to part like that.

'Mac.' I went up to him. I put my head against his chest and my arms around him. He hesitated, then hugged me back. We didn't speak. There was nothing to say.

Chapter Thirty-four

Chloë and I had managed when Mac took the chance to fly home to Ireland for a few nights. But when it came to my turn to have a weekend in York with Bel she became agitated. I had raised the possibility in a vague way before the event but deliberately hadn't told her it was happening until the night before.

'I want to come,' she said.

'Chloë, you can't. This is some time for me and Bel together. I'll only be away two nights. I'll be back here by Sunday lunch. We could do something nice then. Drive into Scarborough for a pizza or go to the cinema. You'll be fine with Dad.'

She pulled out a cigarette.

'Take that outside.'

She stared at me. Lit the cigarette.

'Chloë, take it outside.'

'Fuck off!' she yelled, making me flinch. Then she went outside, slamming the door hard behind her.

I couldn't go. How could I go and leave her?

Mac had overheard. 'You OK?'

'Maybe I shouldn't—'

'Sssh. You're going. She wants us to be prisoners.'

'Mac.' I hated him talking like that because it suggested some volition, when in truth she could no more change her behaviour than a person with epilepsy or asthma could stop having attacks.

'You tell her the script and you go. If you don't, if we can't even have two nights off, we're not going to make it, Lydia.'

The script was the story we told Chloë to reassure her, how we

195

loved her, would never leave her, that she was our daughter for ever. No matter how many times we'd repeated it, she couldn't really trust it to be the truth.

Bel was now running an Airbnb company that specialised in letting accommodation to actors and artists. People who were on tour or in rep or sometimes filming and wanted somewhere to stay other than a hotel.

Through work she'd booked us a flat in the centre of York. She was already there when I arrived.

In an unusual show of affection I got the one-two-three kisses à la France. Then she showed me to my room where I left my case.

'Coffee? Freshly made,' she said.

'Love one.'

'And I booked us lunch – there's this fantastic seafood place. Or has Whitby had you all fished out?'

'Never have too many prawns,' I said.

She looked well, her hair blue-black, cut in a new style, asymmetrical, a long sweep to one side. Similar to how it was when I first met her. I admired it.

'New guy I've found, don't think he realises how good he actually is. He looks about ten.'

'I've given up,' I said. 'Too much grey.' Most of the time I tied my hair back in a ponytail to keep it out of the way. It was dry and split at the ends, the texture of wire wool.

'You can't just give up,' she said. 'We'll sort you out while you're here.'

'How?'

'I have ways.' She was busy tapping on her phone.

'I can't really . . .'

'My treat.'

I knew I was dowdy beside her. Fat and washed-out, I probably looked twenty years older but I didn't care. 'Bel, it really doesn't matter.'

'I know,' she said. 'But it will give you a boost. Sue me if it doesn't. We'll go after lunch. It'll be fun.'

196

I still wasn't sure.

'Come on.' She reached over and shook my shoulder. 'This is your weekend. Consider it a belated Christmas present. Say yes, Lydia. In fact that's the rule: the next forty-eight hours you can only say yes.'

'All right,' I said. I couldn't imagine myself with another hairstyle.

Over lunch I told Bel all about Whitby. 'Things are tough,' I said, 'but it was probably worse before we left Leeds. At least she's not going missing all the time and getting into who knows what trouble.'

'Just a little light arson and the raging meltdowns?'

'Yeah, just that. She asked about her birth-mother, what she was like. I've told her everything we know. But it doesn't amount to much.'

'She can't see her yet?'

'Not until she's eighteen. I've told her she can write. Send a letter with mine and ask questions. It's up to the social workers if they pass that on and if she gets a reply. I don't know if she can handle it, really. Who knows what fantasies she's spinning? Social media makes it so easy for people to trace each other. They find each other on Facebook and just go ahead and reunite without any support or advice. I couldn't bear that.' I pressed my hands to my head. 'We've got a therapist who sounds as though he knows what he's doing. He can start seeing her in March. He's in Newcastle, so it's a four-hour round trip but that's fine.' I sat back. 'And how's Freya?'

'Oh.' Bel snorted. 'Freya's fucking perfect. Taking some exams early, lead role in the school play, volunteering at a charity shop. She's a saint.'

'Give her some credit, Bel,' I said. 'Aren't you proud?'

'Proud? It's nothing to do with me,' she said.

'Go on,' I chided her.

'It isn't. It's in spite of me. She's driving me crazy. Every day's another argument,' she said.

They'd always bickered. Bel couldn't seem to keep her mouth shut if Freya said something she took issue with.

'It's part of the whole becoming-independent thing, isn't it? Hating your parents, arguing,' I said.

197

'She's been like this all her life.'

'Forgive me if I don't feel sorry for you.'

'It's not a fucking competition,' Bel said sharply. The atmosphere soured.

I took a drink. Then another. The wine was cold, fruity.

Bel relented. 'Sorry, it's just like everybody thinks the sun shines out of her arse but she's driving me insane. And I know compared to what you've got on your plate . . .'

'More wine?' I lifted the bottle.

'Always.'

Once we'd finished lunch we went to the salon Bel had found, wending our way through narrow cobbled lanes awash with tourists, a babble of American and Chinese and Australian accents in the air. The pretty stone houses with bow windows were selling silk and wool, perfume and jewellery, handmade crafts and souvenirs.

The salon was in a basement, the walls lined with bamboo cane, a water feature in one corner, a Buddhist statue in another, pools of light over each hairdresser's chair. A door led through to spa facilities and Bel had booked herself in for a mani-pedi and acrylic nails while I had my hair done by a chubby girl with astonished-looking eyebrows called Kyla.

'I've no idea what to do with it,' I said. 'A trim, I guess.'

'Would you consider a colour?'

'Yes. Nothing too artificial.'

'We could start with a nice golden brown.'

'Fine,' I said.

'How much do you want off the length?'

'I don't know.'

She picked up a tablet from the counter and swiped the screen until she found a page of four photographs, headed *Wavy Hair*, and handed it to me. 'This maybe?' She pointed to a beautiful model. 'It's a side part and the length's just to the collarbone. It'll take a lot of the weight off but keep your natural wave.'

'Sounds great.' Though I wouldn't look like the photo in a million years.

'And we'll use a special treatment, an intense nourisher.'

She mixed and applied the colour and left me with a magazine. My thoughts kept returning to Mac and Chloë, though he had promised to ring me in an emergency. It was a novelty to have nothing more to do than sit and flick through the spring trends, articles about Pilates and super-foods.

When Kyla rinsed off and conditioned my hair at the sink she used firm circular motions. It was like having a head massage, the tension melting away.

Bel came back through while Kyla was cutting my hair. Her fingernails were deep purple, frosted with silver tips, like filigree silver. She said her toes were the same. She sat and chatted to Kyla about her training and some of the other treatments they had on offer.

I watched the hanks of hair fall, hoping I'd not made a mistake and that Kyla wouldn't get carried away and cut it too short. She blow-dried it and worked some sort of final polish through it.

When she'd finished I couldn't help but smile.

'You look amazing,' Bel said.

An exaggeration, but my hair shone, it framed my face in soft waves, and having it shorter seemed to make my eyes stand out more. When I ran a hand through it, it felt silky and bouncy.

The lunch had been delicious but by no means hearty and I was ready to eat again by early evening. Bel knew of an Indian on the edge of town, still in walking distance, and we went there for a curry, then to a pub that did craft beers. It was crowded but Bel managed to snaffle seats in the corner as soon as they became free.

'How's your love life?' I asked.

She was usually quick to tell me when she was seeing someone.

'Good.' She raised an eyebrow, pursed her lips in a small smile. I signalled for her to elaborate.

'Barnaby,' she said.

'Barnaby?'

'I know.' She gave a laugh. 'Thirty-something.'

A younger man.

'Lighting engineer. Here.' She pulled out her phone, showed me a picture. He looked like a surfer, hair not unlike my new style, stubble, casual clothes. He also looked younger than thirty-something.

'I don't get to see him much. But when we do . . .' She grinned.

'He away a lot for work?'

'Some. But he's married.'

My heart sank. 'Ah.'

'Yeah. Three kids.'

'Does his wife know?'

'What do you think?'

I thought it was sad.

She stretched. 'Still, doesn't get boring, no fear of being smothered. Suits me just fine.'

Yes, I imagined it did. The transgression of being the mistress adding to the excitement, the time snatched and intense.

'Don't say anything at home. Freya doesn't know. And I'd never hear the end of it.'

'Of course.' I thought of the wife. The love of her life lying and cheating. Imagined the anger and sorrow I'd feel if it was me. Was he a cheat anyway? If it hadn't been for Bel, would there have been someone else? Or had she set out to corrupt him?

Chapter Thirty-five

I woke early on Saturday, force of habit, disorientated for a moment. I checked my phone, no messages, and let myself drift back to sleep, not waking again until almost ten o'clock. Bel slept on while I showered. The local bakery had croissants. I bought some, and a paper from the newsagent's. I made fresh coffee and relished the leisure of it all. The indulgence.

Once Bel was ready we walked through the gardens. The day was mild and dry, cloudy.

Catkins were out and the blackthorn was sprayed with delicate white blossom, the ground scattered with clutches of snowdrops and crocuses.

I told Bel about Chloë's riding and the hope that she'd find work in that field. 'What does Freya want to do?' I said.

'I don't know, she's already talking about studying politics, philosophy and economics. But the fees! She'd come out owing fifty or sixty grand. And they charge interest on it, high interest. It's such a scam.'

'But she'll do well,' I said. 'She's so bright. She'll make more money than any of us have.'

'I can't afford to sub her but there's a trust fund.'

'Since when?'

'It was something my father set up for Freya when she was little. She can only touch it when she's eighteen. But I've told her she'll have to use that to help her manage. It's crazy – she's thirteen and she's already narrowed down her degree course.'

'It's great she knows what she wants to do. A lot of them don't.'

201

'Do you miss your mum?' she said.

I was wrong-footed by the abrupt change of subject. Felt a wave of sadness. 'Every day. You know, when I was a kid I couldn't really see her as anything other than my mum, part of the furniture. More irritating as I got older. It took having Chloë for me to really appreciate her. Not just for bringing us up but as an actual person who existed outside the family. She was born during the war, grew up with rationing still going on when women were forced back into the kitchen. She left school and went to secretarial college. But she had this really strong group of friends – they'd been at school together, then got married and worked and had kids, but they kept the friendships going. I guess it helped that they all stayed in Bradford.'

'No one ran off to Whitby,' she said.

'Hah! What about you – your mum?' I knew Bel's mother had died of liver failure while Bel was in Santa Monica. And by then her father was in a care home. Bel had flown to France for her mother's funeral but had never told me more than that.

'I hated her,' Bel said.

I drew in a breath.

'I probably loved her too.' She caught my eye. 'They're not mutually exclusive, are they?' She looked away. I saw her jaw tighten. She drew back the wing of hair. Stopped walking. 'And I fell apart when she died. I thought I'd be fine with it, not like we were particularly close, didn't see much of each other. Nothing in common.' She blew out her cheeks. 'But I was a wreck.'

'I'd no idea.'

'Ethan dragged me to see a doctor. They threw prescriptions at me. Uppers, downers, sleeping pills. It got me through eventually.'

'Did you try talking to anyone?'

'Oh, you know me, always prefer the chemical solution.' She winked and I laughed. She'd successfully deflected the question. I think she was scared of therapy, of having to open up and confide in someone, exposing her vulnerabilities.

We walked on.

'And how's your dad?' I said.

'Same. I've not been over. No point. He wouldn't know me from Adam.'

'I heard from Colin, about trying to move back from Spain,' I said.

'He can't find enough work. But then, they don't know what will happen with the referendum. If we leave Europe Javier might not be allowed to stay here.'

'That'll never happen,' I said. 'We'd be crazy to leave. It's just the Conservative Party wanting to shut UKIP up once and for all.'

By the end of the afternoon I'd still not heard from Mac or Chloë and was getting stressed about it. I texted him: *Everything OK? xx*

The reply came immediately: *All fine. See you tomorrow x*

Bel and I got drunk that night and staggered back to the flat in fits of giggles.

When I woke the next morning, head thumping, mouth dry, I couldn't even remember what had been so funny. But it had been good to laugh, that much I knew. So good to have time to do whatever I felt like for a few hours. A taste of freedom.

Driving into the yard, the first thing I noticed was a mattress propped up against the wall of the old shed. I felt a clutch of anxiety. Flashcards of horror.

Mac came out of the house to meet me. I read his expression and knew in a second that I'd overreacted.

'Nice do.' He wiggled his fingers at his own hair.

'Ta. What's happened?'

'She got pissed. Half a bottle of whiskey near enough. Sick as a dog.'

'Oh, God. Where is she now?'

'Inside.' He nodded to the house. 'Asleep on the sofa. I got her to shower, drink some water.'

'Shit. At least it was whiskey, not bleach.'

'Jaysus, Lydia. Could you not go darker?'

'I just thought, when I saw it . . . Well, you can imagine.'

'I'd have rung. You know that.'

'I know,' I said. 'You OK? Apart from . . .'

'I'm hung-over.' He made a noise, ironic.

'You want something to eat?' I said. 'Fry-up?'

He shook his head.

'Where are the sheets?'

'In the machine. I chucked the pillow. Good time?' he said, as we went in.

Chloë was curled up on the sofa. Pale and frail.

'Yeah, it was good. Great, actually. Just to be off duty. You know?'

'I do,' he said, with feeling. 'God, I do.'

Chapter Thirty-six

Until the last minute I didn't know if Chloë would get into the car and come with me to see Gregory.

But she did, slumping into the passenger seat and plugging in her earphones.

I listened to the radio, concentrating hard on the driving: there was fog over the moors, grey clouds of it drifting across the road and making it hard to see.

Gregory had experience of working with traumatised and adopted children and treating a range of attachment disorders. The term described emotional and behavioural problems stemming from the failure to form attachment to caregivers in early childhood. Especially an inability to create close relationships, to show affection, to trust.

When I'd first tried to find out about possible psychiatric treatment for Chloë, most of the stuff advertised online for adoptees was something called attachment therapy (which made it sound perfect for problems with attachment). Most popular in the US, it involved holding the child, restraining them, even sitting on them, no matter how much they resisted, with the aim of provoking all their suppressed rage and despair, achieving catharsis and reducing them to an infantile state from which they could then be 'reborn'. They were treated and nurtured as a baby initially and then learned to love their new parents.

The idea had repulsed me. It sounded barbaric, like an exorcism. There had even been cases of children who had died in the process, suffocated. There was no way I'd ever consider it for Chloë.

* * *

We arrived at the Newcastle clinic ten minutes early.

Chloë stood outside the car and had a cigarette. She threw the butt down, crushed it underfoot. She wanted me to reprimand her, ask her to put it in the bin, then she'd explode and sabotage our visit. I didn't rise to the bait.

Gregory saw us together. He asked me to describe what the problems were, how Chloë's distress manifested itself and any previous treatment she'd had. I gave him a snapshot of the current situation. He checked with Chloë if she thought it was a fair description. She agreed. He then asked about Chloë's early life and I told him everything I knew. He encouraged me to talk in more detail, giving him examples of situations we'd found hard to deal with as a family over the years.

Chloë was tense: I could tell from the way she sat, the little movements she made, but I was encouraged that she remained in the room and didn't do anything to disrupt the session.

Driving home, I remembered our preparation days and how we'd been told about the range of problems kids might have. I hadn't ignored it, not exactly, but I think I'd found it impossible to truly imagine. And, anyway, I'd thought love would be enough. That if we gave a child all our love we'd be able to make them better, make them happy. Fix them.

Love was not enough.

Against Chloë's objections the caravan was collected and returned to the company that had hired it to us, and we gave her the option of any of the bedrooms in the house.

After a weekend in meltdown, sleeping on the sofa when she did sleep, refusing to eat with us, marking her arms with cigarette burns, she finally announced she'd have the one at the front on the left side of the house. As far away from ours as possible.

Mac and I moved the furniture across. I fixed up curtains on a pole and encouraged her to pin up some photos on a cork board.

Niall was due to arrive that evening. He wanted to see how the house was looking and talk about the next steps.

I'd made a start on tidying the land at the back for a garden and Mac had ordered stone for a terrace there outside the patio doors from the kitchen. 'He'll want to sell,' I said to Mac, as we marked out the area for the patio with string and pegs. 'That was the deal. If we have to move now . . .'

We both knew it would be catastrophic to uproot Chloë again so soon.

'He won't evict us,' Mac said.

'Do you think he'll let us rent?' I said. 'At market price? Or sell to us?'

'We've not enough to buy,' Mac said. 'Even if we sell the house in Leeds. Somewhere like this, four beds, refurbished, going to be four hundred easily. Our income's tanked. We'll not get a mortgage, no way, not unless you get a full-time job again.'

'Scarborough's the nearest hospital with a haematology depart-ment, but the chance of them taking on staff with all the cuts . . . And me not being around for Chloë . . .'

'We'll just have to see what he says,' Mac told me. 'We'll work something out.'

'Hey, Chloë. How's my favourite niece?' Niall said, when he arrived.

'OK,' she said. A little tense, I could tell from the way she held herself: a result of any shift in the dynamic.

'Will you give me the tour?' Niall said.

'OK.' She walked off. Niall raised his eyebrows at us, then fol-lowed and we went after him.

He was pleased with what we'd done. He'd seen each stage via Skype but said it was ten times better in real life. 'You really have done a grand job here. *Grand Designs* – you seen that show?'

'It was your plan,' I said.

'Ah, but you've made it happen. It's just beautiful.'

We left the hard conversation until after we'd eaten and Chloë had gone to her room.

Mac began. He was running his fingers along the edge of the table and I could tell he was apprehensive. 'Niall, we've been thinking it'd

207

be hard for us to up sticks again right now, hard for Chloë, so we were wondering about renting from you for a couple of years or so.'

'Renting?' Niall's face fell. 'I'd not thought about that. The whole plan was to sell.' There was a horrible pause. 'I'm not ruling it out, it's just I'd be needing the profit from this place to put into another property I've found in Bridlington. I'd have to think about it.'

Oh, God.

'Of course,' I said. 'Maybe we could put something towards that. You know how much it'd be?'

Niall laughed awkwardly and I felt my face grow hot. 'I'm not sure that'd work.'

'No, of course,' I said quickly. I had no idea of all the ins and outs of his business but I saw that our wish to stay on was problematic.

'Give me a few weeks,' he said.

'Sure,' Mac said. I could hear he was disappointed.

'If it's not possible,' I said, 'we'll find somewhere near and Chloë will still be able to go riding and . . .' I petered out, because that was it in terms of positives. On every other front moving house, even a mile or so, would be a nightmare.

I was angry with myself. Why hadn't I thought this through when I'd dragged us all here, when we'd accepted Niall's offer? Why hadn't I thought about the longer term?

I'd been trying to create a future for us, for Mac and me, a way to salvage our family, but I'd led us onto a cliff edge.

Chapter Thirty-seven

The letters I sent each year to Debbie were a challenge, one I dreaded. As Chloë's birthday in April drew closer the obligation to write the note grew heavier. It felt so artificial: I couldn't be honest and talk fully about Chloë's problems as I might to a friend. Besides, this was Debbie's only link to her daughter and it would be hard for her to know how troubled Chloë was. So I had to understate the difficulties and find a way to pick out snippets from Chloë's life that would be good to hear without making it sound like we were living some fairy tale.

I determined to get it done that evening. Mac had gone to the pub. I sat at the big farmhouse kitchen table with my laptop. Outside, the sky was an eerie violet colour and full black clouds were sailing in from the sea. Chloë was getting a drink of Coke so I told her I was writing and asked her if she wanted to put a note in, or a photograph.

'Maybe the one at the whalebone?' she said.

'Not that one,' I said.

'Why?' She was affronted.

'Because it shows where we are.'

'What do you think'll happen? She'll come and kidnap me or something?'

'The rules are there for a reason. She wants to see you, of course she does, and knowing where you are, the temptation, that wouldn't be fair.'

'It's not got our address on, has it? So how could she find me?'

'How about a picture of you on Pippin? I'm going to tell her about your riding.'

'Forget it,' she said, and walked out, slamming the door as hard as she could.

I stared out through the French windows to the shrubs that framed the patio, among them the evergreen fir that had been our Christmas tree. Beyond the terrace the ground was choked with wild bramble and couch grass, which would soon be sprouting new growth. Next on our list of jobs.

The wind buffeted the house and then a fork of lightning split the sky; thunder cracked and rumbled. Even with the triple glazing I could hear the howl of the wind. More lightning, great sheets of it this time, lit the whole sky.

Would there be fishing boats out in this? Would the lifeboat be called?

I told Debbie we had moved to the country, *somewhere Chloë can do more horse-riding, which she really loves. She is learning to jump too and is very good at it.*

There was another fork, a double one, stabbing down to the land, and a crack of thunder that sounded like boulders being rolled above our heads.

The rain came hard and fast.

Chloë also likes . . . what? What else? . . . *going to the cinema. Her favourites this past year have been* Shaun the Sheep, *which she thought was very funny, and also* Selma, *the film about Martin Luther King, which was really good.*

Chloë still finds it hard to deal with new situations and gets very angry at times. Was that too much? *She has kept her hair long. She still has a sweet tooth*. I stared out at the rain, the sky now inky black, the little fir tree bending in the squalls of wind.

She spends a lot of her time online. We had a quiet Christmas, Chloë helped decorate the house and liked her presents. We gave her a tablet computer and riding boots. Did that sound like bragging? I deleted the last sentence and rewrote it to read . . . *and liked her presents, especially her new riding boots*. I didn't mention the fire.

She likes watching TV, programmes like Planet Earth *and* The Great British Bake Off. *Sometimes Chloë bakes biscuits and cakes and tries out the recipes from the show.*

She found it hard to settle at high school and now we have moved I am teaching her at home.

I'd always agonised over how to sign off. *With love* felt inappropriate, *Yours* too cold, *Regards* too formal. I settled with *Best wishes*.

An ear-splitting crack from outside made me jump. A dagger of lightning sliced down far too close to the house, illuminating everything in neon. There was a burst of flame.

I opened the patio doors. The air smelt of burning, pine sap and ozone. The lightning had struck the fir tree. Fire licked over it, making small sizzling and popping sounds. Wisps of smoke curled from the blackened branches. It was carbonised, a black skeleton.

'Mum?' Chloë called out.

'It was lightning. It hit the Christmas tree. Come and see.'

I heard her door close. Then nothing but the rain outside, stones against the glass.

The blasted tree smouldered in the dark.

The ground fell away at the end of our boundary, sloped down to farmland. The fields were different colours, one raw brown earth ploughed in furrows, another left to grass and a third had polytunnels, rippling white. We'd never met our neighbours, weren't even sure where the farmer lived. The farm stretched to the horizon. Beyond, but not visible, was the coast, the sea.

I was planting a pair of tubs for the patio, tapping the plug plants out of their containers, when I saw movement in the sky. Above the fields a great wave of starlings, a murmuration, dived and swooped, twisted and rose. I'd never seen such a big congregation, though I remembered starlings in the middle of Bradford as a child and their chatter filling the air around City Hall.

'Mac,' I called, through the patio doors. 'Come and look.'

He came out, barely glancing at the aerial ballet. 'That was Niall on the phone.'

I set down the trowel and got to my feet, my knees protesting. I didn't need to weigh myself to know that the pounds were creeping on. My clothes were tight. But food was a comfort and I needed something, some small pleasure, a reward or a prop, to help me cope. I baked every couple of days, soft lemon sponges with crunchy drizzle, chocolate cake oozing a dark cream filling, scones and shortbread, the cottage full of the biscuit smell, the tang of lemon zest or the aroma of cocoa.

'He's happy for us to rent until the end of the year but then he'll be putting it on the market. It gives us a few months,' Mac said.

'Seven,' I said, getting to my feet. 'But we should start looking from now, I guess. We don't want to miss out on somewhere in between.'

'Or do we go back to Leeds?' he said. 'The lease on our house is up in September. We give them notice.'

'But Chloë has only just started seeing Gregory.'

'Well, we can keep that going.'

'But it's even further away if we're in Leeds.'

'Jaysus!' He raised his voice. 'I'm just trying to find a way through here for us.'

'So am I. Mac, if we go home she'll be straight back in trouble with that bunch of losers. She'll miss out on the riding. It's too soon. What good could come of it?'

'We'd have friends, some social life. We're marooned here. I go to the pub every few nights. You don't see anyone or do anything.'

'Because—'

'I know why! But what sort of life is it? And what am I supposed to do now the house is finished? I get bookings once in a blue moon.'

The sun lanced my eyes. I turned away, blinking.

'We thought this might help. All we've done is cut ourselves off. None of us are happy,' he said.

'You can't blame this place.'

We were both silent for a moment, the birds twittering. I saw a flicker of movement in the yellow gorse. It was so peaceful here. At first the quiet had made me uneasy but I was growing used to it. Or was it resignation, accepting it along with the lack of adult company, the loss of my job, the shrinking of my world? With a rush of sadness I recognised that I was lonely and bored and low, and I didn't want to be living like this but I would do it as long as necessary, if there was a chance it would help Chloë.

'Maybe you could work with Niall.' I rubbed the compost from my fingers.

'What?'

'Project manage or whatever it's called. Like you have here. If he's talking about another place in Bridlington, maybe you could manage the conversion.'

Mac didn't respond.

'It's worth asking,' I said.

'I never should have let the shop go,' he said bluntly. He dragged his fingers through his hair, greying now. 'That's all I want to do. Run my own studio. Not be a cheap doer-upper for my brother.'

'Perhaps you could find studio space in Scarborough or Filey, then.'

'There's half a dozen there already. And with prime site rents . . . I'd be losing money.'

'What about the Goth festival, Halloween? There'd be a big jump in demand then. Could you . . . I don't know, set up the van in town, talk to the council about—'

'It's clutching at straws,' he yelled.

'At least I haven't given up. I'm trying,' I shouted back, sudden heat flaring across the back of my neck.

His eyes locked onto mine, bitterness plain to see. Then he walked away.

Back over the land the starlings billowed and spun in the late-spring sunshine.

Chapter Thirty-eight

Chloë was in the paddock, practising jumps with Pippin, when I went to collect her. I walked over and stood in the shade of the oak trees that lined one side of the field, batting away the horseflies that landed on my forearms. Chloë rode the horse to the start of the circuit and lined her up. There were two jumps in a row, one like a hedge and the other a five-bar gate.

Chloë settled in the saddle, then rode the horse forward into a canter. I held my breath as they reached the first obstacle and watched them soar over it with ease. The landing alone would have knocked the stuffing out of me, but Chloë rode on, gaining speed again before clearing the second fence.

Clutching at straws, Mac had said. The look in his eyes, the ill-will, I couldn't shake off how worried they made me feel.

'She's doing well. She could compete if she wanted to.'

Barbara. I hadn't heard her approach. Her face was ruddy, and deep wrinkles framed her eyes so they almost disappeared when she smiled. 'I wanted a word,' she said. 'We run a summer riding school in the long holidays, for the tourists. It means there'll be a lot more activity. Group hacking, Pony Club stuff. Family rides. There may be some days when I need Pippin to make up the numbers. Bookings are coming in now, though some people leave it to the last minute. So . . . for Chloë it might mean a bit of shuffling dates and times, and two sessions a week instead of three.'

Across the paddock the horse had completed the circuit. Chloë was leaning forward patting her neck, the physical closeness greater than any she shared with me.

'Some of the visitors get involved in the mucking out too, part of the experience,' Barbara said.

'So the mornings?'

'She'd be welcome to come but there'd be more people around.'

'OK,' I said. Was it? I wasn't sure how Chloë would react.

I felt a sting on the underneath of my arm, rubbed at it.

'I'll do my best to get things firmed up over the next month.'

'Thanks. I'll talk to her about it.'

Chloë led the horse out of the paddock and alongside the barn into the stableyard, where I could hear its shoes ringing on the cobbles.

'You all right?' Barbara said. Concern in her expression threatened to unravel me. 'It's just you seem—'

'I'm fine,' I managed.

'I'm sorry.'

'No.' I swallowed, rubbed harder at my arm and felt the lump harden under the skin. I lifted my arm to examine the red blotch. 'Bite,' I said, moving away.

Driving home we kept meeting coaches and, where the road narrowed, had to pull in and let them pass. With the season well under way, parties were arriving from near and far, Japanese and Italian, American and Polish tourists on excursions with their guides as well as the domestic visitors. The inns, B-and-Bs and holiday parks were filling up.

'Great jumping,' I told Chloë. 'Barbara reckons you could enter competitions if you wanted.'

'Show jumping?'

'Yes.'

I didn't say anything else but my instinct was that she'd rather compete against herself than get involved in having to deal with unfamiliar places, crowds and all the attention.

I talked to her about Barbara's plans for the holidays.

'So there'll be loads of kids around?'

'Yes, and families, teenagers, all sorts.'

'When does it start?'

'The third week of July. I'll check. You have a think what you'd like to do. Yeah? Chloë?'

'OK,' she said irritably.

By bedtime my arm, fat already, had ballooned as a result of the horsefly bite. The itch was maddening, the desire to scratch impossible to resist. A scab formed, weeping yellow pus.

I woke in the early hours, swimming up from a nightmare. Watching Chloë ride, the horse a white stallion, far too large for her and out of control, foaming at the mouth, wild-eyed. I was running, trying to catch them, reach the reins. Chloë like a rag-doll, her hair flying out in a fan of white, as the horse hurtled towards the high brick wall ahead. Clods of earth flew from its hoofs, hitting me in the face and eyes. The horse leaped into the air, flanks steaming, and Chloë was flung from the saddle, hurtled through the air, falling to land hard on the ground.

Limp.

Still.

I ran to her but a crowd formed tight about her, their backs to me, blocking my way. 'It's my daughter,' I shouted. 'Let me through! That's my daughter. Please! Chloë?' The crowd roared with laughter, kept their backs to me, unmoved, as I clawed at their shoulders, tried to force a way through.

The residue of the dream, the fear, clung to me like grime. Mac slept on.

I got up, put on my dressing-gown and went to the kitchen.

The night was still and clear, stars visible, the crescent moon an arc of light high in the sky.

I ate a slice of coffee and walnut cake, then another.

I caught sight of my reflection in the glass doors. Pitied the woman sitting there, careworn, alone, stuffing her face in the middle of the night. I thought about texting Bel, arranging to Skype soon, but it felt like too much of an effort. What had I to say after all but more of the same old same old? While Freya was taking English and maths GCSEs two years early and Bel's business was going from strength to strength, we were flailing.

I ate the last piece of cake. And dabbed at the crumbs with my fingers. My arm throbbed and I scraped it against the table's edge.

I knew I ought to try to sleep, I had to drive Chloë to see Gregory the following morning, but I was still too tense.

Everything changes – that was one of the truths I clung to. It's a universal truth, in science, in all of life: nothing stays the same. It's supposed to give us hope.

I felt as if we were frozen now, locked into an existence fraught with conflict and frustration, with disappointment. My love, for Mac, for Chloë, was deep as ever. Loving her wasn't a choice. It was what I did, what I felt. The same as I did with Mac. She was in my heart. Love for her ran in my blood. And somehow I was able to see that, however bad her behaviour, it was a response to the pain she was in. To the trauma that was resurfacing as she became a young woman in a world where she was constantly anxious and angry and frightened.

But my love was beset on every side by exhaustion and dread. I could feel the dullness and darkness of depression creeping through me. I thought of seeing the GP. Put it off.

Everything changes. Yes, things would change inexorably.

But what if the change was for the worse?

Chapter Thirty-nine

In August we got a letter through from the NHS Health Trust. Chloë's CAMHS appointment had come through, for a Monday in October, almost a year since the GP had made the referral.

Gregory was on holiday for the month but I wanted to check with him if it was all right to have the two therapies going on simultaneously, assuming CAMHS offered Chloë counselling after her assessment. Cognitive behavioural therapy seemed to be the most common treatment. From what I'd read online it was debatable how appropriate it was for children with problems of attachment and trauma. I'd be guided by what Gregory said.

Mac had gone over to Wicklow, visiting his dad Brendan, who was recovering from a heart bypass operation. I was on the patio, resting after a busy day, and had been scrolling through the local estate-agent sites, looking for any new listings of rental properties.

It was a sweltering day, the horizon beyond and the crops in the fields rippling in the heat haze. The air was thick with insects, flies and bees. A dragonfly, even, though we had no pond. Skylarks fluted high above. From the outside it must have looked idyllic.

My email pinged, a message from Bel headed *Postcard from Corsica* with a selfie of her and Freya on their balcony. I made a Skype call straight away, hoping she was still online, and told her about CAMHS. 'I'll have to see what her therapist says,' I told her. 'If he says it won't be helpful, we'll decline it.'

'Even though it's free.'

'I know. Gregory's costing us a small fortune.'

'Is it working? Her seeing this guy?'

'Yes. No. I don't know. I lose perspective. There's not been any

218

clear improvement yet, but he said it's a long process. He's away all month and she's not going riding – it got too busy and she was over-whelmed. She's withdrawing, just shuts herself in her room. Barely communicating.'

I didn't know which was worse: the rages or the silence.

'Sounds like a normal teenager,' Bel said. Which really didn't help.

'So how is Corsica?' I said.

'*Très jolie,*' she said. 'Apart from the prices, which are *incroy-able*. Fucking outrageous. Freya's got her face on because the veggie options come down to omelette or tomato salad.'

'Yummy. Well, while you've been swanning around the Riviera—'

'Not strictly Riviera.'

'OK. I've been hacking through the wilderness.'

'What?'

'Clearing brambles. We're hiring a rotavator to dig up the big patch of ground at the back and put turf down. I'm scratched to pieces.'

The area where I'd cut back the tangle of blackberries, nettles and thistles now looked even worse, the ground bristling with broken stumps and clumps of couch grass. My arms were laced with scratches, beads of blood dried along them. I thought of Chloë's arms, the tracery of scars. Would there ever come a time when she didn't need to cut herself to deal with the pain she felt? Would those scars fade?

Down the phone I heard Freya calling, 'Mom.'

'We're off for a swim,' Bel said to me.

I groaned with envy.

'You could go there,' Bel said. 'Or is it pissing it down?'

'No, it's beautiful. Maybe I will.' I said goodbye.

It was nearly teatime so a lot of the visitors would be leaving the beach, off for fish suppers or burgers, the coach parties convening to travel back to their hotels or onward to their dinner reservations. I put away my laptop, cleared up, and locked the patio doors.

'Chloë?' I knocked on her door. 'I'm going for a swim, down the beach. Do you want to come? Get an ice cream on the way back?'

No sound.

I knocked again. Then opened the door.

The room smelt sour, slightly sickly, overlaid with the reek of cigarettes that clung to her hair and clothes.

She was sprawled on the bed, earphones in, tablet on her stomach. She looked up sharply, touched her screen, took one earphone out. 'What?'

'Come for a swim. We can get out for a bit.'

She shook her head.

'You can wear a long-sleeved T-shirt, and some leggings,' I said, in case she was worried about exposing her arms and thighs. 'We won't be long. And it's so hot, a swim will be lovely.'

'You go.'

I was disappointed even though I hadn't really expected her to say yes. 'Bring you back some ice cream?'

She shook her head. 'It's all right.'

I couldn't reach her.

'You know we love you,' I said. 'If you want to talk about anything or . . .' I faltered.

She glanced at me, her grey eyes flat, blank, not even spiked with irritation. 'I don't. Just go.'

It was a struggle to get my swimsuit on: the straps dug into my shoulders, the top of the legs bit into my thighs and rolls of fat spilled over. I almost bottled out. Chiding myself for being such a wimp, I slathered on sunscreen, pulled a dress over my swimsuit, then collected a towel and my sandals.

Town was humming with tourists, music blaring out from the amusement arcades. The whelk and cockle stands, the candy-floss and toffee-apple stalls were ringed by queues.

The tide was halfway in. People promenaded along the piers and there were others sitting fishing on the lower gangway; a group of children dangled crab lines into the water.

A pleasure boat headed back into port, pennants flying.

I went down the access ramp, took off my sandals and walked along the beach. I could smell the bladderwrack on the rocks by the cliff, a salty vegetable pong, and now and again I caught a whiff of coconut or melon from someone's sun lotion.

The beach was emptying, families gathering up buckets and spades, lilos and cool boxes.

Reaching a clear stretch, I lay on my towel and closed my eyes for a few minutes. The sand was hard under my hips and I wriggled to get a little more comfortable, listening to the suck and sigh of the waves, to the rhythm of their approach. Horns sounded from one of the boats. And somewhere a bell was clanging. The light through my eyelids was the colour of blood oranges. The cuts on my arms tickled in the heat.

No matter how much I tried to empty my mind, to concentrate on my breath, to relax and let go, the thoughts scurrying around my head were like vermin scratching and gnawing for entry. I sat up and took off my dress. Feeling self-conscious, I walked down to the water's edge. I stepped in, ankle deep, and felt the cold drill into my bones.

The hardest part was always getting in. Wading out, I sucked in my breath as the water rose and when I was up to my waist took a gulp of air and launched myself in, stifling a shriek. My skin contracted and tingled with cold. My scratches stung. I swam breaststroke hard against the incoming tide, breaching the dips and troughs of the waves.

I swam until my arms and lungs burned and cramp chewed at my calves. Then I turned to look back at the beach. The pull of the tide had prevented me going as far as I'd thought. I lay back and let myself float, the cold sea cradling the back of my head. Tasting salt on my lips.

Above me the sky was a deep summer blue, criss-crossed by gulls, their silhouettes, the arc of their wings and their long bills dark against the sky.

Rocked by the water, gazing up into the blue, finally I was peaceful. Empty. When I got goosebumps I swam again, parallel to the shoreline west towards Sandsend at the far side of the bay. Level with the village, I turned and swam back as fast as I could.

Coming out of the water my legs were unsteady, my lungs felt scoured, my skin sticky from the brine, which had raised puffy white welts along the bramble cuts on my arms. A pinch of sunburn stung my neck.

I must do this again, I promised myself, as I walked back along the tide line through the foam, with its cargo of torn seaweed and shingle.

I will.

Every sunny day.

Chapter Forty

Chloë came into town with me – I wanted to do a supermarket shop. Getting out of the car I was surprised, and pleased, when she said she'd look round the shops, waving a hand towards the maze of streets.

How long would I be? We agreed on forty-five minutes.

She had a little money and I gave her a twenty-pound note in case she saw anything she'd like to buy.

I'd finished loading the bags into the car and there was no sign of her. The car park was close to the harbour and I wandered down there. It was a hot day, more like August than September. Halyards were clinking in the breeze and people were busy about their boats, one man mending nets on the harbourside, another hosing down plastic fish trays. A yacht was leaving the marina, flying an Irish flag. In the water a mob of seagulls were fighting over something floating there, diving, screaming and mewling.

The sun made the skin on my shoulders tingle. I hadn't any sunscreen on.

I was wondering if I should ring Chloë, when I saw her crossing the bridge. The sight of her always made my heart swell. I watched as she wove among the people strolling past. She was nimble, slight, her hair glowing in the sunshine.

I met her back at the car.

As soon as she got close I could smell it on her, the bitter, burning-rubber smell of skunk.

Shit! Was that what my twenty pounds had gone on?

'Buy anything?' I said.

'No,' she said, narrowing her eyes against the light. I waited a moment but she didn't offer me my money back.

How had she got hold of the cannabis? How had she found someone who was dealing?

We didn't speak on the drive home. I was too busy trying to work out what to say. How to tackle her.

Once at the house I told her to give me a hand putting everything away. We carried the bags in and put them on the kitchen table. I didn't wait any longer. 'Chloë, I know you've been smoking weed.'

'I haven't.'

'You reek of it. Don't lie to me. That stuff messes with your head, especially someone as young as you. It's not safe.'

She picked up a can of pineapple, turned away from me, and put it in the cupboard.

'Never mind that it's illegal. I don't want you smoking it. People get psychotic. Your brain is still developing and that stuff is really strong. It can make you paranoid.'

'No, it won't,' she retorted.

'You don't know what you're doing,' I said.

She picked up a jar of honey. 'Stop going on at me. I'm not a kid.'

'You are! That's exactly what you are.' I slammed my hands on the table. 'Why won't you listen to me?'

'Fuck off,' she shouted, and hurled the jar across the room. It smashed into the big mirror over the bookcase. My mum's mirror, and her mum's before it. The silver glass splintered, shards crashed onto the bookcase and the floor. The honey jar, cracked in places, rocked on the top of the bookcase.

'Now look what you've done!' I screamed. 'You stupid idiot! Why can't you just . . . That was Grandma's, and now you've broken it. You're so selfish, so bloody . . .' I could feel my face hot, contorted, spit flying out of my mouth as I shouted. 'I'm sick of it, all of it. You just don't care about anybody else. Have you any idea of how hard it is?'

She stood rooted to the spot, her face blank, unblinking. Then she smiled, a grin getting ever wider, taunting me.

'You treat me like shit,' I said. 'You're driving me mad. You just . . . you . . . how . . . I can't—' I became inarticulate. Tears of rage burned my eyes. 'Go to your room,' I yelled at her. 'Get out.'

I sat and wept, drowning in the sorrow and fury, beating my fists on my head, banging at the table. Not caring if she heard. As my crying subsided, I felt shame rise in its wake.

Fuck. What had I done?

Numbly I went and washed my face, then made a cup of tea and put the rest of the shopping away. The frozen food packets were sweating, the contents softened.

I was so ashamed about losing my temper: there was no sense of catharsis or cleansing. Instead I felt soiled. Chloë had tested me yet again and this time I had failed spectacularly. I'd exploded and given her exactly what she felt she deserved: rejection, criticism, cruelty. I had sent her away.

I knocked on her door and went in.

She wasn't there. The stench of skunk hung in the room, pungent and cloying. Tiny streaks of blood marked the duvet cover.

I looked around outside, then tried her phone, panic bubbling inside me.

Years of accommodating her, of staying calm, giving her space, acting consistently, and now I'd trashed it all. What did I expect?

Before I could decide whether to go off in the car looking for her, Mac arrived home. He'd been to pick up more logs for the stove.

'That should last us—' He broke off, saw the mirror, the spill. 'What's going on?'

I told the story. 'And then I blew up,' I said. 'And now she's missing.'

He stared up at the ceiling, hands on the small of his back. 'There's no end to it. It's like a hole, digging and digging, and it gets wider and deeper . . . Ah, shit.'

'She's fourteen, she's struggling. We knew the teenage years would be harder. All the stuff about identity, working out who she is.'

225

'She breaks everything. She's . . . And it'll go on until she's destroyed us. Don't you see?'

'Not if we don't let it.'

'How, Lydia? How in the hell? I'm not a saint. And I'm not made of stone either. I can't do it. We can't keep her safe any more. She needs to be with people who can.'

Back in care. 'No, Mac, please—'

'Whatever hell she went through, it's part of her. It's never going to go away. Nothing's changed, Lydia. We agreed to try this but . . . She can't change.'

'We don't know that. With the right help—'

'Don't be so naive,' he yelled.

'I'm not. I won't give up hope. I won't give up on her.'

'At any cost?'

'Four years and she'll be an adult—'

'Four years? Christ, I don't know if I can cope with another four weeks, let alone four years.'

'She's our daughter.' I thought of that first meeting, her hair all fluffy, her determination. 'Remember? She was so fierce and tiny, and I wanted to protect her. I wanted to save her. But most of all I loved her. And she needs us.'

'That's not love, that's pity.'

'No! Don't say that. I love her. In spite of everything. I'm her mother.'

'You've done your best. You've nothing left to prove. But all you've got is unrequited love. A roller-coaster nightmare. Pretending any of this is halfway normal—'

I glared at him. 'I don't give a fuck about normal. And I'm not pretending. I can't turn my love on and off like a tap. Yes, I hate what she's doing, how she makes me feel. And I'm angry with her but I'm the adult here. I'm not the traumatised child.'

'She's brought it all with her, we know that. It's on all those web-sites you're so fond of, isn't it? That dysfunction, she's recreating it with us. Forcing us to dance to her tune.'

'I couldn't stop loving her, looking after her. It's unconditional. I couldn't stop any more than I could stop loving you.'

226

'Sometimes you have to let people go – if you really love them.'
He stared at me.

Was he talking about Chloë or himself?

'What if she'd be better in care? What if that's what she wants?'
he said.

'No,' I said. 'She's never said that.'

'You won't even think about it? Not for five minutes?'

'I couldn't bear it, Mac.' I swallowed, determined not to cry.

'It shouldn't be about you, though,' he said.

'She's acting out. That doesn't mean I react by taking away the
only things I can give her.'

He drew his hand over his face.

'We're just going round in circles,' I said. 'Maybe *we* need to talk
to someone, you and me together.'

'I think it's too late for that,' he said.

Oh, Christ.

'She might manage with help from Gregory and the CBT, and
if we hang in there . . .' I knew I was pleading, begging. 'She's so
unhappy.'

He levelled his gaze at me, steady, despairing. 'Aren't we all? I
won't be a martyr any more,' he said.

'She can't help it,' I said.

'Then what fucking hope is there?'

Silence hung between us, thick and heavy.

He gave a shake of his head, paced away from me. 'I'm done,
Lydia. When we leave here, I'll find a place on my own.'

'No! Please.'

'I can't be with her. I cannot.' He exhaled loudly. 'Ah, what a
fucking mess. So what now? We report her missing?'

'Give it till dark,' I said.

He walked away.

'Where are you going?'

'To look for her.' He slammed the door, making me jump. Dust
motes rose, spiralled in the beams of sun coming through the windows.

227

The honey gleamed, dripping down shelves of books, pooling on the floor around the fragments of silver glass, its sweet smell cloying in the room.

He was back within the hour, and stayed just long enough to drop Chloë off and tell me not to make him any tea.

The argument, the ultimatum, an ocean between us.

I spoke to Chloë before we ate. Her eyes were bloodshot but dry. I assumed it was from the cannabis. Her face stony.

'Chloë, I'm sorry I shouted. I was frightened and cross and upset. I love you but I'm worried. All I want, all I ever want, is for you to be happy.'

She angled her head away, bobbing slightly, one of her feet twitching, the picture of long-suffering at the tedium.

I was sick of it. That much was true. Mac was the love of my life and the thought of losing him ripped me in two. But if I chose to keep him and sacrificed Chloë I would never forgive myself. As long as I drew breath and my heart pushed blood around my body I would do all I could to care for my girl.

Chapter Forty-one

With the holidays over, Chloë started back at the stables. I'd feared she'd refuse to go, using that as a new area to battle over, but I was wrong.

I was driving back from there, following a tractor through the fog, relieved to be free of her for a few hours, when my phone rang. I let it go to voicemail and checked it when I got into the house. Bel.

'Hello?' I said, when she answered my return call.

'Hi. You still asleep?' she said.

'Very funny. Been up for hours. So?'

'We're coming to visit.'

'Well, I'm not sure that's—'

'No objections,' she said. 'Dying to see the place and Freya will love all the second-hand shops. It's months since I've seen you.'

'Chloë's not great,' I said.

'What's new?' Bel said. 'And you could do with some company, couldn't you, with everything else?' Bel knew about Mac's decision to leave but we hadn't had a chance to talk about it much.

'It's just that—'

'I won't take no for an answer,' Bel said.

'When are you thinking of coming?'

'Today. Be there about five.'

'Mac's away tomorrow, stag night. His brother's getting married again. And we've only got an airbed so—'

'Fine. We'll bring duvets and pillows. Booze. Send a text if you need anything else fetching. See you later.'

I felt like I'd been ambushed. I considered calling her back and insisting she postpone. But perhaps she was right and the visit would do me good. It would be lovely to see her again, to have the chance to talk frankly about everything once the kids were in bed.

Mac came out of the bathroom.

'Bel and Freya are coming for the weekend. Just been informed.'

'I'm at Luke's stag.'

'I know. At least you'll get to see them tonight. Where's the airbed?' If they didn't want to share a room, I thought, Freya could always sleep on the sofa.

'In the shed.'

'Great.'

'Right, I'm off.'

Since his decision to leave me I'd felt such sadness. Between us there was a sense of something drawing to a close. At the same time I couldn't actually imagine it happening. It was unreal. I hadn't tried to change his mind. We'd barely talked more about it. But how would it work? Would he and I still have a relationship of any sort? Would this end in divorce? Would he still see Chloë? What would we say to her? The questions burrowed in my mind as I made things ready for our visitors.

The bedroom next to ours had become a place where we dumped stuff, shoes and boots, shopping bags and suitcases, cushions from the garden chairs. Now I moved all that into the spare room on the other side at the back, which was home to tools and packing cases and drying racks.

I brought the airbed in from the shed, brushing off cobwebs, then unrolled it and unplugged the valve to let it self-inflate. A stool would serve as a bedside table, or alternatively as somewhere to put clothes. There were no blinds over the window but Bel and Freya would just have to put up with the morning light. It looked very stark, but at such short notice I didn't have a chance to make it more homely.

I bought extra fruit juice, beer and wine, bread and cheese, fresh vegetables, ice cream and yoghurt on my way to collect Chloë. The fog persisted, swathing the coast and pegging the temperature at eleven degrees, colder than the rest of the country. Down in the south-east they'd had a heatwave. Here it was cold enough to light the log burner.

Chloë's mood hadn't improved with the ride. The set of her shoulders, the angle of her head as she approached the car spoke volumes. When she climbed in, her animosity vibrated like the hum of an electric fence. Stay away.

She was clicking her lighter, over and over again, staring ahead as I drove us home.

When she'd had a cigarette and some tomato soup I told her about our guests.

She darted a look of dismay at me.

'If you want you could—'

'Don't tell me what to do,' she yelled, shoving herself away from the table. I had been going to say she could help bake biscuits. A jolt of resentment shook me. *Fuck!* I took a steadying breath, then another. I got out the scales and the ingredients I needed.

Mac was packing for his stag do, when I heard Bel's car approach and went out to meet them.

'You find it OK?' I said to Bel, as she got out.

'Missed the turning,' she said.

'Twice,' Freya said. She was taller than I was now. She had a trilby on, a wool coat and ankle boots. All grown-up.

'I could have done without the *Hound of the Baskervilles* special effects,' Bel said, waving her arm at the fog.

'Wrong moors,' I said. 'Come in. Give me something to carry.'

Inside they shed bags and coats and I admired Freya's style. She wore a stripy Breton jumper, ripped navy leggings and a gold brocade waistcoat with a gold and blue scarf.

'Hipster,' Bel said.

'I like it,' I said.

'All second-hand, apart from my hat,' Freya said. 'Recycling.'

'Good for you,' I said. 'I'll make drinks. Your room's that one at the front.'

'This is amazing.' Bel spun round. 'I love the beams. Loo?'

I pointed.

We settled round the kitchen table. Mac made coffee and answered all Bel's questions about the conversion.

I set some biscuits aside for Chloë, and Freya and I made short work of the rest.

Freya was quizzing Mac about whether we'd used sustainable materials for the refurbishment while Bel rolled her eyes at me. Chloë appeared to say hello without prompting, then went out to smoke.

'Do you want juice?' I asked her, when she came in. 'There's cookies.'

She nodded. Sitting next to Freya, she looked like a child. She'd only just started her periods and had no bust to speak of.

'I thought we could go out to eat,' Bel announced. 'My treat. One of your famous fish-and-chip restaurants.'

Chloë blinked, pressed her knuckles against the table. Tiny gestures. I doubted Bel could sense the shift in the atmosphere.

'We're as good getting take-out,' I said. Chloë would be struggling with having visitors but taking her out to eat, to be in an unpredictable situation, an unfamiliar public environment, would add to her anxiety.

'I'm veggie,' Freya said.

'That's OK,' I said.

'No, they use beef fat.' She curled her lip.

'Not all of them. But I'll check.' I'd soon found the website for Robertsons. 'Here we go. They use vegetable oil and you can have a mushy pea fritter or spring rolls and chips. Have a look. And when it says medium portion it actually means enormous. What do you want, Chloë?'

'Just chips.'

Mac phoned the order in and set off soon after to fetch it.

Chloë stood. I expected her to shrink off back to her room, but Freya brought up some website on her phone, animals in ridiculous situations, and Chloë leaned in, laughing, a short single 'hah' at each new clip.

'Haven't you seen it before?' Freya said.

'No.'

'It's a whole channel. This one here, with monkeys, I love it. It's *sooo* random.'

'I'll get my tablet,' Chloë said.

I was lightheaded. That engagement, to hear her laugh, it was so precious. The girls had never clicked before but now it was like they were just two teenage mates chilling out.

I was so glad they'd come.

Mac arrived back with the meal and we shared it out.

'Oh!' Bel jumped up, went to their room and returned with a magnum bottle of spirits. 'Vodka. New distillery in Leeds.'

'Not sure it goes with fish and chips,' I said.

'You are so pedestrian. What do you think all those Russian sailors lived on? It's a match made in Heaven.'

'I'll wait.' I smiled. 'I still remember my hangover from York.'

Mac joined her in a glass and proclaimed it was all right if you'd no whiskey in the house and had to make do.

'Ingrate,' Bel said.

Chloë looked puzzled. 'It means an ungrateful person,' I said.

After we'd eaten, the girls went to Chloë's room, and the three of us sat round the wood burner in the living room and chatted over drinks. Mac was more relaxed than I'd seen him for ages, entertaining Bel with a story about a hellish journey back from Ireland. Was this how he was down the pub? And which was more real? The happy man with a tale to tell or the frustrated one, exhausted and ill-tempered, whose life was so far from what he wanted it to be? The man who was leaving his family.

Mac wanted to get to bed early – the stag party was due at a whiskey tasting at ten in the morning in Edinburgh – and Freya had said she'd rather sleep on the couch so we all turned in when he did. I'd not had a chance to talk to Bel on my own but tomorrow night we would.

I opened our bedroom windows before getting into bed. It was still hazy out there, a damp wool smell in the air.

233

I kissed Mac goodnight and asked him to wake me before he left.

I imagined life without him, his side of the bed empty. In the quiet I heard the call of an owl out hunting, tracking its prey, alert to every snick and rustle in the undergrowth.

When I came through for breakfast Freya and Bel were mid-argument.

'You said we could go shopping.' Freya put down her spoon and leaned forward.

'I said you could go,' Bel snapped. 'Why would I want to traipse around a load of junk shops?'

'I can't go on my own.'

Should I offer to take her? I allowed myself a brief fantasy, Freya and I rummaging through clothes, me offering encouragement, waiting for her to try pieces on. Stopping for hot chocolate and flapjacks. All the things I never did with Chloë.

'Oh, for fuck's sake. Take Chloë,' Bel said.

'Mom! No!'

'I don't think it's Chloë's scene,' I said. 'She hates shopping.'

'And everything else,' Freya said.

My cheeks burned. 'Freya?' I'd thought they were getting on so well.

'Sorry. But she's . . . well, she's weird . . . Sorry.'

'And you're a nasty little bully,' Bel said.

'Wonder where I got that from,' Freya said, her voice wobbling.

I felt deeply uncomfortable.

Bel banged the table. 'Get ready, then,' she said. 'We'll go now if it'll shut you up.'

Freya slid her chair back noisily and went off to the bedroom.

'Hormones!' Bel said.

'Yours or hers?'

'Hah! Do you want to come with?'

'What – and referee? No, thanks. You go. It is a lovely place,' I said. 'We could all go somewhere this afternoon. It's not beach

234

weather but we could do some sightseeing.' Outside, the grey sea fret still smothered the landscape.

'OK.'

While they were out I put the radio on and cooked some vegetarian dishes for our evening meal: spicy chickpeas and spinach, curried dhal and onion bhajis. The smells of cumin and garlic, fenugreek and fresh coriander filled the kitchen in spite of the work of the extractor hood.

Chloë hadn't surfaced by midday and I knocked and told her it was time to get up.

'What for?' she said.

I opened the door. Clothes littered the carpet. There was an overripe fruity smell, which I struggled to place until I saw a wine bottle on its side by her chair, and glasses on the drawers.

'Who said you could drink wine?'

Stupid question. She raised herself up on her elbows, face sullen.

'Please don't take wine or beer or anything else without asking. That's stealing. You know that.'

She wasn't looking at me. Her hair was tangled, almost knotted at one side.

'And I want you to clear all this up.'

I didn't wait for a response knowing there might not be one.

Going back through to the living room my heart jumped at a loud smashing sound. The sound a glass bottle would make if you threw it against a stone wall.

Leave it, I thought. But then I imagined her standing, rocking on the shards of green, feet bleeding. Little mermaid.

I wanted to throttle her.

Chapter Forty-two

'Smells good,' Bel said, coming in with Freya.

'Success?' I asked.

'I got two blouses and an amazing suede jacket,' Freya said.

'I thought you were vegetarian,' Chloë said.

'I'm not gonna eat it. Duh!' Freya said.

On alert, I was ready to get Chloë out of the room, if needed, but she just gave a laugh, cold and curt.

'*Ghostbusters* is on,' Freya said, 'the new one. We saw a poster.'

'God, I loved that film,' I said. 'The first one.'

'This is all women,' Freya said.

'Shock horror,' Bel said.

'Have you seen all the crap on social media?' Freya said. 'It's like they're going mental. All these men, they're like, *it's an abomination, women can't be funny, you ruined my childhood, dudes.* Knuckleheads! I'm going to try these on again.' She held up a canvas shopping bag.

Chloë went out to smoke.

'Chloë was drinking last night,' I said to Bel. 'Wine. I don't know if Freya was too.'

'Oh, probably.'

'You don't mind?'

'Have you forgotten what we were like?' Bel said.

'Not at fourteen.'

'Speak for yourself. Besides, anything that tarnishes the halo is fine by me, I tell you.'

I shook my head. 'Bel, we have to be careful with Chloë. It's—'

Bel's phone sounded. She read the text and pulled a face. 'Oh, God. I knew this would happen.'

'What?'

'Work. I've a big client based in Newcastle but he spends most of his time abroad. I've been trying to arrange a meet-up for weeks. It's small fry to him but for me it's a big deal. I could be looking at a whole portfolio of properties to add to my books. Anyway, he's back in the country and he wants me there this afternoon.'

'In Newcastle?'

'Yes. I can't say no.' She sighed. 'I'd better get moving.'

'But Freya . . .'

'She'll be fine. Take them to the movies?' She was rummaging in her shoulder bag, checking things.

'We'll save you some tea.'

'I'll have to stay over. These meetings, you're expected to social-ise. Takes hours. And I don't want to be driving back in the dark.'

She went to tell Freya, and to fetch her overnight bag. And was back almost straight away. 'At least Freya can have the bed tonight.'

Bel was almost running. *Her bag was packed and ready.*

My mouth went dry. I felt a shiver, then a flush of heat. She was lying to me. 'Bel?'

'I'll be back for lunch, maybe sooner. Make an early start.'

'It's not work, is it?' I said. 'It's Barnaby.'

'Don't be daft.'

All of this, the visit, the jollying me along, so she could dump Freya and go to shag her secret lover. Had she run out of people in Leeds to leave Freya with? Had there been some uncertainty whether Barnaby could make it so she'd engineered this trip and waited for his signal?

'Show me your phone.'

'Oh, for fuck's sake, Lydia.'

'It's not fair. You lied to me.'

She made a 'gah' sound, lifted her bag and headed for the door.

'You selfish bitch,' I said. My tongue felt fat in my mouth, my ears were buzzing, and my head was full of wasps, angry, stinging.

237

'That's all I am, is it?' I followed her. 'A bloody babysitter? A cover story?'

Bel opened the front door and went out, raising a key fob and triggering the lock release on her car. The lights flashed, just visible through the fog.

'All so you can go shag your toy-boy? Have you ever thought about his poor bloody wife?'

She didn't answer.

'No, of course not. You never think about anybody but yourself, do you?'

'Don't be so bloody melodramatic.'

I thought she'd defend herself, maybe even apologise, try mollifying me, admit that she was out of order and ask for my understanding, but she just got into the car, switched on the headlamps and reversed out of the yard. I was biting my cheek, the back of my eyes burning.

There were footsteps. Chloë coming back in. How much had she heard?

Bel had betrayed me. The anger rose like a storm inside me, making me tremble. Just like when she had got pregnant and I'd been so hurt.

She'd gone too far this time. Yes, people had affairs, lots of people. Marriages ended or didn't, new ones started. It wasn't her seeing the man that rankled, it was her lying to me, using me, pretending their visit was anything other than a ruse for her to get laid.

As I went inside, Freya said, 'What do you think?' She'd put on her new suede jacket, caramel-coloured, fringed, and with it some black skinny jeans and a broderie-anglaise blouse. She tipped her hat back, face open and smiling.

'Great.' I cleared my throat. 'It all looks lovely. You look lovely.' I felt a stab of pity for her. At least I could walk away from my friendship with Bel. And I would. Once and for all. But Freya was stuck with Bel. Bel would always be her mother.

238

Chapter Forty-three

There were only two tickets left for the evening screening of *Ghostbusters*. I almost let the idea go then. Chloë's mood was so very volatile, her behaviour unpredictable. Freya had seen her rages when they were younger and understood, I think, that she was unable to control her emotions at times, but it wouldn't be fair to expect Freya to have to deal with it.

But Freya was so crestfallen when I told them about the tickets that I reconsidered. Chloë loved the cinema: we'd never had to leave early, unlike other social occasions, because interaction with other people was minimal. And the girls would only be unaccompanied for two and a half hours while they were absorbed in the film.

'You two could go,' I said. 'I can drop you off and pick you up. Chloë?'

'OK,' she said.

'Yes!' said Freya.

Patches of fog obscured the road, forcing me to drive slowly, and when we began the descent into town it thickened, muffling the whole valley. The coloured lights that zigzagged over the main streets were fuzzy blobs of red and blue and green coming into and out of view.

It was just dark as I pulled in and let them out on North Terrace opposite the cinema. I could see a queue at the entrance. Chloë had a backpack with her.

'You really need that?' I said.

'Yes,' she said.

'Right, I'll be back at ten. Have fun.'

I watched them cross the road. A gap between them, no linking

239

arms or nudging shoulders, Freya with her trilby on, and Chloë looking like her little sister, her bright hair catching the light from the streetlamps.

At home I put the leftovers in the fridge and cleared up the kitchen.

I tried watching television but couldn't concentrate, my thoughts distracted by Bel. I wished Mac were here to talk to about it. He wouldn't be back till Monday, though.

I imagined Bel swanning back in, blasé and lying through her teeth. Of course I wouldn't do anything to undermine her in front of Freya and she probably knew that. No doubt she would engineer it so that we had no time alone together before they set off back to Leeds. I'd been such a fool thinking she was coming to support me, have a heart-to-heart, help me deal with the prospect of my marriage falling apart.

Maybe I'd have to write her an email or a message. Or a letter. A good old-fashioned letter. Something she couldn't just delete with the click of a mouse or a swipe of her finger. Dear Bel. A dear-John letter. Postmarked Whitby. The prospect saddened me. After all these years. Thirty – I worked it out. After everything we'd shared together. They say that there's an imbalance in every marriage, that one party loves more, but perhaps that's true of friendship as well. That ours meant less to Bel than it did to me. That she loved me less. That I loved her more.

The fog was lifting as I drove back down into town. I caught glimpses of the church and the abbey across the valley, and a full moon, large and creamy, rising above. A harvest moon: there'd been a feature in the paper about it, named because its light allowed farmers to work on into the night gathering their crops. It would make a striking photograph, the last rags of mist on the hillside, the large white disc, the bones of the abbey, like a whale.

I parked and waited.

The streets emptied. I turned the radio on and caught the news, headlines about flash-flooding and disruption in the southern counties, ongoing reactions to nuclear testing in North Korea. I turned it off again. Then I became impatient.

I rang Chloë, but there was no answer. She'd perhaps have switched it to silent for the film but I'd have expected her to turn it back on by now.

I left a message.

Were they still inside? Gone for a milkshake or something? Though I wasn't sure the café would be open at this time.

Locking the car, I crossed the road and went into the foyer.

'We're closed,' the woman said, the only person in the lobby.

'I'm collecting someone. My daughter and her friend. They might be in the loos?'

'Have a look if you like.'

No one there.

Walking down to the whalebone arch, where steps switch back and forth down towards the beach road, I could see there were still people out and about on the piers, and along Marine Parade. The tide was up, the waters slapping at the harbour walls. The lighthouses flashed, one red, one green, marking the harbour entrance.

I couldn't see Chloë or Freya.

Beginning to feel anxious, my breathing uneven, I rang Chloë again, swearing when it cut out.

And I didn't have Freya's number.

I tried Bel. The phone rang out, then went to voicemail. I could imagine her looking at the display and deciding not to answer, returning her attention to Barnaby, who was solicitously refilling her champagne glass. Or in bed, oblivious. Losing herself in the sex. Her phone discarded along with her clothes.

A fog horn sounded out to sea, mournful.

At least they were together, Freya and Chloë. If it was Chloë on her own I'd be more worried, already thinking about reporting her missing to the police.

A pair of herring gulls landed a few yards from me, searching for scraps. All along the harbourside there were signs advising against feeding the seagulls. The creatures raided bins and had been known to dive at unlucky individuals, sometimes causing injuries. The birds' shit splattered everything in town.

Where were the girls?

Could they have misunderstood our arrangement?

I rang Chloë a third time. A wave of relief washed through me when I heard her speak. 'Mum?'

'Where are you?'

Silence.

'Chloë? Where are you?'

'In the graveyard.'

'Jesus! You were supposed to wait at the Pavilion. Come down the steps now. I'll drive round to the Co-op car park. Chloë?'

There was a shudder of breath. My blood ran cold.

'Chloë?'

'I didn't—' She broke off. There was such anguish in her voice.

'Is Freya there?' I said. 'Let me talk to Freya.'

The phone went dead.

And I ran.

Chapter Forty-four

Something was terribly wrong. Running, I didn't think, couldn't think, what might have happened. Whenever my mind inched towards possibilities it veered away, like approaching a force field, a black hole, primed and ready to shock me into oblivion.

My thighs chafed, my breasts hurt as I raced over the swing bridge and into Church Street. I kept bumping into people who were moving between the bars and eateries. The cobbles were slippery, treacherous underfoot.

There was a stab of pain in my heart. Sharp as glass. Forcing me to stop, sipping breaths, one hand on the wall of a shop-front for balance.

A group of young people stared at me as they passed. Thinking me mad or drunk, I guess.

The pain eased a little, an icicle melting, and I carried on, half running until I reached the bottom of the old steps. High above hung the moon with its senseless smile.

I froze. Dread at the ascent crawled up my back and through my blood, thick as tar.

Chloë.

I began to climb, the metal rail was cold to touch, slick with dew, the broad stone steps gleaming in the moonlight. They were worn smooth, concave in places, from all the centuries of use. All the parishioners climbing to demonstrate their faith, the burial parties who would carry the corpse of the departed up to the top for the funeral.

I couldn't stop shaking. Every few steps, I paused for a moment, panting, my heart a wild animal, cornered and frantic.

On I went, sweat prickling under my arms, on my scalp. My breath ragged.

The bitter tang of grass was in the air and wood smoke from someone's stove. The steps wound up the hill. Soon I could see St Anne's church listing towards me. And all around it the ranks of gravestones stood sentinel, highlighted by the silver of the moon.

She was there. By the iron gates, sitting on the step.

Just Chloë.

I reached her, ignoring the chittering fear in the back of my head, terror at what I would see if I turned to face the drop behind me matched by the fear of seeing her alone.

'Chloë?'

She looked catatonic. Unseeing.

'Chloë? Where's Freya?' I touched her, she didn't even flinch as I crouched and held her by the shoulders. That wasn't right. That lack of reaction. I could smell alcohol on her.

'Chloë? Where's Freya?'

Nothing.

'Chloë?'

I shook her. 'Where's Freya?'

She finally looked at me with dead eyes. 'She's gone.'

'What do you mean "gone"?' Hysteria edged my voice. 'Gone where?'

Chloë breathed out. A tired sigh. Tears sprang into her eyes and spilled down her cheeks.

'Chloë?'

She turned her head, looked to her right and nodded to the far corner where the graveyard met the cliff's edge. Where barbed wire and warning signs cautioned danger, and bunches of flowers in cellophane marked a place of sudden tragic deaths.

'She fell,' Chloë said.

Oh, my God. I pulled out my phone, hit 999.

'How did she fall?'

The fog horn howled again.

'Chloë, how did Freya fall?'

Chloë bowed her head to her knees, her hair luminous in the moonlight. I had no trouble making out the words.

'I . . . Mum . . . I pushed her.'

'Show me.' She sat still as stone.

'Show me. Show me where,' I screamed. Then I used all my energy to moderate my voice and repeated the question. 'Come and show me.'

She got stiffly to her feet. Sniffing.

We walked along the edge of the graveyard. It was muddy underfoot.

The operator answered and I said, 'There's been an accident, on the cliffs by the abbey. Someone's fallen.' I hung up.

The land rose up high towards the far corner. There was a broken gate and a narrow strip of clifftop hemmed in by wall and wire fencing. Little more than a passageway. At the far edge I could see a bottle, the vodka Bel had brought, and Chloë's backpack.

'That's where?' They'd have had to climb over the wall or the gate and avoid the barbed wire.

The pain came back in my heart and I was holding my breath.

I had to look. I had to see. I had to try to find Freya. I kicked the gate again and again, the wood splintering and snapping until I could get through. Holding onto the stone wall I edged along the little tract of land. I was shuddering, great waves. I'd never been so cold. I stopped when a sudden rush of nausea made me vomit, the bitter liquid spewing through my nose and mouth. Nearing the very edge I could no longer walk but had to get onto my hands and knees and crawl forward.

Where the cliff dropped away, the raw earth was exposed, falling down to the ink-black sea.

I could see nothing but the water, ruthless and unforgiving.

The police alerted the coastguard, the lifeboat was deployed, and Chloë and I were taken to the other side of the graveyard where an ambulance waited.

A police officer recorded our details and asked us to stay where we were, perched in the back of the ambulance.

Was Freya a good swimmer? I'd no idea. The fall itself . . . hypothermia . . . She had been close to the shore, near enough to swim to the rocks or the barriers of concrete boulders at the corner of the harbour. The moon would help show her the way.

A distant clattering sound grew louder and a helicopter came swinging over the headland, creating turbulence in the air above our heads, blowing our hair out of control.

The helicopter dipped and flew down over the water, cones of light beaming onto the sea.

I rang Mac. He didn't answer. He'd be in a bar somewhere, music on, the group shouting to be heard. Laughing and joking.

I texted him. *Ring me*.

Bel. What could I . . . how on earth . . . ?

'Lydia.' Someone was talking, a trim man with a neat moustache. He was wearing a suit.

'We're taking you and Chloë to the police station in Scarborough,' he said.

'Why?'

'We need to establish what happened. And whether a crime has been committed.' *A crime*. He said it so calmly, matter-of-fact, like he was talking about something insignificant.

'Please, can we wait till they find Freya? Please?'

'You have to come with me now,' he said.

'But if we're not here,' I said, 'her mum's away and—'

'As soon as there is any news we'll get word.'

'You need to understand. Chloë – she has a disorder, an attachment disorder, she was adopted—'

A blur of movement and Chloë was running up across the grass towards the coastal path along the edge of the plain. She ran like the wind.

'Chloë!' I yelled, darting after her.

Several of the police officers ran too, gaining quickly.

Someone grabbed her and put her on the ground; another bent to hold her. She was face down, bucking and twisting.

I was calling as I ran, 'Don't hurt her, please don't hurt her.'

She was screaming, a terrified high-pitched sound.

'Let her go. Leave her alone,' I shouted.

'She needs to calm down.'

I reached them. 'She will, but only when you stop touching her. Please take your hands off her.'

The officers looked to the detective who gave a nod.

They moved back, one rocking on his heels and standing swiftly, the other getting up slowly, coughing and spitting.

Chloë was still screaming. I sat on the grass. 'I'm here, Chloë. Come on now, I'm here. I'm going to stay with you. We'll go together.'

Chloë's spasms weakened. The screams quietened at last. She got up. Mud on her face and hands.

We walked back to where the detective had parked his car.

Behind us the giant moon illuminated the great skeleton of the abbey. A behemoth in stone.

And the helicopter bobbed and wheeled over the cold dark sea.

Chapter Forty-five

At the police station I felt numb as I answered all the questions they needed for their forms: Chloë's personal details, current living situation, any health issues. I told them about her emotional and behavioural difficulties, trying to make them understand how vulnerable she was. Chloë sat quietly beside me, apart from moments when I didn't know what to say. Then she spoke. Yes, she'd been drinking, yes, she'd taken drugs, cannabis.

Which meant they couldn't interview her until she was sober.

They removed her phone, her cigarettes and lighter, the money she had in her pockets, and asked her to change her clothes. They would provide clean ones and spare shoes.

'Why?' I said.

'They may offer evidence as to what happened,' DI Cartwright said.

'We know what happened. She said what happened.'

'And that evidence may help confirm Chloë's account.'

Chloë continued staring down, her face smeared with mud, fists balled tightly on her lap. I could see the old cigarette burns that spotted the back of her hands, pale discs of silvery skin.

'Chloë's only fourteen. We don't want her to have to stay here overnight if we can find her a bed somewhere more suitable,' DI Cartwright said.

'I can take her home,' I said. 'We can come back in the morning.'

'Chloë is considered a flight risk,' DI Cartwright said. 'She ran away earlier tonight.'

'She was frightened,' I said.

'Yes,' he agreed. 'But there's a risk she might do that again. We need to ensure Chloë's safety. It wouldn't be appropriate to send her home and expect you to keep her contained. It wouldn't be fair to Chloë either.'

I wanted to cry. I pressed my tongue to the roof of my mouth.

'Now we'll get that change of clothes arranged,' DI Cartwright said. 'Meanwhile do you want anything to eat or drink?'

'A cup of tea, please,' I said. 'Chloë?' She didn't answer me. 'Some Coke, as well,' I said.

It was another hour until DI Cartwright said he'd been able to find a bed for Chloë in a children's home and had arranged for an escort. 'We'll start back here tomorrow at eleven,' he said to me. 'If you can be here for then.'

'Yes.'

'Chloë? Do you want to say goodbye to your mum?'

I didn't want them to take her. I wanted to grab hold of her and run and hide her away.

'It'll be OK, Chloë,' I said. 'I'll see you in the morning. I love you.' I kissed the top of her head.

She shivered and moved away.

'See you in the morning,' I said.

When the two of them had gone, my eyes flooded with tears.

My beautiful girl.

My beautiful, broken girl.

DI Cartwright arranged for someone to drive me back to Whitby.

'Is there any news?' I asked him.

'Nothing yet.'

'Please, would you ring me, please, if there is? And Bel . . . tomorrow . . . If she doesn't answer her phone and she gets back and I'm not there . . .'

'We'll arrange for a family liaison officer to be at your house from nine o'clock. They'll inform her of the situation.'

'Chloë's never hurt anybody before,' I said. But that wasn't strictly true. 'What I mean is, whenever there's been a fight, incidents at school, it's been her trying to defend herself. People touching her, invading her space, it can be a trigger.'

249

'We'll talk to Chloë in the morning. If you do hear from Bel, this is my direct number.' He passed me a card.

Getting into my car, still parked opposite the cinema, it felt like days since I'd dropped off the girls.

Oh, Freya. The reality kept rocking me, hitting me like waves, knocking me down whenever I tried to stand. Freya with her jaunty hat and her keen opinions. Her glossy dark hair, that full face always expressive.

Why hadn't they gone into the film? How had they ended up in the graveyard? Had Chloë really pushed her? Why?

She couldn't have survived so long in the sea, I knew that.

The cottage was in darkness, the yard and the roof lit by moonlight. In the distance I thought I could hear the thrum of the helicopter.

Inside the house was still warm but the stove needed feeding.

It was two thirty in the morning.

My stomach was gnawing with anxiety, and hunger. I made toast and honey, tea. All I wanted was to wake up from the nightmare.

My phone rang, loud in the still of night.

'Mac?'

'I got your text,' he said.

'Come home.'

'What is it?' Alarm alive in his voice.

My breath caught. 'Freya . . . she . . . There's been . . .' *An accident?* I couldn't lie. '. . . Freya fell from the cliffs.'

'Oh, Christ.'

'They're still searching for her.'

'OK, I'll set off—'

'There's more.' I gulped back tears. 'Chloë was there. She said she pushed her.'

'No,' he said. 'Fuck, no. Oh, Lydia.'

'I know.'

'What the hell happened?'

'I don't know. They shouldn't even have been there. Chloë was

250

drinking, and smoking weed. She hasn't really explained. The police are interviewing her in the morning. They've found a place for her overnight.'

'Ah, Christ,' he said. Then, 'OK. Be there are soon as I can.'

The sun rose over the horizon, a big peach-coloured ball, climbing into a soft blue sky, washing the fields pink. I watched the light spread, I was dizzy with fatigue, crippled by backache, my eyes scratchy. I hadn't slept, hadn't tried, but I had lain on our bed for a couple of hours in the dark, my eyes closed, phone in hand. Terrified that Bel would call.

Now the sound of Mac's van on the lane sent me running outside.

He pulled up in the yard and jumped down. Came and held me.

I could smell his sweat and cigar smoke. Felt his chest heaving, heard him gasp a sob.

My phone rang and we broke apart.

'Lydia, it's DI Cartwright. I wanted to let you know that a body has been recovered from the water near the west cliffs.'

'A body,' I said, my mouth dry.

'Yes. A girl. I am sorry. We won't be releasing the name until next of kin have been able to confirm the identity.'

Bel. 'Yes. Thank you for . . . Thank you.'

Mac was gripping his brow bone, a thumb and finger pressing into each temple.

I took his arm to go inside and a flock of gulls passed overhead, yelping and shrieking, bound for the boats coming in with the night's catch.

Chapter Forty-six

Bel wasn't back by the time we left for Scarborough, though the police liaison officer had come. We gave her a spare key so she could let Bel in to collect their things.

We drove there separately, not knowing what the day would hold.

Mac and I were shown to a waiting room at the police station. Shortly after, a woman arrived and introduced herself as Naseema, the duty solicitor. She wore black jeans, a yellow jumper and a gold-coloured scarf over her hair. 'I've just been talking to Chloë. She's OK – ah—'

The door opened and Chloë came in then, escorted by a police officer.

'Hello,' I said to her, trying to smile.

'Dandelion.' Mac's voice was gruff.

Chloë blinked and looked away. She sat down, her heels raised, knees moving, dancing on the balls of her feet. She was terrified.

'I'm here to represent Chloë, to advise her,' Naseema said. 'I'll attend all interviews, and everything will be filmed and recorded. We need either you or your husband to be there as an appropriate adult.'

'Me,' I said. Mac nodded his agreement.

'You are there to make sure Chloë understands everything that's said. If you think she's confused or not clear about anything, you ask the detectives to repeat it or put it more simply. If she becomes distressed or tired we can request a break. I'll be representing her from a legal point of view, if you can focus on her welfare.'

'Yes.'

'OK. Did you follow all that, Chloë?' Naseema said. Chloë nodded. 'I wanted to check, does Chloë have a social worker?'

'No.' I almost laughed. 'We've asked for help. Never got it. But she is having counselling, privately. She's being treated for an attachment disorder.'

'Is she on any medication for that?'

'No.'

What if she won't talk? I thought. What if she flies into a rage?

I expected we would be going to a small bare box of a room but it was more like a relaxed office space or a work lounge. Low easy chairs and a table. A video camera and a separate recording machine.

DI Cartwright unbuttoned his jacket and sat back in his chair, looking relaxed, calm and sympathetic. He invited Chloë to describe in her own words what had happened.

Chloë said, 'We were up on the cliffs and I pushed her and she fell.'

'You pushed Freya?'

'Yes.'

'Why did you push her?' he said.

Chloë didn't answer. She had her left hand on her right forearm, pinching the skin there.

DI Cartwright smoothed his moustache with finger and thumb, and said, 'It's my job to build up a full picture of what happened to Freya, and I need your help to do that. Let's start with earlier on. Your mum dropped you both at the cinema. What happened next?'

'We went to the cliffs.'

'You didn't go into the Pavilion?'

'No,' she said.

'Why was that?'

Chloë shrugged.

'Whose idea was it to go to the cliffs?' he said.

'I didn't want to see the film. She could go if she wanted.'

'Freya could go on her own. And were you planning to do something else instead?'

'Just hang out,' she said.

'With anyone?'

'Don't know,' she said.

253

'Did you meet anyone that evening?'

'Yeah.'

I was startled.

'Can you tell me about that?' DI Cartwright said.

'Don't know.'

'Who was it?' DI Cartwright said.

'Don't know his name.'

'Is he your friend?'

'No.'

'Why were you meeting him?'

'To get some weed.' An edge in her voice. Defiant.

I closed my eyes for a moment.

In dribs and drabs Chloë's story came out. Bare and perfunctory at first, a sketch. Then the detective elicited elaboration and went over it again. And as Chloë coloured it in, I could see it all in my head, like a film.

Freya is furious when Chloë wants to go off and leave her to watch Ghostbusters *on her own. She threatens to tell me. Chloë doesn't care one way or the other. She walks off towards the steps that lead down from the whalebone arch and Freya, I guess not wanting to be on her own in an unfamiliar town, goes after her.*

Down on Pier Road, near the bandstand, Chloë meets the dealer and buys weed from him. He disappears.

Freya wants to know what Chloë's going to do and Chloë tells her she's going to chill out. 'Have a picnic,' she says, waving the little glassine bag. 'Up there.' She points across the harbour to the abbey, floodlit on the west cliff.

I don't know whether Freya goes along because she feels an obligation to stick with Chloë or because she decides to make the best of the situation.

The girls cross the bridge to the other side of town, take the lane and climb the steep steps. They walk through the graveyard and scale the wall to the small tract of land on the prow of the cliff's edge. Sitting there, they are out of sight. They can see the waves, the North Sea, churning below.

They smoke some weed and take turns drinking swigs of vodka from the bottle Chloë has stolen and carried hidden in her back-pack.

The skunk is strong and after a while Freya gets very giddy. Then she feels sick. She stands up. She wants to go home. She wants Chloë to ring me so I can go and fetch them.

Chloë refuses.

Freya asks her again. 'Don't be a cow.'

Chloë ignores her.

Freya lunges for the bottle, snatches it.

Chloë scrambles up. 'Give it back.'

'It's not even yours. You're a thief.'

'Give it back.'

'Or what? You'll have one of your tantrums? You're like a little kid. You're pathetic.' Freya is furious, all righteous indignation.

Chloë smiles.

'It's not funny. Ring her now.' Freya doesn't realise the wide smile is not a sign of humour. It's a warning.

'No,' Chloë says.

'I'll ring my mom, then. Tell her what you did.'

'I didn't force you. She won't care, anyway,' Chloë says.

'Just cos you're adopted, you expect everyone to feel sorry for you. I don't feel sorry for you. You're a little freak and you just make life horrible for everyone.'

'Fuck off.' Chloë is laughing. Her eyes are cold.

'You've ruined their lives, you know. Your dad wants to send you back into care.'

'Shut your fucking mouth.'

'Ask him. Your mom can't work because she's got to home-school you. They had to leave Leeds because you were crazy, out of control. If your mom won't put you back in care your dad's bailing. Dumping both of you. My mom told me.'

'She's a liar and you're talking shit,' Chloë says. She spits on the grass.

'Whatever.'

255

'You think she's at work, your "mom"? She's not at work,' Chloë says. 'She's off fucking her boyfriend.'

'You are so full of shit.'

'He's married. He's got kids. You're not supposed to know.'

'That's crap. You'll say anything—'

'It's true. I heard them shouting about it. That's why you came for the weekend, so she could dump you and go shag her toy-boy.'

My own words in Chloë's mouth.

'She can't stand you anyway. She probably wanted a break.'

'Shut up, you bitch.' Freya ditches the bottle. She grabs at Chloë, catches her shoulder. Chloë rears back. Freya moves in, seizes her again. 'You loser, you fucking weirdo.' Chloë feels the spit on her face. She wrestles to break free.

'You ruin everything, you just mess up. They don't love you – how could anyone love a fuck-up like you? They're stuck with you. They should never have said yes to you. They should have given you back soon as they realised what a retard they had. What a total psycho.'

Chloë doesn't speak. With both hands she shoves Freya hard in the chest.

Surprised, Freya lets go, staggering, grunting as she tries to keep her balance. She rights herself and springs at Chloë. 'You bitch.'

Chloë, rage boiling through her, shoves Freya again. Once. Twice. Freya goes flying, tumbling back, kicking out her heels searching for purchase, for solid ground. As she flails, arms flung out, the earth drops away. There is only air. Down she plunges, like a stone. Swift and silent.

Chloë kneels on the grass, breathless. Freya is gone. Far below there is nothing but the roar of the waves against the crumbling rock.

Why did I let them go to the cinema? The unease I had, the concern about Chloë's behaviour, why didn't I listen to my instincts? Act on them. *Christ!*

I felt sick, my stomach ached. I was holding myself together, calm on the surface, but it was as if my bones were brittle, my skin paper-thin, and only willpower kept me from breaking apart.

256

I went to the toilet and splashed my face with cold water. I met Naseema on my way back to the waiting room. 'Please, can you find out if Bel is back? If she knows about Freya?' I said.

'I'm not sure if that information can be—'

'Please. If you could just ask, please?'

'Let me try.'

Naseema came back to me very soon and said, 'She's been notified. She's here.'

A spike of fear ran the length of my spine. 'At the police station?'

Her face softened. 'In Scarborough. They'll want her to make a formal identification.'

I pressed my hand to my mouth, saliva clogging in my throat.

Oh, Bel. 'Could I—' *What? See her? Send her a message? Talk to her?* My thoughts collided, fractured. I shook my head.

During the lunch break Naseema explained to us what was likely to happen next. The police would present the evidence they had to the Crown Prosecution Service, who would decide if it was strong enough to press charges.

I didn't want to hear it, didn't want to know. It wasn't right. None of this was right.

'She didn't mean to hurt Freya,' I said. I glanced at Chloë. She didn't appear to be listening.

'Intent, or lack of it, will be part of any defence. They may not go ahead if they decide—'

'I want a cig.' Chloë stood up, legs jiggling.

'You can't smoke here,' Naseema said. 'We can see about getting you some Nicorette, or a patch. But I'll have to get a doctor to agree. It might take a while.'

Chloë fell back into her chair in disgust.

I wanted to yell at her then: *Freya's dead and you're having a tantrum about cigarettes!* It was a horrible aspect of her disorder, the inability to show remorse. But she wasn't a stone-cold killer, she was a damaged child, and I had to make them understand that.

* * *

DI Cartwright's colleague, DC Gidley, read back Chloë's statement out loud and Chloë and I were asked to stop her if there was anything we wanted to hear again or anything we thought was inaccurate.

Neither of us spoke. Chloë was fidgeting, flexing her arms and messing with her hair. Was she really listening? Did she understand the severity of what she'd done?

Chloë signed the statement and we were taken to the waiting room again.

I stepped into the corridor and rang Mac to tell him what was happening.

'And if they charge her?' he said.

'There'll be a trial. Naseema says it will be up to the magistrates' court, the youth court, what happens in the meantime.'

When I went back in, Naseema left to buy another parking ticket.

I sat down next to Chloë. 'It's so sad, all this. Freya didn't deserve what happened, no matter what she said. I can't believe she's—' I sighed. 'Chloë, those things Freya said, that wasn't right, she should never have said that to you. We love you, Chloë, we always have. We always will. You're our daughter. Nothing can ever change that.'

She rocked back in the chair, staring at the ceiling.

'I know it's hard for you to trust any of that but it is the truth. We did talk about whether we could manage, your dad and I, and that's why we moved. Because we'd do anything to make it work, keep you safe with us. We love you. I know you never set out to harm her. I know you're sorry and I am too, I'm so sorry.'

'Don't be,' she said.

'Chloë?'

She glanced at me and gave a half-smile, rocked in the seat again.

'I know you're scared.'

'I'm OK.'

She went to the water-cooler and messed with the tap. Her back to me. Shutting me out.

It was late afternoon when the detectives came back and we all assembled in the interview room again. The camera and recorder

258

were set running. Once a note had been made of who was present, DI Cartwright said, 'We've spoken to the CPS and it's been agreed that we may proceed to charge.'

I swallowed and braced my feet on the floor.

'Chloë, I'm now going to read the charge. Chloë Kelly-Ross, you are charged that on the seventeenth of September 2016, at Whitby, North Yorkshire, you did murder Freya Radcliffe contrary to common law. You do not have to say anything but it may harm your defence if you do not mention when questioned something which you later rely on in court. Anything you do say may be given in evidence. Do you understand the charge?'

'Murder? But it wasn't murder,' I said. 'It was an accident!'

DI Cartwright ignored me. He leaned forward and said, 'Chloë? Do you understand?'

'Yes,' she said.

'You'll be going to the magistrates' court in the morning and they will refer the case to the Crown Court. They'll also decide where you'll stay until then. What we call remanded. It may be into the care of the local authority.'

'They'll put her in care?' I said.

'Either care or youth custody. A young offenders' institution.'

'No, they can't—' I wanted to stop them. 'She couldn't—'

He signalled for me to stop talking. 'The escorts are here. If you want to say goodbye, you can take a minute in the next room,' he said.

''S OK. I'm ready now,' Chloë said.

DI Cartwright and Naseema exchanged a glance and I sensed the ripple of discomfort in the room at her indifference. I'd become resilient to it over the years but now it pierced me anew.

'I'll be there tomorrow,' I said, keeping a steady voice. 'Me and your dad. We'll see you in the morning. Love you.'

She put her hands into her pockets. Moved towards the door.

I watched her go. Holding myself rigid and resisting the temptation to run after her.

Chapter Forty-seven

Bel's car was at the house. A wave of guilt turned my insides to water. What could I say? What did she want? What would she do?

I steeled myself to go inside, only to find that Mac was there on his own. Apparently the police had driven Bel to Scarborough, leaving her car in our yard.

'How come Bel wasn't here last night, anyway?' Mac said.

Where did I start?

'Lydia?'

'Is there coffee?'

'Sure.'

I told him everything from the time Bel got the text about a supposed client in Newcastle to Chloë being charged with murdering Freya, and then I went back over everything compulsively until my voice was croaky and the moon had risen in a cloudless sky. 'You were right,' I said to Mac. 'We should never have moved. Now we've lost her. And Freya, dead.' I started crying. 'How could she be dead? How can this be happening?' I rubbed the tears from my cheeks. 'If I hadn't taken them, if Bel hadn't gone off . . . It felt wrong but I still—'

'I wasn't even around,' he said. 'I was rat-arsed, leaving you to it. And Freya telling her that, about me wanting her back in care, about me leaving—' His voice broke. 'Shit. How did Freya know? You told Bel that?'

'I tell her everything. But I don't expect her to tell anyone else.' I rocked forward and back. *Oh, Chloë.* 'It was just a moment,' I said. 'A second's loss of control. If Chloë had not been drinking, if she'd not been off her face, if she hadn't heard Bel and me arguing . . . Freya, she'd got this lovely jacket, one of the vintage shops. She was so pleased with it—' I broke off, remembering Freya, here in our house, modelling her bargains for approval. 'Oh, Mac. What has she done?'

The colour had gone from his face and he looked drawn. Exhausted, like me. 'What they say about adopted kids believing they're bad in some way, to be abandoned they must have done wrong, they're to blame. And now she's done something terrible. It's a confirmation for her.'

I thought about Debbie. Would she have to know what had happened?

'I feel dirty,' I said. 'I feel sad and scared and so guilty.' I put my head in my hands. 'I should have—'

He hushed me and moved to hug me from behind.

I dragged myself to the shower and afterwards we picked at leftovers. I ate the ice cream I'd bought and some fudge. Nothing tasted right. Nothing could fill the chasm of emptiness inside me.

Travelling to the magistrates' court the next morning I had a weak, shaky feeling as though I'd left my bed after a bout of flu.

Because it was the youth court it was a private hearing. I was expecting to see a panel of magistrates but a district judge was hearing the case on his own. Naseema explained this sometimes happened. The judge didn't wear a gown or a wig.

I had to stop myself crying out when Chloë was brought into court. I felt a tug of pity and a rush of love when I saw how tiny she looked, bruises on her cheek and chin where she'd been tackled to the ground. She sat with her head bowed and spoke only to confirm her name and address. The case was referred to the Crown Court in Leeds. She would appear there the following day. Meanwhile she would be sent back to the children's home.

They took her away straight after that. We couldn't see or talk to her. Nothing. It felt barbaric.

When we got home Bel's car had gone and so had Freya's case, the spare key pushed through our letterbox.

* * *

The next morning, as we waited in the Crown Court at Leeds, I saw a woman taking notes over to one side of the room; she didn't appear to be a member of staff.

'Who's that?' I asked Naseema. 'I thought it was private.'

'Reporter. It's a matter of public interest so the press will be covering it but they won't be allowed to identify Chloë because of her age.'

There had already been headlines in the papers, *Police treating death of 14-year-old girl in Whitby as suspicious.* And later, *Police charge 14-year-old girl over death of girl in Whitby.*

When Chloë was brought in I could see the bruises were darker now, blue smudges.

'And how do you plead to the charge of murder?' the judge asked her.

'Not guilty,' she said.

'I'm remanding you into the care of the local authority while you await trial,' the judge said. 'I need to warn you that if you breach any of the conditions set, make any attempt to abscond, or if your behaviour becomes unmanageable, you can be sent into custody. Do you understand?'

'Yes,' Chloë said.

'As a looked-after child, you will be allocated a social worker and they will be involved in helping you from this point on.'

She was back in care. If I'd listened to Mac the year before, if we'd asked for her to be taken into care then, if I'd just admitted we couldn't cope any more, that life with Chloë was intolerable, that we could no longer be responsible for her, that the adoption had broken down, then Freya would be alive and Chloë would be free.

Again Chloë was taken away, without any chance for us to meet with her.

I cleared my throat, asked Naseema, 'What do you think will happen?'

'I've learned not to predict in this business,' she said.

'But you must know what's most likely,' Mac said.

'It's most likely that this will come to trial. I'd be very

surprised if she was found guilty of murder but manslaughter is a possibility.'

'And would that mean prison?' I said.

'Again it's hard to second-guess. Manslaughter can range from a suspended sentence or community service to a life sentence. It would be up to the judge. She's very young, it's a first offence, and those factors will be taken into account along with social-work reports, psychiatric reports. We'd do everything we can to make sure that whatever happens to Chloë is proportionate and that all factors are taken into account.'

I thought of Gregory. I'd cancelled Chloë's appointments but not spoken to him yet about what was going on. He could explain Chloë's behaviour, how her condition meant she sometimes couldn't control what she did.

'It could be up to six months before trial. As soon as we have some dates through we'll let you know,' Naseema said.

She must do this every day, I thought. Deal with ruptures in people's lives, in moments of no return, helping people whose world had stopped turning.

That evening Colin rang.

'Lydia, I just heard. Oh, God.'

'You heard from Bel?'

'Yeah. Oh, God.'

'How is she?' I said.

'You can imagine.'

'Yeah. It's a fucking nightmare, Colin. Freya . . . I just—'

'How's Chloë?'

'She's been taken into care, until the trial.'

'What happened? If you can talk . . .'

'It's fine,' I said.

'Only Bel didn't say much.'

'They were up on the cliffs, drinking, smoking weed. There was an argument. They both said some really nasty things and it got physical. Chloë lashed out. She never meant to—' I broke off.

263

'Oh, Lydia, I'm so sorry. What can I do? I know – stupid question.'

'Look after her,' I said. 'Bel – look after her.'

'I'll try. You still in Whitby?'

'For now. The funeral?' I said.

'Next Friday but I don't think that—'

'No, of course. Of course not. I just wondered.'

'I'll give you a ring. Later. After,' he said.

'Yes. Thanks.'

I put my phone down and went to the windows, gazed out at the night, fully dark with stars glittering brightly. I thought of Freya in some funeral parlour, Bel choosing coffins and flowers. It was unreal. Horribly unreal. Sorrow lapped at me and I let it come, my vision blurring, obscuring all the stars in the sky.

Chapter Forty-eight

The children's home was in Darlington. We went to visit her every day. I ached to see her but dreaded the reality of those visits. Sometimes Chloë would engage a little, playing Connect 4 or Jenga. At others she ignored us and wanted to go back to her room or the lounge.

Towards the end of her first week she started ranting at us as soon as we arrived, shouting that someone had stolen her cigarettes. A warning from one of the staff who heard the commotion led to a full-blown meltdown with Chloë kicking at furniture and banging her head on the wall and we were asked to leave while she was restrained.

To see her flailing and screaming and the staff, all so much bigger than her, surrounding her, tore my heart in two.

The next day we met Chloë's social worker there, before seeing Chloë. She referred to Chloë's challenging behaviour but said the staff were very experienced and were dealing with it. 'One advantage of her being a looked-after child is that she's a priority for accessing specialised therapeutic services via CAMHS. Although I'll be honest, cuts have affected availability of provision.'

Mac gave a hollow laugh and I shook my head.

She gave me a questioning look.

'We've been trying for years. Asking for help. For specialised therapy, for respite. It's come to this. She has to be back in care to get any—' I couldn't go on.

'I'm afraid it's not uncommon.' She pulled a rueful face.

Anger exploded through me. 'Not uncommon? It's a fucking disgrace, that's what it is. All those families, struggling with . . . We

265

adopt and that's it, everyone washes their hands, leaves us to it. Our daughter has been traumatised, she is damaged, she is fucked-up beyond belief. We're just expected to get on with it. Sink or swim. If that help had been there from the start then maybe our daughter wouldn't be charged with murder and Freya, my friend's little girl, would still be alive.' I was trembling as I finished, my face burning hot.

'I know,' she said. 'I agree with you. I wish it were different.'

That evening as we went into the cottage, I said to Mac, 'It's awful, but . . . just knowing it's not our job to be responsible for her day and night, that it's not up to us any more, there's this sense of relief. Then I feel so guilty, so horrible, thinking that.'

'But it's true,' he said, moving to feed the stove. 'I feel exactly the same.'

'You knew—' I felt like crying.

'What?'

'That it was too late, that we weren't coping, and I wouldn't listen and I dragged us here and now . . .'

'Hey.' He came over to me, wiping the wood dust off his hands. He cupped my face and locked his eyes on mine. 'I didn't know anything. I was just freaking out with it all. And I came here because I thought it might help. We tried. It's not our fault, Lydia.'

Isn't it? So why did I feel so horribly guilty? Tainted and dirty and ashamed, the blame infecting every part of me, like a virus.

I came close to phoning Bel so many times. To say I'm sorry, to say I miss you, to beg forgiveness for Chloë. Would Bel know what had been said that night? And why Chloë had struck out? Would the police have told her?

I stared at my last text to her, imagining what it must have been like when she arrived back at the cottage to find a police officer. Did she feel guilty like I did?

I thought I might write: *Dear Bel . . .* The words were ashes in my mouth . . . *Thinking of you . . . so sorry for your loss . . .* All

266

was overshadowed by the elephant in the room. *My daughter killed yours.*

In the end I focused on Freya:

Bel, I am so desperately sorry. It's hard to know what to write. Freya was such a wonderful girl, so bright, so talented and full of energy, passionate about making the world a better place. Mac and I used to love our Sundays with her when she was little. She was a joy to be with.

My heart is breaking for you. For you and your beautiful girl. I am so very, very sorry. Her future should never have been taken from her like this. You have been a part of my life for so long, Freya too. I love you.

Lydia

She can tear it up, I thought, if it's not welcome. Burn it. Or put it in the bin unopened. She'd know my handwriting just as I know hers.

'Fancy a walk?' Mac said. It was a day when we weren't making the trip to Darlington. 'I'll go crazy if I just sit here any longer.'

'Walk where?'

He shrugged. 'The beach?'

'No. Not town.' I felt cold.

'You can't blame the place.'

Why not? How could I see the abbey, the graveyard, the towering west cliff with anything but dread in my heart? I couldn't avoid town indefinitely but it was too raw, too soon.

'The moors. I'd rather go there,' I said.

'OK.'

The North York moors are often bleak, especially in winter, but this time of year, in clear weather, the hillsides were bright, thick with purple heather, green moss and sedges.

The wind was fierce and I tucked my hair up into my woolly hat. Now and then grouse scolded and chucked in the heather.

267

We passed other walkers, many with dogs, some people riding mountain bikes, and even someone on horseback. I'd rung Barbara about Chloë, the coward's way, saying she was having problems at the moment and wouldn't be coming riding any more. Barbara had thanked me, and wished us well. Had she any idea? Did she figure out that Chloë leaving coincided with the death of another fourteen-year-old in the town?

A skylark sang high out of sight, a joyous sound that made my heart tighten.

A memory unrolled, something I'd not thought of in years. My parents used to take us walking in the Yorkshire Dales in summer – it wasn't far to drive. We'd pack a picnic and share it sitting at the top of whatever ridge we'd ascended. Peeling hard-boiled eggs to eat with bread rolls and ripe tomatoes from my gran's greenhouse. That particular day, I was about nine and Steven five, my dad had got the flask out and dropped it as he was passing it to my mum. There was the telltale sound as the inner lining smashed.

My dad swore but my mum laughed. She stood up and began to sing 'The Girl From Ipanema' in a mock Spanish accent, moving the flask like a cocktail shaker. She was so funny I choked on my egg and had to spit it out. How I missed her now. The grief came back sharp as glass. If only I could see her, talk to her, feel her love and comfort.

But then again, it was best she'd never know what Chloë had done.

I'd rung Steven and he'd been so shocked. 'God, I'm so sorry,' he kept saying, over and over again. Mac's family had been the same. What else could they say?

'Hawk,' Mac said, pointing across the valley. I saw the bird riding the thermal. Looked across the wide gorge, worn away not by glaciers but by the seep and weep of water.

We stopped to read a plaque: there were barrows here, burial mounds from the Bronze Age.

People who'd lived and died here thousands of years ago.

I pictured Freya, pale and still, her dark hair wet from the sea, eyes unseeing. Her funeral tomorrow. Bel would have made all the

268

arrangements. Would she be buried or cremated? It would be on the news, some reference to it. The death of one girl at the hands of another so unusual, so rare and shocking, that it commanded public attention.

I'd be there if I could, shouldering that burden with Bel, taking part of the blame too. But I was a pariah.

We walked on and a sudden movement caught my eye. A brown daub, dot of white. A rabbit. Black pellets scattered along the edge of the path.

We crossed a brook, the water copper brown. The sound made me thirsty.

I got our water out of Mac's rucksack and we drank. The wind was colder now, with a keen edge that made my nose run.

'I think we should go back to Leeds, move before Christmas,' I said. 'We can give notice to the tenants.'

'Yes,' Mac said. No need for discussion. He looked up at the sky: dark clouds were coming in from the coast. 'Home?'

I nodded.

Then my phone rang.

It was the children's home.

Chloë had run away.

Chapter Forty-nine

The hours dripped by, water torture. I imagined Chloë wandering round Darlington, unfamiliar streets, strange estates, looking for somewhere to hide. Or somewhere to buy weed. Looking for new friends, kids like her, on the edge, off the grid. Had she any money?

I imagined worse: offers of a roof for the night, food or cigs in exchange for sex.

And worse still: Chloë on a railway line, Chloë walking into traffic, Chloë poised on the roof of a multi-storey car park.

I didn't know what to do with myself but I was unable to sit still. Mindlessly, I made a start on chores we'd neglected, filling the washing-machine, sweeping the floors, cleaning the hob.

'You hungry?' Mac said, when it got to six o'clock.

'A bit. There's probably something in the freezer.'

We had just started eating chicken pie and chips when my phone rang. A Leeds number. I looked at Mac, put the speakerphone on.

'Is this Lydia Kelly?'

'Yes.'

'Your daughter is Chloë Kelly-Ross?'

'Yes.' *Tell me.*

'My name's Harry Stokes from the West Yorkshire Youth Offending Team. Chloë was apprehended by British Transport police at Leeds station for travelling without a ticket. I understand she's been remanded in care of the local authority and has absconded.'

'Yes. Is she all right?'

'She appears to be. I've no immediate welfare concerns. Chloë's at the Crown Court here in Leeds and the judge in chambers has just now remanded her into custody.'

Christ. She was going to prison.

'Yes. Thank you,' I managed.

'I'll be back in touch when we know where Chloë will be placed. I'll need to talk to you some more about Chloë's situation, find out what I can from you, her background, history and so on. And I can explain what happens next from our end.'

'Thank you.'

'She's all right,' I said to Mac, when the call was over. 'I kept thinking she might have done something . . .' I didn't need to spell it out. 'But they're sending her into custody . . .' I shook my head. 'Mac, those places. The reports come out one after another. She's meant to be looked-after, how can she be looked-after somewhere like that?'

'There's nothing we can do,' he said, 'except make it clear to them that she needs a lot of help and that she's vulnerable.'

The young offenders' institution was part of a women's prison an hour and a half's drive south of us on the way to Hull. Visiting time was between two and four in the afternoon, except Monday and Friday. The youth justice officer had advised us how to book in. He gave us Chloë's prisoner number and emailed us a list of clothing we were allowed to bring in at our first visit. He stressed we had to bring photo ID with us or we'd be refused entry.

'It's not a nice place for anyone. We always try to avoid people being remanded in custody but, unfortunately, it's too late for that. However, Beck Bridge does have a good reputation compared to some units. Big emphasis on support between the residents and on education. You'll meet Chloë in the visiting hall. There's no privacy, really. It's going to take time to adjust, for Chloë and for you. But the team there know all about our concerns and she will be monitored as a vulnerable person. Chloë will be allocated a youth remand officer. Within the next ten days they'll hold a remand hearing at the facility, involving you and social services. And after that they will be seeing Chloë on a monthly basis.'

When I thought of her locked up in her cell, I couldn't shake the image I'd always had of her as a baby in her cot, cold and hungry, alone, ignored. Howling. Until she'd learned the lesson that when she cried no one came.

The route took us up and over the moors, then down into farmland, the flat terrain divided into fields ploughed for the winter. We drove through a series of small villages, passing garden centres and country pubs, the occasional caravan site along the way.

We arrived early and went to the visitors' centre where we were checked through a metal-detection scanner, like the ones at the airports. We had to put all surplus belongings in a locker.

There was a spaniel. I thought it a nice touch, pet therapy perhaps, before realising with a jolt that its job was to sniff out any drugs.

The large visiting hall had machines for refreshments along one wall and opposite that a section with toys and books for children. Comfortable chairs in threes and fours were placed around tables in the central area.

The prisoners came through. Chloë was one of the last. My heart gave a thump when I saw her.

She looked tired out. There were dark circles under her eyes and her lips were chapped. Her hair looked brittle; it had lost any lustre.

'Are you all right?' I said.

She nodded.

'Do you want a drink?' Mac said. He bought chocolate, Coke and coffee from the machines.

I tried to focus on the practical, telling her what clothes we'd brought, asking if there was anything else she wanted.

'We put some money in your account for cigarettes and snacks,' Mac said.

'What's your room like?' I asked.

'OK.'

'Small?'

'Fairly.'

'Have you got a telly?' I said.

'Yes. We can't have phones.'

'And you'll be doing lessons every day.'

272

She nodded.

Across the room a woman in her twenties, wearing a tabard to show she was an inmate, laughed as she picked up a toddler. The woman had discoloured teeth, and tears in her eyes. The child was crying, red-cheeked, teething perhaps. How she must miss him.

Another woman, a prisoner with grey hair, was talking to an old man. He had a walking stick and hearing aids. I wondered what had led her there and how long he'd been visiting.

'I spoke to Gregory,' I said. 'He'll be happy to write a report for the court.'

She didn't react to that.

She finished her chocolate bar.

'We were so worried about you, Chloë. If you feel bad while you're here, if you start thinking about hurting yourself, you must tell someone.'

'They check on you,' she said.

'That's good.'

'There's a window so they can see in at night.'

'Good.'

The conversation ignited again briefly as she told me all about the latest episode of *The Great British Bake Off*. Then it sputtered and died. She turned her attention to the chocolate wrapper, tearing it into ever smaller pieces.

I kept talking. Dredging up questions about food, how many girls were in her lessons, what subjects they had to do. Getting monosyllables back at best.

I could feel her mood, which had been muted, start to tighten and darken.

'You can ask about medication,' I said. 'I'll mention it too. There might be something they can give you to help you relax, or help you stay calm. And I'll chase up the social worker about counselling.'

She met my eyes for a moment. Hers were jaded, sceptical.

Around us people were saying goodbye, picking up children, exchanging quick hugs and kisses.

'Think of what you'd like to do when this is all over,' I said.

'Maybe we could go abroad, do a trekking holiday. Or if there's a course you'd like to do. Some things you can study online. It'd be good to have something to look forward to.'

'I want to see my birth-family, my mum.'

It was like a slap in the face.

I blinked. 'Yes,' I said. 'Of course we can help you do that.' I was fumbling with the buttons on my cardigan.

'Look after yourself,' Mac said. 'We'll see you on Saturday.'

'We love you,' I said. 'It'll be all right, you know.' I stepped forward, stooping to kiss her head but she leaned away. I reached out my hand, let it hover over her forearm.

She looked around, as though bored, and moved to the door that would lead back to the prison.

And we went out through a series of heavy metal gates to drive home through the flatlands, in the pouring rain.

Chapter Fifty

That night I dreamed of Freya. Freya teetering high on a mountain top and me at the foot of the slopes calling to warn her: 'Go back! Get away!'

She couldn't hear. The wind snatched my cries. She saw me but stepped closer, perilously near to the edge, turning her head, hand to her ear.

'Go back!' I thrust out my arms, palms facing up at her, to demonstrate.

But she took another step forward.

I jolted awake, screaming.

I told Mac about it over breakfast. 'I can't stop thinking about Freya,' I said. 'All those things she'll never do, never be . . . It's so awful. And for Chloë . . . Do you think she's sorry? Truly sorry?'

'I'm sure she is, as much as she can be.'

'I'd like to do something for Freya, I think, to remember her.'

'What like?'

'I don't know. Make a memento or something. Leave it for her,' I said.

'Where? We don't even know where she's—'

'Here on the cliffs. I'm not sure what. She'd hate anything tacky. But something natural. Could you draw her, make a picture? I've got photos,' I said.

'Sure.'

'Would it last?' I said.

'We could get it engraved, use brass or slate,' he said.

'Slate. There's that place in town does engraving.'

'I could do it myself but I'd have to buy some tools,' he said.

'You design it then and get them to make it. Nothing too big.' I held my thumb and finger a few inches apart to show him.

He did the sketch that evening and we agreed on words to go around the edge: *Remembering Freya, with all our love, Lydia and Mac.*

I had a moment's doubt. 'I'm just . . . what would Bel think about it?'

'Will she ever see it?'

'I don't know.'

I pictured her wrenching it from the fence, stamping on it until the slate cracked.

'And what if it came out, our names, who we are?' I said.

'How would it? Chloë's identity is protected.'

'I just don't want to hurt anybody.'

'It'll be fine,' Mac said. 'I think it's a good idea.'

It was a glorious autumn day, the sun warm, the air clear and still, when we went to place the engraving on the fence.

We drove up to the car park, which was as busy as ever with tourists visiting the abbey.

As we walked down the road towards the graveyard, I felt sick with tension; sweet saliva filled my mouth. I stopped. Head full of that night. Chloë on the top step by the graveyard gates, me shaking her, demanding to know where Freya was. Seeing the bottle of vodka and Chloë's backpack on the ground. The moon's dazzling light. Chloë tackled to the ground. The beat of the helicopter blades thudding inside me.

'I can't,' I said.

'Let's sit down.'

I went with Mac to one of the benches on the grass outside the graveyard wall. I was shuddering, blowing my breath out, riven by panic.

Mac took my hand and held it, rubbing his thumb in stroking motions, soothing.

'This place,' I said, 'I know it's beautiful but—' I looked up at the abbey, its ribs and columns honeyed by the sun. The outline of the great windows patterned against the blue sky. Gulls weaving in and out of the ruins.

'Eight weeks and we'll be gone,' he said.

A trio of people came walking up from the 199 steps. Goths. Two girls and a boy. Black clothes and pale faces, silver-buckled boots and frock coats. Laughing and smoking. Full of life.

'They're early,' Mac said. The festival wasn't for another fortnight. They were beautiful.

We sat on, and slowly my terror ebbed away, leaving just a wash of sorrow.

'OK,' I said to Mac.

We walked through the graveyard with its huge tilting headstones, its biers and family plots, to the top corner by the cliff's edge. I saw someone had repaired the broken wooden gate and a new sign had been fitted, warning of the danger.

Mac held the picture up, suggesting a place.

I nodded my agreement.

I let the tears come, soundless, tasted salt at the corners of my mouth.

He clipped it onto the wire fencing with the bracket we had brought.

My vision was blurred as I looked at the image of Freya. I shut my eyes and said a silent prayer, then stepped back a little.

The horizon was clear, an indigo stripe marking the point where the steel grey of the sea met the bright blue sky. Closer in, a trawler was coming back to port. Down to our left, along the harbourside, people thronged the promenade and the piers. And further into town a puff of steam, a plaintive whistle, marked the arrival of the train from Pickering. 'Rest in peace,' I whispered.

We walked back slowly to the car. Mac's arm around me. The sun on our backs. Past the vast stone shell of the abbey.

Chapter Fifty-one

Once we'd agreed to move back to Leeds I searched for haematology jobs in West Yorkshire. My old department were advertising for maternity cover, six months starting in January.

The irony was not lost on me.

I filled in an application and was invited for interview.

'What if I blank out? Just freeze?' I said to Mac, as I tried on outfits a couple of days before.

'You'll smash it,' he said. 'You've over twenty years' experience.'

'Twenty-five. But my head's gone to mush. My concentration. With everything that's going on . . . And I've not really done interviews before, not since I started out. I've never needed to, working in the same place. And what do I say about moving back?'

'You miss work, miss city life,' he said.

'Green or the cream?' I held up the tops in front of me.

'Yes,' he said, teasing me.

I turned back to the mirror. 'If I can get into them.' I look so old, I thought, with dismay. Grey hair unkempt, dull eyes. My face was plump enough to mask wrinkles but there were deep grooves above the bridge of my nose, frown marks, worry lines.

Waiting to be called into the interview room, I sat wound up tight, trying to practise answers to potential questions in my head, worrying that my face was shiny, my clothes not smart enough.

But within minutes of starting, I was actually enjoying myself. I had no difficulty explaining what I might do in certain clinical scenarios or talking through the advantages of various diagnostic tests and the merits and disadvantages of different anticoagulants. My boss had retired but the new one was welcoming, and there hadn't been many changes since I'd left. It might have felt like years but it was only thirteen months.

I didn't stumble over the more personal questions about availability and they didn't even ask me why I was moving back to Leeds.

I came out on a high. 'It was amazing,' I said to Mac, on the phone, before I set off for home. 'It was like – I can do this, I'm good at this.'

The interview had lasted thirty minutes. Thirty minutes when I hadn't thought about Chloë once. And that was how it used to be, once we'd had Chloë: work was a safe space; it was constructive; there was validation there. I could exist there, breathe, do well.

'Jaysus, I hope you get it,' he said.

'They'll let us know tomorrow. But if not I can try other hospitals, even if I have to commute a bit.'

I rang Colin to let him know we were moving.

There was an odd tone to his voice when he answered the phone. I was trying to decipher it as he said, 'Bel's not well. She's in hospital, a psychiatric unit. She . . . It was an overdose. She took a load of stuff, coke and pills, and she was drinking.'

My stomach turned over. 'Oh, Colin. I'm so sorry.'

'They want to keep her in but I don't know if she'll stay. She's there voluntarily at the moment. She's been in a bad way. Just . . . impulsive, destructive.' He sighed. 'You knew about Barnaby?'

'Yes,' I said.

'Well, she showed up at his house, made a scene.'

Fuck. I could see her, high and vengeful, lashing out at whoever she could. Wanting to hurt someone like she was hurting.

'Oh, no,' I said.

'He's taken out a restraining order,' Colin said. 'His wife was there. And the kids.'

'What a mess.'

'I know. Anyway, how are you?' he said.

'Not great. Just getting on with it. Still waiting for a date for the court case.'

'And Chloë?'

'Well . . . just about coping. It's so hard.'

'I can imagine,' he said.

'We've no idea whether they'll convict her or what sort of sentence she might get.' If she was released, would she come back to live with us? I thought Mac would leave if that were the case.

'We're moving back to Leeds in December.'

'Oh, that's good,' Colin said.

'It'd be lovely to see you, if you . . .' I had a moment's pause. Would Colin feel the need to pick sides? To support Bel and so avoid Mac and me?

'That'd be great,' he said.

'How are you doing? And Javier?'

'Yeah. Not bad. I've applied for an Irish passport.'

'Really?'

'We still don't know if he'll be able to stay here. It's such a car crash. All that crap about £350 million a week for the NHS. Taking back control. Of what? It's economic suicide. Never mind the cultural side of things.' He groaned. 'Sorry, soapbox over.'

'I'm with you on that . . . I'm just so tired, Colin. It's hard to feel hopeful about anything.'

'There's always Jeremy,' he said, with a smile in his voice. 'Our wonderful leader. I've joined the Labour Party. Words I never thought would leave my mouth.' He laughed. A spark of the old Colin.

I wished us back in time. Colin and Bel and me, three kids in a bar with fake IDs. Full of promise and adventure. The thrill of sex and drugs and rock 'n' roll. A world all of our own.

In the first days of November the weather turned bitter and the roads on the way to the prison were slick with black ice in the dips and hollows where the winter sun hadn't reached.

I was full of a head cold, my throat peppery, my nose clogged, mind sluggish.

We were discussing Christmas. There was no prison visiting on Christmas Day or Boxing Day and Mac suggested we go to see his family. My immediate reaction was to reject the idea. I wanted to hide away, lick my wounds, not be in company with people who'd inevitably want to talk to us about Chloë, and how we were bearing up.

'But we'd want to see her on Christmas Eve,' I said. 'And on the Tuesday.'

'We could fly over to Dublin on Christmas Eve, straight after visiting.'

'Where from?' I said.

'Leeds-Bradford or Newcastle.'

Ahead of us on the road a tractor was pulling a trailer stacked with hay bales. Mac was waiting for an opportunity to overtake.

'You're not keen?' he said. 'It'll be a really long day either side but—'

'It's not the travelling,' I said. 'It's . . . I'm not sure I can face—'

'What?'

'Being with people, talking about it.'

'So we should lock ourselves away too?'

Stalks of hay were flying free of the bales, puffs of golden dust rising whenever the trailer bounced over a bump in the road.

'Maybe it would actually be good to talk about it,' Mac said. 'With people who care, people who know her. People who understand what it's been like. Besides, most of the time it'll be chaos at my dad's, kids and presents, too much food. There might not even be time to get to that.'

We passed a farmhouse, smoke curling from the chimney, geese in the yard. The smell of silage. A wooden sign read 'Potatoes and Eggs'.

Mac indicated and accelerated as he drew out to pass the tractor. 'Be good to just do something normal,' he said.

'OK. I'll think about it,' I said.

Chloë had a cold, too, her nose red at the end, eyes bleary. She kept coughing, a raw, hacking sound.

She had been taking a sedative for the past week to tackle her anxiety and seemed subdued and sleepy. Yawning and scratching at her arms and her neck.

Our conversation was sporadic. Mac passed on news about her Irish cousins and she listened and nodded now and then, but her gaze kept drifting off as though another conversation was going on out of sight.

I told her about my going back to work, about getting the job. 'But I'll still be able to come and see you,' I said.

It was noisy in the hall: there was a family with very loud voices close by, two men and a woman visiting a young prisoner. One of the men kept bursting into shouts of laughter that interrupted my concentration.

At another table a prisoner was crying, a black girl with her hair braided in a circlet around her head. She kept swiping at her face and the woman visiting her was leaning forward and talking, nodding, as if to reassure her.

'How've your lessons been?' I asked Chloë.

'Same.' She took a breath and coughed, wincing.

All the things I would do if she was back home – give her cough sweets, Olbas oil to help her breathe, Vaseline for the sore patch on her nose, hot honey and lemon to drink.

'What have you done this week, then?' I said.

She sighed.

Talk to me. Even some sarky comment about how boring it was would be better than nothing.

'You know you said you wanted to meet your birth-mum,' I said.

Her eyes moved, stopped. Swerved up at me, then away.

'I was thinking, before then, maybe we could ask for a picture of her. A recent one. Would you like that?'

'Yes,' she said.

I sensed Mac stiffen in the chair beside me. We hadn't discussed this. Before arriving I'd had no idea I was even going to suggest it. It was an attempt to reach her, to break through the fug of her

282

withdrawal. And if meeting Debbie was something for her to look forward to, then we should encourage that, no matter how nervous it made me.

'You look so alike,' I said. 'She loves you, you know. She says that in every letter. And we love you.'

Chloë slid her feet forward under the table, sloped back in her chair, affecting boredom. Until a coughing fit forced her to sit upright.

'I'll get drinks,' I said. 'Coke? And some Galaxy?'

She gave a nod.

When I came back and passed them to her I saw her hand was trembling. Was that from the medication? 'How've you been feeling this last couple of days?' I said.

'Tired,' she said.

'Are you sleeping?'

'Who cares?' I saw a flash of pain in her eyes.

'We care,' Mac said. 'We want you to be . . . comfortable, to feel safe.'

'In this place?' She smiled.

A chill slithered through me. 'Are you thinking of hurting yourself?' I said.

She shrugged.

Before I could ask more, the man with the laugh roared again. Chloë dropped her Coke. One of the prison officers came over. I think they imagined she had thrown it until we explained.

The buzzer sounded. Time to go.

'Let me give you a kiss,' I said, almost begging as we stood.

An expression rippled across her face. Reluctance or resignation. She ducked her head and I planted a kiss on the top of it. Inhaling the smell of her skin, salty, slightly metallic, mingled with cigarette smoke and the sweet aroma of the chocolate she'd been eating.

'I love you. See you soon.'

Mac held out his fist and I was relieved when she tapped it with her own. 'Love you, Chloë,' he said. 'Be safe.'

* * *

'Thanks for the heads-up,' Mac said, as we got into the car.

'Sorry, it just came out. But it's better we're on board, helping manage her expectations about any contact with Debbie. Supporting her with it. I know it's still four years away and there are risks involved.' There were plenty of stories on adoption-support-group sites of children returning to their birth-families at the first opportunity, abandoning their adoptive parents. Drawn back looking for answers, acceptance, love and belonging. Stories of lives imploding with kids replicating the pattern of their early lives, neglect or violence, having their own children put on the at-risk register. Of the overarching pull of nature over nurture.

'It scares me shitless,' he said. 'You'd think after this nothing else would.' He tipped his head back to the prison building.

'I know. But we're her parents, Mac, we always will be. We show her we're strong enough as a family to let her explore her identity.'

'Are we? She knows I was going to leave.'

'That doesn't stop you being her dad, wanting what's best for her.'

'No.'

We were quiet for a moment. I watched other relatives get into cars, or taxis, or begin the walk to the nearest bus stop.

'How did she seem to you?' I said.

'Fragile,' he said. 'Angry and depressed.'

'Yes. But she let me kiss her. And you did the hand thing. That's good.' I was trying to be positive but unease was gnawing at me. 'Still, I'm worried. I'm going to talk to the careline.' The unit had a system where friends and relatives could report any welfare concerns. It was part of their effort to reduce self-harm in the facility.

'Hello,' I said, when they answered. 'I'm ringing about Chloë Kelly-Ross.' I gave my name and date of birth and Chloë's prisoner number.

'How can I help?'

'We've just had a visit with Chloë and she seemed very low. And when I asked if she was thinking about hurting herself she didn't really answer.'

'Did she talk about making any plans to hurt herself?'

284

'No. But we had to leave, you see, before I could ask her more about it. She has a history of self-harm, and she's vulnerable.'

'Thank you for letting us know. I'll make sure everyone is aware of that.'

'And the medication,' I said, 'can someone review that? I'm not sure if it's helping or making things worse.'

'I'll pass that on,' she said.

'Let's go out,' Mac said, once the car began to climb the road to the moors.

'What?'

'Tonight. We can please ourselves. Have a meal, couple of pints.'

I sneezed. 'Mac, it's a lovely idea but I'll be dead on my feet by nine.'

'We'll go now, on our way home. Stop in Scarborough to eat, hold the drinks for when we get back. Saves cooking.'

'Go on, then,' I said.

It was dark already. The road quiet. Our headlights glanced off the hedges, lit the row of cat's eyes down the centre of the road. At intervals we were dazzled by the lights from oncoming drivers before they dipped their beams.

'I do love you,' I said.

'You'd better.'

And he put on the music player, linked to his phone. Michael Kiwanuka's soulful voice, riven with heartache, singing us 'Home again'.

Chapter Fifty-two

Niall had arranged for an estate agent to measure up and take photographs of the cottage on the Saturday morning at ten. They'd be finished before we had to set off to visit Chloë. On Friday night we were up late, de-cluttering and cleaning, moving as many of our personal belongings out of sight as possible and taking everything we didn't need out to the shed.

I set my alarm that night. I was usually awake by seven thirty but I didn't want to risk oversleeping.

My nose was blocked and my mouth parched, my head aching when the alarm woke me. I thought I'd slept right through, then realised the sound wasn't the alarm: it was my ringtone.

4.12. Private number.

'Mrs Kelly?'

'Hello.'

'I'm ringing from Beck Bridge young offenders unit.'

The hairs on my arms, on the back of my neck, rise. My blood thickens and stops in my veins. 'Yes?'

'I'm so sorry, I have some very bad news.'

'Yes?' I say again. Stunned into stupidity.

'Chloë was found to be unresponsive in her cell a couple of hours ago.'

'No!' *No no no no no no no. Please no.*

Mac moves beside me, waking.

'She was transferred to hospital in Hull and was found to be dead on arrival. I am so very sorry.'

'What?' Mac says. 'Lydia, what is it?'

I wail, a high keening note.

He takes the phone from me.

I have to go to her. I pull on clothes, stumbling, fumbling. My hands won't work.

I rush downstairs.

Mac follows. 'Lydia.' He grabs hold of me. 'Lydia.' I'm hitting him, tugging, trying to get away. He pulls me close. I try to push him off, to escape from his embrace. I'm howling, sobbing. Inchoate.

'Hey,' he keeps saying. 'Hey, I'm here. Lydia, I'm here. We can't see her yet,' he says. 'They'll call us.' There is such anguish in his voice.

He steers me to the sofa, sits me down, rocks me.

Later I hear him in the kitchen, the clink of crockery. Him weeping, soft and gruff.

Chapter Fifty-three

The sun comes up. Light steals into the room. How can the sun still rise?

We identify her from behind a wall of glass. The sight of her, her frame so small on the table, bright hair, delicate face, is a punch to my heart. Shatters it into pieces.

And then I, too, am dead. For a while.

At the funeral parlour in Leeds, Mac and I sit vigil. The urge to pick her up and hold her in my arms, to sit and rock, to hug her tight and shower her with kisses is visceral. I could not hold her, not in life, and cannot now, but at least I can touch her. The funeral director was very understanding when we explained what we would like.

She has made sure that I can wash Chloë's face and brush her hair, no matter that these things have already been done.

These rituals are foreign to me. I don't know where the need to do them has come from but it is vital.

I bathe her face with liquid and a small cloth. Her eyes are closed. Small veins on the lids. I remember nights lying beside her after she'd wept herself to sleep, watching her, studying every inch of her, the line of her chin, the whorl of her ear, the shape of her mouth. My mapping a substitute for the familiarity of touch.

I cannot sing. That would unravel me, like it did when I tried it with my mum.

I talk to her in my head. There's no need to say anything aloud. She cannot hear, I know. The life has gone from her. Still I talk to her, fishing for the happy moments, rare jewels to share.

288

Her hair is soft, fine, still long. They've treated it so it gleams and there's no static as I brush.

Occasionally a tear falls and lands on her hair, a raindrop, a diamond that melts away.

The funeral director has prepared Chloë so we are able to hold her hands. Not just stroke them but hold on. Like you would crossing the road with a small child. Like lovers do. The trolley has been adjusted so we can sit comfortably beside the coffin, Chloë just slightly below.

Sitting with her hand in mine, I trace the scars and marks. Don't cover them, we told the director, they're part of her. We're used to them.

All except the dark ring around her throat, left by the ligature.

My hand aches from the cold, stiffens. Her fingers, her palm feel so dense, as if she's full of sand, ground rock where her blood once flowed.

My baby girl.

It is hard to leave. To leave her there. To walk away. But she's gone already.

I part from her with kisses. A kiss on the forehead, smooth now, no scowl. A kiss on each cheek. On the palm of each hand. One on her lips.

My beautiful child.

My sleeping beauty.

My daughter.

We could not keep her safe. Could not save her. Love was all we had and love was not enough. We entrusted her back into the care of the state and they failed her. They failed us and they failed her other mother.

Chloë is cremated. All our friends, our families come. Everyone but Bel. I am mute most of the day. Tranquillisers from the GP help me to put one foot in front of the other.

We haven't decided what we will do with the ashes. It's hard to know where she was happiest. The stables, perhaps. We will keep her with us for now. There is no rush.

Or maybe have her ashes mingled with ours when the time comes.

Who will there be to do that for us?

I contact the social workers and let them know that Chloë has died. A promise made at the time of the adoption, there in the small print that no one ever expects to consult again.

I write a last letter to Debbie. Saying how sorry we are, how one of the last things Chloë asked for was to meet up with her, how we were going to help make that happen. I enclose a photograph.

Packers help us move.

Mac starts up a studio near the Piece Hall in Halifax.

I return to work. It's a lifeline. It gets me out of bed, through each day.

My heart is broken, my soul bruised and burned.

Chloë has gone. I absorb that with each breath, every morning when I wake, every time I walk through a doorway, and every time I see a baby, a teenager, but especially a toddler.

She's gone. I know that. And I rail against it. From the hair on my head to the marrow of my bones. With each beat of my heart.

I will live with the loss of her until the end of my days.

Her death is part of my life. Day after day. The grief more savage, more chaotic and deeper than the gentle grief I bear for my parents. More shocking and profound than the grief I felt after Freya's death.

I have Mac. And Mac has me. I am blessed in that.

We are kind to each other, the love we have a cradle for our grief.

But in the troughs of night and the pitfalls of the days, in moments of reverie, and the ambush of memory, I meet Bel.

Chapter Fifty-four

It is Chloë's birthday. An icy Saturday in April. She would have been fifteen.

Her birthdays were always freighted with extra meaning, a stark reminder that she had had a life before her life with us, a family she was taken from. Some families celebrate adoption day, marking the date when a child arrived in her new family. Should we have done that? Would it have helped? All we knew about her birth was Debbie's brief account. *It were hard. They give us an epidural but it still hurt. She were born at midnight, near enough.*

Too often I find myself trawling back through the years, visiting the turning points, the forks in the road, the decisions that led us here. To Chloë's death, to Freya's. All the might-have-beens.

If I'd never met Bel, if we hadn't decided to adopt, if Chloë had had therapy sooner, if we hadn't moved to Whitby, if Bel had broken up with Barnaby, if social services had given us respite, if I hadn't lost the twins, if my mum hadn't died when she did, if I'd listened to Mac, if Chloë hadn't heard Bel and me fighting, if Freya hadn't provoked her, if they hadn't been drunk . . .

I call Bel's number. She doesn't answer. She never answers. I'm not sure what I'd say if she did.

We haven't spoken since she left the cottage that day. My last words to her, 'You never think about anybody but yourself, do you?'

I ring her again. She's still living at her house in Meanwood. I know that from Colin. She's been out of hospital for a while. She's not working.

I picture her glancing at the phone, seeing my number and feeling

. . . What? Outrage or pity or hatred? I've no idea. Just like I've no idea what I want to say to her.

Still, I call her a third time.

And when she does not answer a flash of anger lights through me, hot and sharp.

She has never acknowledged the death of my daughter.

I put on my coat, hat and gloves, lock up the house and go to find her.

It's a fifteen-minute walk. The sky is brooding: pewter clouds crowd low and a perishing wind buffets me and soon numbs my nose and the tips of my fingers.

When I try to rehearse what I might say the words slide around and scatter like quicksilver.

The skies blacken and hail beats down, stinging my face, bouncing off the pavement, collecting like polystyrene balls in the gutter and along the bottom of the garden walls.

I have a moment's pause, waiting for the traffic lights to change. It would be easier to go home. But then I'd never know.

I am breathless by the time I reach her door at the crest of the hill, my lungs on fire.

The hail has stopped but the wind still slices through me.

I bang the knocker, three loud raps that ring through the cold air.

She opens the door.

Catches sight of me.

Slams it shut.

The expression on her face, shock and then animosity, is emblazoned on my mind.

I bang on the door again, a volley. When she ignores that I push the letterbox open. Bending to peer through the horizontal slot I can see the hallway is empty. The doors to the living room and kitchen are ajar; the stairs rise from the right.

'I'm not going away, Bel. Not until I've seen you. Let me in.'

I'm not sure where she is but I know she's listening.

'Let me in,' I shout. 'What are you scared of? Hearing the truth? Do you even know what happened that night?'

There is no noise from inside the house. Someone nearby has

wooden wind chimes in their garden. They clank with each fresh gust, a melodic clatter. It's the loneliest sound.

'Do you think I should be punished?' I say. 'Is that it? You cutting me dead. Because, I tell you, there's nothing you can say or do that will make me feel any worse than I do. I'm here, Bel. I'm not hiding any more.'

I see movement out of the corner of my eye. A neighbour looking out of the bay window next door to see what all the shouting is about. I ignore him.

I bang on the door. 'Let me in. I'm not going away until you let me in. You owe me that.'

Teeth gritted, I hammer the knocker over and over again. Pounding it as hard as I can.

The door is yanked back, wrenching my fingers.

'Fuck off,' she spits. 'I don't owe you anything. My daughter is dead because of yours.' Her eyes needle hate.

'I could say the same.' I make to step over the threshold but she blocks my way. 'Get out.'

'No.' I push forward. 'You always ran away. Whenever things got too hard to handle, too close for comfort, you'd bolt. Move house, switch jobs. I used to think that was brave, that you were a free spirit. That you didn't need anyone. But you were just scared, weren't you?'

She grabs my face in her hand, fingers stabbing into my cheeks. 'Why are you here?' I smell alcohol on her breath, see the pores on her skin, the deep blue wheel of her iris.

'Because no one else can understand,' I say.

She lets go, spins away, raising her arms to clutch at the top of her head.

I shut the door behind me. 'I wrote to you,' I said.

'I burned it.'

'Do you even know what happened?'

She turns back. Her face livid with hostility. 'Your demented feral bitch of a daughter pushed mine to her death.'

My cheeks glow hot. 'Do you know why?' I say.

'Because she could?'

'Don't be fucking flippant.' I want to slap her.

'They argued. What does it matter? It won't bring her back.'

The heating is on, the house stifling. I pull off my hat and gloves.

'Chloë heard us rowing when you were leaving to see Barnaby. She heard it all, the whole charade you'd cooked up, visiting us. Married man with kids. When Freya got mad with Chloë, when she wanted to go back to the cottage and Chloë wouldn't, Freya laid into her, told Chloë how she'd ruined our lives, how Mac wanted her back into care, that he was leaving us. Stuff you must have told her.'

Bel is shaking her head as I speak, lips pinched tight.

'Chloë retaliated, told her where you'd really gone, what you were really doing. Freya went crazy.'

Bel jerks her head up towards the ceiling, dismissing what I'm saying.

'Freya grabbed Chloë and Chloë freaked out. She couldn't stand being touched, you know that. She was trying to get Freya off her. That's all. She never meant—'

'She killed her!' Bel roars. The cords of her neck stand out like wires, her eyes blaze.

'It was an accident,' I say. 'No one is to blame. Or maybe we all are.'

'You are so self-righteous.' Bel gives a laugh, devoid of any humour.

'No! Some of this is on you.' I'm trembling. 'You weren't there for Freya. You lied to her, you left her. Your daughter fell to her death. Mine took her life in a prison cell. We lost our girls, Bel. Both of us.' My eyes burn. 'And I'm so sorry.' My voice breaks.

She flies at me, screeching, 'Go! Get out! Fuck off!' Her fists hitting out. A blow to my cheek and a jolt of pain sears through my temple. I see stars.

I grab her wrists, hold on tight. She struggles to break away. 'You used me, Bel. Maybe that was it all along. I was useful. Did I make you look good? The fat girl? I trailed after you . . . Why me?' I clear my throat, release my grip. 'I loved you. I thought you were amazing. You were . . .' My thoughts trip and fragment. 'Why?'

Her throat ripples. 'You—' She swings away. Her hands grasp the nape of her neck. She turns back to me.

'You were there, Lydia. You made me . . .' She presses her hand against her chest. 'You made me better, everything better.' Tears glitter in her eyes. 'I liked you. You were my friend. You held onto people. Mac, your family. You had everything.' *What about the IVF?* 'And you didn't really need me.'

'But you never wanted all that.'

'And I don't. But I always had you.' Her face creases. She is crying. She presses a fist to her mouth. 'You were my friend.'

She moves slowly into the kitchen and I follow, unbuttoning my coat.

She sinks onto a chair, folds her arms on the table, lays her head on them. Her shoulders and back rise and fall with her cries.

How close were we, really, over the years? How do you measure that? I don't know.

I sit.

Time ticks by.

Her breathing shudders, slows.

She rouses herself. Sniffs and snorts, wipes a hand across her face.

She gets up and fetches a bottle of gin out of the fridge, another of tonic water. Without looking my way she brings two tumblers, mixes drinks.

Mothers' ruin.

Neither of us speaks. The drink is cold and astringent. It goes to my head and I feel a lightening, a blurring.

I think of Chloë and Freya drinking vodka.

Of Bel that New Year's Eve, dancing on the ice. Her sharp style, her vivid beauty.

I don't know what happens next. Where we go from here.

But we can't go back.

I take Bel's hand, and her fingers, cool, weave through mine.

The wind pitches hail scattershot at the window.

We sit hand in hand.

Holding on.

Not letting go.

295

Afterword

Adoption is often thought of as a fairy story, a happy-ever-after for those concerned. But at the heart of every adoption is loss, the loss of family and identity and legacy for the child, the loss of a child for the birth-parents, the loss of the possibility of having a biological child for most adoptive parents who come to adoption because of infertility.

I was one of half a million babies adopted in the 1950s, 1960s and 1970s in the UK. The majority of us were adopted because our mothers were unmarried at a time when both Church and state punished such women for transgressing, deeming them morally depraved and unfit to be mothers. There was social stigma and shame attached to being pregnant and unwed, and huge pressure on women to give up their babies. I've been fortunate enough to have had a successful reunion with my birth-mother and to form strong relationships with her and my seven birth-siblings. My adoptive parents met my birth-mother, brothers and sisters and that was a hugely positive experience. Reunion alongside counselling helped me heal emotionally, and my birth-mother said the same. An important part of that whole process was to acknowledge the grief, insecurity, guilt, even the anger that came with being adopted.

Thankfully, times have changed. Nowadays women have more control over their lives and more choices about contraception, reproduction and sexuality. Families come in all shapes and sizes. Few babies are relinquished for adoption. In this century people who adopt are more likely to be creating a family with a child who has been taken into care, a child who has had a damaging start to life. Friends and acquaintances of mine have adopted and some have encountered serious difficulties with the behaviour of their children, especially as they reach adolescence. Barely any of those families, or the ones I've read and heard about, have been able to get access to the sort of support they needed when they needed it. A survey carried out by BBC Radio 4's *File on 4* programme and Adoption UK in 2017 found that more than a quarter of adoptive families were struggling, facing challenges so serious that the adoption was at risk of disruption. It's not an issue that is widely aired – it's almost taboo. What is heartening is that nine out of ten respondents were still glad they had adopted. And adoption *does work* for the majority. But the most vulnerable children in our communities need unstinting assistance, and their families deserve backing to the hilt with resources put in place for those who require them. Our adoptive parents may give us all the love in the world but sometimes love is not enough.

Acknowledgements

Thank you to the people who kindly gave their time to help me research this book: Clare Wigzell, Dave Leeming, George Wigzell, Janet Finucane, Marion Lindsay, Richard Honey, Simon Cregeen, Tim Leeming. Thank you to Marie McLaughlin, head of Youth Justice Manchester, and colleagues Michael Grant and Louise Prince. As always any mistakes are down to me. There are many websites about adoption that I learned from: https://thepotatogroup. org.uk/ was particularly valuable. Thanks again to my writers' group – Anjum Malik, Livi Michael, Mary Sharratt and Sophie Claire – for stellar feedback and lively chat. Thank you to all the team at Constable, especially Krystyna Green, Jess Gulliver, Amy Donegan and Ben Goddard. Thanks to copy-editor Hazel Orme for making it a more coherent read. And a big cheer for my wonderful agent, Sara Menguc.